The Cross You Bear

By: Da'JonC
Copyright 2020 By: Da'JonC
Published By: Legacy Publishing LLC

About the author:

Author Da'Jon C is a 25-year-old writer who currently resides in Cleveland, OH. The Cross You Bear is the first published book of many to come from author Da'Jon C. A certified personal trainer, Da'Jon has spent the last three years of his life incarcerated in which he has read numerous books of all genres and has written various forms of content including poems, short stories, and music. Da'Jon's love for creative writing began in grade school where he enjoyed writing short fictional stories, poems, and essays. Stay tuned in to read more books from Da'Jon in the future.

Acknowledgements:

All praise to the most high! My family, friends, and others who have supported me during this crazy journey. My beautiful daughter; Leeahna who gives me all the motivation that I need to reach my full potential and beyond. Taylors Legacy Publishing LLC.

Dedications:

7L- Live, Life, Lavish, Large w/Laughter, Love, and Loyalty

Chapter 1
How it all began

Tires screeched as Kobe and Tiffany rushed to the hospital. She had been in excruciating pain for hours and more pain to come. The couple drove a 1982 GMC safari van that looked like it could break down at any moment. Kobe drove through a stop sign of a four-way intersection that nearly caused them their lives. Instead, they smacked the back of an elderly woman's 1990 BMW coupe. This still didn't slow them down as they continued to haul to the hospital. The couple pulled up to the hospital's emergency entrance around 2:30 a.m. Nurses rushed to the sliding doors to help Tiffany out of the vehicle and into the wheelchair. They pushed her quickly into the first available room. Tiffany's pain began to get worse and worse, causing her to scream out loudly. Kobe grabbed her hand while the nurses brought in pain medication.

After hours of screaming, pushing, and breathing, Tiffany and Kobe welcomed their beautiful fraternal twins into the world. Neveah Queen Matthews was born first at 12:44 p.m. Just a few minutes later, Adoree' King Matthews was born. Tiffany and Kobe looked each other in the eyes and smiled in relief that the pregnancy had finally ended.

They'd been together for seven years, but married for two. Overall, they had a great relationship. In 1984, when they first met each other, Kobe had a girlfriend named Leslie Johnson. Their relationship was full of ups and downs. At the time, Tiffany was just someone he vented to. In a way, they were best friends but aware of the feelings they shared. So, in 1986, Kobe decided to end his relationship with Leslie to be with Tiffany. They were so inseparable that you would never see one without the other.

In 1989, before the two were married, Kobe got involved in the drug game. The 80's was the start of the crack-cocaine era, and the potential profit that you could make from dealing it was enough to grip Kobe's interest.

Initially, he just wanted to deal until he was able to buy Tiffany the wedding ring that she wanted. Once he saw how fast he made the first ten thousand, he wasn't ready to stop. He kept his family in mind, which was what helped him decide. But just months after buying the engagement ring, Kobe began to use the drugs himself and became addicted. His addiction got so bad, that he and Tiffany lost their home and vehicles.

A year leading up to the loss of their properties was during a time when the only income entering the home was Tiffany's. Her hair salon business was doing well, and she was making close to fifty thousand a year working as a registered nurse. Both incomes combined wasn't enough to keep the three-million-dollar mansion they lived in, however.

Kobe was a retired NFL player, whose career ended after a year due to a major back injury. He was a promising athlete throughout his high school and college years which helped him land a one-million-dollar deal with Reebok and a five-hundred-thousand-dollar rookie contract for the Baltimore Ravens, his hometown. Post retirement, Kobe lost motivation to carry out tasks in the real world. He also didn't listen to Tiffany when she told him to make smart investments with his money.

They both filed for bankruptcy in 1992, a week after they found out they were expecting. Kobe's sister, Christine, was the one who came up with the idea. She was a bank accountant for one of the most popular banks in the Baltimore area. She was very experienced as she was an accountant for former and active professional athletes before Kobe was drafted.

Tiffany didn't want to file for bankruptcy because she knew that it would take a while for the whole process to be completed. They needed stable income for their unborn children, but she listened to Kobe, who was usually good at making smart decisions. He decided to file based on several loans that he received from his former teammates. His best friend, Zeus, gave him fifty thousand dollars and other close friends lent him ten thousand dollars altogether. With the money, he was able to buy everything the twins needed. Even with that, Tiffany was able to work until she was seven months pregnant. When she was unable to be present at the salon, she allowed Jane to take control of it.

Jane was a recovering drunk and alcohol addict, who had been clean for some time now; she was the oldest sibling of the two, but she looked at Tiffany as her role model. Their parents passed away when they were just nine and eleven years of age in a house fire. The two sisters were lucky enough to have been at a sleepover with their cousins during the night of the fire. Sadly, the rest of the family abandoned Tiffany and Jane after their parents died, which resulted in them being placed in foster care. They stayed there until around ages fifteen and seventeen.

Tiffany's plan was for them to stay only a year longer than they did, but those plans were halted when their foster family found drugs that belonged to Jane in the home. When they were confronted about it neither said a word. At first Jane tried to come clean about it, but Tiffany wouldn't allow her to. She was afraid that they would split up which was what she told Jane when she asked her why she wouldn't rat her out to the family.

After they were kicked out, Jane's boyfriend moved the sisters into his one-bedroom apartment. Tiffany continued high school while Jane dropped out and spent all her time getting high and drinking with her boyfriend and his no good friends.

Tiffany was never really at the apartment. Instead, she spent all her time at the nearby public library because it was the only place where she could receive quietness to complete homework for both high school and the early college program that she had been enrolled in. One night, after a late library session, Tiffany arrived at the apartment to find Jane lying on the ground unconscious with her mouth wide open. She called the ambulance and Jane was rushed to the hospital. Since they were both minors, the ambulance wouldn't allow her to ride in the back of the truck. One of the policemen, who showed up to the home before the EMS truck, did allow Tiffany to ride with him. She cried the entire ride and even harder when she found out that she couldn't be in the room with her when they tried to revive her. Thankfully, they did. In the process, they noticed that she had been raped by multiple men. Shortly after, they were able to dodge the police and child protective services who tried to get them back in foster care.

They ended up going to a motel, where they would live out of for the next year until Tiffany went off to school at Morgan State University. In just three years, Tiffany graduated with a bachelor's degree in the science of nursing. The next school year, she went to a Morgan State's homecoming game against the University of Michigan with a few of her friends who were also alumnus. Michigan's star player was having one hell of a game as they were up by forty-two points late in the fourth quarter.

Instead of getting out of the game, like his head coach insisted, he decided that he wanted to return one last kickoff. He began in the middle of the field and worked his way down the left sideline as raindrops began to fall from the sky. It clouded his vision some as he tried to cut in closer to the inside of the field after making one defender miss. As he planted his right foot inward, his left foot got stuck in the mud and he was tackled from behind. He landed on the ground in extreme pain. Even though he was on the opposing team, the whole crowd got silent, especially being that this could have potentially been one of the last games of his immaculate college career before entering the draft. He was the team's best player in every aspect of the game since coming in as a freshman at 5'10," one-hundred and seventy pounds. Now standing at six feet, and weighing close to two-hundred and ten pounds, he was projected first round pick in the upcoming draft.

Still lying on the ground, his team and some of Morgan State's teammates took a knee to express their sympathy. None of Michigan's medical staff were available and to assist him and Morgan State's medical staff had already left the stadium. While everyone waited for medical assistance, Tiffany and her friend made their way down to the field where the injured player was laying.

At first glance, Tiffany's first thoughts were how handsome he was even with a disgruntled expression and awkward position. Tiffany was beautiful herself, but she never had a boyfriend or even another male that she had gotten close to. But laying eyes on him, she knew there was something about him. As she stood there mesmerized by him, the star shouted.

"Damn, you just going to stand there or are you gonna do something?"

The pain in his voice helped Tiffany snap back to reality and she began to calm the player down. She asked him where was he hurt and he answered, "my fucking knee, this one," he replied while holding his left knee with both hands.

Tiffany had seen the play and guessed that he tore his ACL. Once they were able to get him to the hospital, they did an MRI and told him that it would take a few days before they knew the severity of his injury.

Later that night, Tiffany received a call from Michigan's athletic department. They were calling to thank her for her volunteer service on the field. During the conversation with the president, she recognized a concerned male's voice in the background. That voice made his way on the other end of the phone. He started by telling her how great of a nurse she was. He then tried to offer her money, but she declined knowing deep down that she could use some extra cash. At the time, she didn't owe any money for bills or student loans, but she was living paycheck to paycheck and barely making ends meet. After she refused, the man finally told her his name, in which she remembered the last name from the back of his jersey. Her heart began to beat fast. The star player peeped the nervousness in her voice, so he offered to take her out for dinner. She happily accepted. After the phone call ended, she was surprised that she heard from him again. In her head, she just questioned why the future professional athlete wanted to take her on a date out of all people.

Tiffany called her friends immediately to tell them and they were just surprised as she was. None of them watched sports, but since the he was from the same city that they were, they heard about all the hype surrounding him. Also, her friends knew that she was super shy and had self-esteem problems, but they believed her because she was so beautiful and had great qualities.

Saturday seemed to come so fast for Tiffany. She was excited to see him, but she had never been on a real date with a real man before, so she had no idea of what to expect. Hell, she didn't even know who to call. She decided on a red and white dress with a black pair of heels. To top off the outfit was matching jewelry, jacket, and purse. After she picked her whole outfit, she went to her get her hair and nails done. Once she made it back home, she just so happened to walk in to the phone ringing.

"Be ready at p.m.," the voice said. Tiffany hung up. She was confused because it didn't sound like the man she helped at all.

She was fully dressed by 7:30 p.m. and waiting near the phone for another call. At 7:56 p.m. she heard a knock on the door. She jumped up and peeked out the window to find a limousine parked in front of her apartment. She was so nervous that she didn't even go outside to see if the driver was for her and was even more stunned when she heard a knock at the door. With her heart racing, she slowly went to the door and answered it.

"Evening Miss. I'm looking for a Tiffany Anderson," the chauffeur said.

How the fuck does he know my government? she thought to herself. "Yes, how can I help you sir?" she asked him.

"Your date for tonight, Mr. Kobe Matthews, is waiting for you in the limousine. You guys will be eating at Lee's Eastery," he responded.

"Damn that's one of the best restaurants in town," Tiffany mumbled as the chauffeur chuckled and signaled for her to follow him.

She quickly locked the door and sat in the backseat where Kobe was sitting there with a bottle of Dom Perignon and two glasses in his hand. It took every muscle in her face and stomach to refrain from smiling ear to ear. She wanted to seem nonchalant about the whole situation.

"I wanted to thank you again for your help on the field earlier this week," Kobe began.

"You're welcome. *I knew it,* she thought in her head.

"Well, it's nice to formally meet you. How has your week been so far?" he asked.

"Ehh, it's been fine. I didn't do much," Tiffany responded.

"Ok. I see you don't talk much huh?" he said smiling.

It wasn't that she didn't want to engage in a conversation. She was just nervous, shy, and inexperienced with dating. She never verbally answered his question. She just shook her head no and looked away.

"Well, you look very nice today. Oh yeah we're going to have dinner at Lee's Eatery. Eaten there before?" he asked.

"I haven't," Tiffany said.

"Neither have I so that's great," said Kobe.

The limo pulled off and headed toward the freeway. The restaurant was about twenty-five minutes away. When they arrived, the chauffeur held the door open for them to get out. Kobe held his hand out for Tiffany to hold onto while they walked to the entrance of the restaurant. He held the door open for her so he could see her ass as she walked. Tiffany looked around amazed at how nicely decorated the establishment was. There were animal statues all over. The floors were marble, the antique eating utensils were elegant, and even the waitresses were beautiful.

The one that greeted and seated them was Persian. Kobe asked Tiffany what she wanted to drink. The waitress finished taking their orders and left.

"So Tiffany, I see you had on a Morgan State University alumni sweatshirt. I know you were pretty upset about the outcome of the game?" Kobe joked.

"Yeah yeah. Y'all were supposed to win," said Tiffany.

"Yeah you're right. So how long ago did you graduate from there?" he asked.

"I graduated last spring with my BSN," she said.

"Oh, that's amazing. So, you must be like 22,23, something like that right?" he asked.

"No, I'm 19. I graduated from high school when I was 16 and I was taking college courses then," Tiffany responded trying to not sound like a geek.

Kobe looked at Tiffany with his eyebrows heightened. He had never heard of anyone doing that before in addition to being thrown off about her age.

"Wow, that's sweet. I would have never guessed that you were only 19. You carry yourself well," he added.

"Thank you! Now let me hear about you. Do you plan on graduating from Michigan or are just going to enter the draft?" Tiffany asked.

"I'm going to declare for the draft soon. We only have two games left and I'm excited to get them over since I'll be on sideline watching. This injury has already lowered my draft stock from a top ten pick to a late first round or maybe even an early second round," he answered.

"Well, why not play another year to raise your stock back up. That way you can graduate and get drafted both in the same year," Tiffany suggested.

"It doesn't always work like that. I can get injured again next year and this time it could end my career before ever getting the chance to step foot on an NFL field," he explained.

"Yeah, I understand what you mean. I never looked at it that way. But I wish you the best and I know you'll do great," she said.

"Ok good, so you do talk?" he said with a smile. "I appreciate it. So, what's your future plans Ms. Graduate?" Kobe asked.

Tiffany gave a big smile back. "I'm trying to get a job at Devi-Jane Hospital on Basil Street. I also want to open a beauty salon. I love doing hair, nails, and make-up," she responded.

"With your drive, you'll be able to achieve anything you want. But damn where the hell is the food?" he asked.

"I was just thinking the same. I'm starving!" Tiffany concluded.

The food arrived a few minutes later. They enjoyed their meal while talking and laughing over a few drinks. Tiffany became more comfortable as the night went on and with the drinks. Kobe paid for the food and asked her if she had to be somewhere in the morning.

"Nope, this is my weekend off. Why you ask that?" Tiffany asked.

"It's still kinda early in the night. It's only 9:30, wanna hang out a little longer?" he asked.

"Uh, what do you have in mind? I'm usually getting ready for bed around this time," Tiffany said laughing.

"It's a cool Saturday night, let's catch a movie," Kobe said.

"Alrighty," she responded.

The driver took them to Kobe's apartment lot so that they could get into his truck before heading to the movies. The movie had already started when they arrived. It was a fairly new movie that neither had seen. Tiffany looked at Kobe and told him that she was really enjoying the night. Kobe smiled and agreed with her as they continued to watch the movie. Kobe leaned his seat back and briefly glanced at Tiffany without being seen.

Damn, I wonder if she has a boyfriend? Wow, why didn't I ask? he thought in his head.

He turned back and watched the movie for a bit, but the question still lingered in his head. He wanted to start a conversation before jumping to that question so he looked over to ask her what she thought would happen next in the movie, just to find out that she had fallen asleep. He finished watching the movie and then headed home afterward. When he was back in his parking lot, he tapped Tiffany's leg to wake her up. She woke up and looked around in confusion. Kobe put his hand on her shoulder and told her how the movie had ended.

"Yeah, I saw that coming," she responded to his conclusion of the movie.

"It's late now. I should be resting my leg for real. Wanna stay the night and I'll bring you back home in the morning?" Kobe asked.

A little hesitant at first, she replied.

"Ok that's cool,"

Kobe showed her around when they got inside. You would have thought he had a job. He showed Tiffany the guest room then went and got in the shower. He let the shower run shortly before getting in as he usually did. While rubbing the bar of soap into the wash rag, he noticed the shower curtain peel back. Tiffany's naked body was standing there with perfection. Kobe was completely caught off guard. He couldn't do anything but stare and feel his dick rise in excitement. Tiffany stood and watched it rise before joining him in the shower. She got in and reached for a bar of soap, but Kobe slowly grabbed her by the waist, and they started kissing.

This was the most intimate she had ever been with a guy, but Kobe couldn't tell. Tiffany kissed back with passion while he grabbed both her ass cheeks and caressed them. Then his kisses went down to her neck, then to her breast as she began feeling sensations in spots she never had before. Next, Kobe rubbed his hand down her butt until he was between her legs and he reached under to feel her clit. She let out a soft gasp while he felt how wet she was.

Forgetting that he currently had an injured knee, he lifted Tiffany up in the air high enough to taste her. Just seconds in her juices covered the bottom of his face. She tried not to be loud, but she couldn't help it. A loud moan escaped from her mouth when she felt the sensitivity of her first sexual orgasm approaching. It was like it was taking over her body and she couldn't control it any longer. As she was cumming, she pushed down on Kobe's head at the same time. He carried her to his bedroom. Her body was drained from her first orgasm, but she needed to feel him. He laid her down on the bed and they both stared at each other for a moment before Kobe walked up closer to her. Tiffany licked her lips, grabbed his dick, and started to suck it. He looked down at her while she did her thing. At the moment, he was still unaware of her being sexually inexperienced.

He laid her on her back and slapped his dick on her pussy a few times while kneeling over her. He held her breasts and started kissing her from the neck down to the bottom of her inner thighs and back up to her stomach. Tiffany's legs started shaking uncontrollably. She wrapped her arms around his neck as he tried to slide into her, only the tip went in and that was a struggle. He took his time and kept trying until he was finally able to make baby strokes and how wet she was aided in his progression. Kobe was persistent until the baby strokes became deeper. Her moans became louder to the point that he pulled out and flipped her on her stomach. He placed his left hand on the top of her back and tried to go right back in when he heard Tiffany say, "go slow, this is my first time,"

He looked down and saw the blood on the both of them.

Chapter 2

Time for a change

Neveah and Adoree' were brought home for the first time three days after being born. They came out of the womb with very light skin like most babies. Tiffany and Kobe were exhausted from the intense labor and lack of sleep, so Kobe had arranged for Jane to help with things around the house. The first thing she noticed about the twins was that Neveah resembled Kobe and Adoree' resembled Tiffany. Adoree' was born fourteen ounces heavier than Neveah. Jane made a joking comment that the sibling bullying had already begun in Tiffany's stomach. Kobe and Tiffany laughed, and he added, "no bullying would be tolerated" as he recalled being bullied by his older sister as a child. Tiffany nodded her head in agreeance.

"Unity will be one of our most valuable teachings to them," she said.

The three talked and reminisced about the past few years before Kobe suddenly told them that he had to make a quick run. His wife was obviously thrown off by his spur of the moment move as Kobe was able to view through her array of questions on his whereabouts.

"Really Kobe? We haven't even been back for five hours and you're leaving?" Tiffany shouted. She didn't care that her sister was there to help with kids. She just wanted him there with her and the kids together, as a family.

Kobe pulled up to a gas station and parked. From there, he walked to an alleyway where he usually met up with the same two guys. Each of the three men looked around before indulging in their *medicine* as they called it. Their hands felt frozen while they tried to breathe in them. It didn't take Kobe long before he got high out of his mind and walked back to the gas station. He stood in the parking lot stuck with his brain cells racing around in a random assorted pattern. He finally made up his mind to go inside the gas station to buy a pack of cigarettes. Before pulling off, Kobe lit his cigarette and took two puffs.

At this point, he was so high that he shouldn't have been behind the wheel. But being the risk taker that he was he did so anyway. Before stepping out of the car, he grabbed the cologne from his glove compartment and sprayed both his hands and neck. He noticed Jane asleep with the twins. Tiffany was in the bedroom watching tv when she noticed Kobe walk into the room. He went to join her as she pulled the cover back for him to lay down.

"Where were you Kobe? I needed you, we needed you, your family,"

"I just went out for some fresh air and some smokes," Kobe assured her.

"Fresh air, Kobe? It's fucking December!" she yelled with frustration.

"Yeah, I'm aware of the time of year, Tiff. I just didn't want to smoke near the babies. Secondhand smoke is a motherfucka ya know. But everything cool right?" he asked.

"Whatever! And yes, everything is cool. I just spent 9 months pregnant with OUR TWO BABIES, not one, and you can't spend a full day at home without getting high?" she continued.

"Babe relax. You're right, I should have been here with you and I apologize. But I swear I wasn't getting high. I told you that I was done with that shit baby," he said calmly.

"Ok baby. I'm about to nap. I haven't slept in days. Can you get the kids from Jane when they wake up?" she asked.

"Of course," Kobe said.

Kobe knew he was still high as hell, but he knew he couldn't commit. After some hours went by, the twins woke Kobe and Jane up from their crying. He went in the kitchen and warmed up their bottles to feed them. He had no paternal instincts, but it came natural to him. As he held their bottles up to their mouths, he thought of how the little freedom he did have was now over with. He couldn't even think of one person he could call besides Jane that would help babysit while Tiffany was at work whenever she started back. The thoughts were saddening in a way because they wouldn't have neither grandparents in their lives. He didn't talk to his parents and Tiffany's were deceased.

Kobe's father was a retired professional baseball player, and his mother was a physical therapist. At the age of sixteen, Kobe told his parents that he wanted to play football and only football, so they cut all ties with him. At the time, they didn't believe that his skillset was well enough to get a full ride scholarship to play college ball. They assumed that they'd have to pay out of pocket tuition and that meant that Kobe would have to do whatever they wanted him to do.

The next morning, Tiffany came to the living room and spotted her husband asleep holding a twin in each of his arms. She smiled and tears began to fall from her face. They were tears of joy that everything they had experienced together in the last nine years had finally paid off. She stood there, admiring the three of them sleeping as it was a special to her.

"Aww, look at the beautiful family," Jane said, walking into the living room.

Kobe woke up to the sound of her voice. He brought the babies to Tiffany and headed upstairs to the bedroom.

"Good morning, ladies. I'm finally going to bed!" Jane and Tiffany bust out laughing because they already knew his pain. The two sat down to watch the news when their eyes captured a headline that read; 7 overdoses on Baltimore's southside in 20 days. The only thing Tiffany could think of were the words that came out of Kobe's mouth last night when he got in the house.

'I told you that I was done with that shit baby,' played over and over in her head. She couldn't picture life with the twins without Kobe being there and with that vision she believed the statement that he made to be true.

A month later, the couple took the twins to their first month checkup. The doctors told them that they were very healthy, and all their vitals looked good. There was now only a two-ounce difference in their weight, and they were the same height.

"Maybe they'll both be baseball players like your father," Tiffany said.

The thought of both his children being athletes excited him. Also, Adoree' and Neveah were extremely smart. Both had already began to clap at things and nod their heads yes or no. They were two of the cutest babies. Everywhere they went, people stopped them to tell them how beautiful of a family they were.

Tiffany started working out with Jane at the local gym to snatch her body back while Kobe found a job working for Morgan State University's athletic department as a recruiter/scouter. The football and track team were extremely interested in him just from his name. He never ran track because his football coach knew he would be competing for the Olympics after graduating and he didn't want that to take away from his promising football career. During his freshman year, his coach gave him an ultimatum to play football and just football, but if he wanted to play any other sport then he wouldn't allow him to play for the team. Yeah, it was selfish of his coach which is why Kobe never told anyone. But Kobe was lightning fast when he did play so they assumed he knew a little something.

Tiffany and Kobe agreed to start saving. They still had money left over from the loans that Kobe had gotten from his friends and the twins were loaded with everything they would need for the next few months. Tiffany hours at the hospital picked back up so she saved every penny that she could. Kobe promoted her beauty salon heavy while he was out scouting. Jane continued to help at the salon in addition to babysitting the twins as needed. When neither was available to watch the twins, they went to a daycare and that's when Kobe and Tiffany met a parent that suggested they put Neveah and Adoree' into baby modeling.

Kobe was totally against the idea of his son being a model, but he was all for Neveah doing it. He and his wife agreed to think it over, considering that they were both busy as hell. By June, Neveah was already beginning to stand up on her own for seconds at a time. The daycare staff told Tiffany and Kobe that they never saw babies who were so smart. They also mentioned how well behaved they were. Overall, the staff enjoyed keeping them because they didn't need as much attention as the other babies their age and even ones older did.

Tiffany got happy when one of the staff told her that Adoree' says *ma* throughout the day. Another time when Kobe came to pick up the twins, they told him the twins said *da* a lot and even repeated it consecutively. Tiffany and Kobe couldn't help but wonder just how smart they'll be.

Chapter 3

Chances make?

Already running late, Kobe stopped at the house again to freshen up a little. He was supposed to meet his wife at the schoolhouse for Neveah's parent-teacher conference by 5 p.m. and it was already 4:55 p.m.

When he first arrived back from Cleveland, OH, where he was recruiting players from Glenville High School, he had a few hours to spare before the conference at the school. About an hour before, he got that urge. He jogged over to the alleyway to make a quick purchase. It was always one or two guys who he bought from but this time it was someone different.

"What's up, bra? Chris sent me, he's out of town re'ing up," the dealer said.

"Alright what's good, bra. Is it some better shit? Cuz that last batch was weak af," Kobe inquired.

"Haha, yeah man. I tried it out last night, it's fire!" the dealer assured Kobe.

"Shid, imma take yo word on that," he responded.

"Same as usual?" the man asked.

"Yeah. Well shit if you're saying this shit fire like that, I wanna get a bulk," Kobe said.

"Smart man, so what you thinking?" he asked.

"10 of em," he said.

"10 what?" the man asked.

"10 bricks, bra," Kobe responded.

"Damn, bra. I ain't know you buy like that but I know you got it Mr. Reebok," he laughed. "But of course I don't walk around with that type of work on me. Back up here in an hour?" the dealer asked.

"Yessir," Kobe responded.

Kobe drove back to the house. He went upstairs to him and Tiffany's savings that was stashed in the attic. He stood there and pondered on it for a while with mixed thoughts floating in his head.

"I can make a killing off this. But what if I get caught? I can't put myself in that type of predicament, but for a flip like that, it may be worth it," he mumbled under his breath.

He thought about how Tiffany would go crazy if he spent their entire savings on something of that sort. After carefully thinking, Kobe went downstairs and called his right-hand man, Issac, who arrived in less than ten minutes. Kobe discussed the deal he and the guy organized then they headed to the gas station. Issac stayed in the car while Kobe walked over to the alleyway with his family heavy on his mind. One thing he always wanted was for them to have money so their lives could just be that much easier. He was willing to risk a whole lot so that they'll be set for a while.

The alley was empty. Not even a stray cat in sight.

"Fuck, where is this motherfucka," Kobe mumbled.

His paranoia was weighing heavy on him. He leaned up against the brick wall, and to make things worse, he saw a police car drive past. He took that as a sign from the man above and started to walk back to the car.

"Yo, where you going?" a voice asked from behind. Kobe turned back around.

"Man, I thought you weren't gonna show big dog," Kobe said

"Hell naw man. Anytime it's money involved, I'm there. Ya feel me?" he said back.

"I know that's right," Kobe finished.

Kobe examined the man to see where he had the work tucked at and he saw he was wearing a large bookbag. He opened the duffle bag he was carrying around his shoulder and showed it to the man.

"That's all of it?" the man asked.

"All two-hundred thousand of it. That's cool, right?" King responded. The man nodded and began taking off his bookbag. He was just about to unzip it when he suddenly felt cold steel on the back of his head.

"Drop the bag and lay the fuck down. Now! "he heard a voice say. He looked up and saw Kobe, who was still standing in front of him.

"Really dude?"

"Come on motherfucka you heard what he said!" Kobe yelled. The man did as instructed and put his hands in front of him. Isaac picked up the bookbag from the ground and grabbed Kobe by the shoulder.

"We out, bra," Isaac said.

He made it to the schoolhouse at 5:15 p.m. When he walked in the classroom, where the conference was being held, he saw Tiffany, who shook her head when she saw him walking toward her.

"I'm sorry, babe. Got back from Cleveland later than planned," Kobe exclaimed.

"Luckily, the meeting isn't until 5:30. I told you 5 so that you'll be here on time. I was testing you and you failed, miserably," Tiffany responded with an eye roll.

"You know what, girl, you are something else," Kobe said smiling.

"Only for you, baby. How'd it go?" she asked.

"It was great actually. The top players at Glenville high school looked even better in person than on film. Oh, and I ended up catching another game from a high school called John F. Kennedy. Not a big football school like Glenville but they had an amazing player there. I got a chance to talk to him after the game. He was very well mannered and down to earth. He said he's running track this winter and spring. And guess what's crazy? He wears my old jersey number which is?" he responded.

"Come on, dude. Everyone knows your favorite number is 8," she said.

"That's why I love you girl!" Kobe added.

Tiffany sat there, blushing at Kobe's reply. Her love for him had only increased from the moment they had gone on their first date and so had his. The additions to their family was the icing on the cake for Tiffany because this was everything she envisioned. Not so much for Kobe though. The twins were definitely a plus for him, but he knew that if they struggled financially then he wouldn't feel that his family was complete.

Neveah's teacher came into the room a few minutes prior to 5:30. She was a heavyset woman who wore pigtails like a child but was in her mid-forties. Ironically, she was the wife of Adoree's teacher; Mr. Thomas, who'd met with the parents a week prior. That conference left them in disappointment, so they were looking for some better news today.

"Hello Mr. and Mrs. Matthews. How are you guys?" Mrs. Thomas asked.

"We're doing good and yourself?" Tiffany responded.

"Long day but I'm doing well. Thanks for asking," the teacher said back.

"Ok, let's get straight to it. How is Neveah doing in school?" Kobe asked anxiously.

"Kobe!" Tiffany yelled.

Mrs. Thomas chuckled.

"No he's right. I'm tired and I know you guys probably are too so let's jump straight in. Neveah is doing great. Her grades are excellent, and she behaves well. Her and her twin brother are just the cutest. They eat together during lunch and they talk about everything under the sun.

It's actually great that you guys are here because I met with Principal Rodgers earlier this week to discuss Neveah's academic level. Following the meeting we both agreed that she is well beyond a kindergarten's level," she explained.

"Where exactly are you getting at Mrs. Thomas?" Kobe asked.

"Well, Mr. Matthews, we are proposing to bump Neveah up at least two grades," said Mrs. Thomas.

Tiffany and Kobe looked at each other. They knew she was smart but getting skipped two grades was something they didn't expect to hear, and Mrs. Thomas knew it.

"You guys don't have to give an answer right now. There's still three weeks left in this marking period so we would need an answer by then. Just think it over, discuss it together, and let me know. Cool?" she asked.

"I don't even know what to say. Both Neveah and Adoree' are smart. In my opinion, they are both equal academic wise," Tiffany replied.

"Technically, I'm not supposed to share other students that aren't in my class information but since you're his parents too, I'll tell you. Principal Rodgers met with my husband yesterday regarding Adoree' getting skipped as well. Academic wise he's way ahead of his peers but his behavior is questionable. My husband doesn't think his maturity level is there yet," Mrs. Thomas added.

"Maturity level? He's only 5," Kobe said sounding confused.

"Right. How can a 5-year-old be mature?" Tiffany added.

"Well, that's kind of the point I'm trying to make. Most 5-year olds aren't smart. Actually, most children in general aren't which is what makes Neveah so unique," the teacher said.

The conference lasted for a few more minutes. On the way back home, Kobe and Tiffany discussed their thoughts on the possibility of Neveah advancing two grades. It was something for them to think about which put even more on Kobe's mind with the episode he had prior to the conference. When they pulled up to the house, they noticed Jane's car in the driveway.

"I thought Jane was keeping the kids there tonight?" Kobe asked his wife.

She looked at him just as confused and he was. Neveah got out of the car and ran to Kobe to hug him. Jane got out of the car, shaking her head, so Tiffany asked what was wrong and where Adoree' was.

"He's at the police station. They wouldn't release him to me because I'm not his legal guardian," Jane she said, gesturing legal guardian with air quotes marks. "Hell, I might as well be," she added.

"How the hell did he end up at a police station?" Kobe asked.

"We were in the science museum and Adoree' grabbed one of the security guard's gun and aimed it at him. Then he aimed it at some of the kids in the class and even tried to pull on the trigger after saying 'freeze punk.' Luckily, the gun's safety was on security said," Jane explained.

Kobe started laughing, but neither of the women found it funny so they shook their heads. Kobe realized that this was a serious matter and they headed to the Baltimore police station. Jane stayed in the car with Neveah while Tiffany and Kobe power walked into the station and up the stairs.

"Hi, I'm here to pick up my son Adoree' Matthews," Tiffany said to the officer at the front desk.

"And you are?" the female officer asked.

"I'm his mom and this is his dad," Tiffany responded.

"And your names?" she asked.

"Dude, Tiffany and Kobe Matthews! Damn you want our fucking life stories too?" Kobe yelled.

"Ok, I need to see some identification from the both of you and then I need one of you to sign here," said the officer.

"Yes ma'am. Where is Adoree'?" Tiffany asked sounding concerned.

"He's in the back with the sheriff. After you sign, I'll have the Sheriff come talk to you and let you know what's going on," the officer said.

"Ok, thank you, Tiffany said.

The few minutes of waiting was torture. Tiffany was concerned that Adoree' was going to have to seek some form of discipline, but Kobe told her over and over that everything was going to be fine. While he sat there trying to explain to her that Adoree' was just a little child they heard the door opening so they both stood up to face it. The sheriff walked out standing beside Adoree' who had his head down.

"Pick ya head up," Kobe calmly said.

Adoree' lifted his head revealing the frown on his face he had since the female officer told him that his parents were here.

"Boy fix your face!" Tiffany yelled. Adoree' relaxed the frown a little and started looking over at the door.

"We underst…" Tiffany started to say before being cut off.

"Before you finish that sentence, I just want to start by saying that you have an extremely bright kid here. Mr. Matthews held a conversation with me better than a lot of the adults that come through here. He was very cooperative and knew exactly what and what not to say. I think you all might have a lawyer here in the making," the sheriff said laughing.

"We appreciate your positivity sheriff, but this isn't a delicate situation, and we apologize for our son's episode. Adoree' has never done nothing like this before so we're beyond disappointed. We hope he can move forward with just a warning," Tiffany pleaded.

The sheriff signaled for Adoree' to go and sit with the female officer. Then he turned to the couple and broke out laughing.

"Mrs. Matthews, we wouldn't prosecute a toddler, but we do want him to know that there are consequences for actions like that. I'll leave that up for you and your husband to take care of," he explained.

"We appreciate it, sheriff," Kobe responded. Tiffany walked over and grabbed Adoree' by the arm as they headed to the car. He was quiet the entire ride back mainly because he knew that he had messed up big this time. Once Kobe finally got the chance to lay in bed, he stared up at the ceiling and mumbled to himself.

"What a fucking day,"

Tiffany agreed as she laid down on his chest and rubbed the hair on his lower stomach. They ended the night holding each other tight as if it were their last day on earth.

Chapter 4

Envisionment

The beautiful Florida weather graced the Matthew's family. It was the twins' seventh birthday and the family had taken a vacation trip before the New Year. Tiffany and Kobe grossed close to seventy-five thousand combined for the year. Aside from that, Kobe flipped the 20 bricks and made a fortune. He bought his wife a 2000 Mercedes Benz car for her 35th birthday a few months prior. Tiffany just assumed that Kobe had got another loan from one of his many wealthy friends. The family was doing great. The twins loved how much space they had in their new home. Adoree's friends came over almost every weekend. Tiffany made a promise to Kobe that he would allow Adoree' to play football soon. They figured that a sport would be great for him to exert his energy since he had so much. Neveah was similar but she had more discipline. She was just about to start school at Isaiah Lampkins school for the gifted and talented. Her infatuation with education was so high, her parents sent her to an advanced educational program on the Saturdays.

On the weekends, Adoree' usually went outside and played with the kids from the neighborhood. His favorite outside activities involved running, racing the other kids, playing tag, and playing football. One time, the family was just coming back from the grocery store and Adoree's school bus was driving down the street. When the driver spotted Adoree' and his family, she quickly stopped in the middle of the street and got out of the bus to tell Kobe and Tiffany how Adoree' sometimes walked in the middle of the street in an attempt to race the buses. Tiffany grounded him for a week in addition to taking away his tv and gaming systems.

Today was the last of the family's vacation trip. Kobe made a call to his friend who was also a retired NFL player. He and Kobe arranged something nice for the family while they were all still asleep that morning. Tiffany was the first to wake up because she had to go pee bad. She turned the shower on right after she peed. Kobe came in behind her and helped her take off her clothes. He rubbed his face on her breasts while taking off his t-shirt that she was wearing and leaned her up against the sink. Tiffany leaned her head to kiss Kobe's neck, but he already kneeled for his morning meal. He knew her body so well that it wasn't even a minute until she was about to cum before Kobe stopped quickly and pulled her body closer to the edge of the sink while Tiffany directed him inside of her. He instantly began stroking rapidly as if they had not a second to spare. Tiffany leaned back with her legs spread wide enjoying every stroke. She wanted to watch his every stroke, but it was so much pleasure that she couldn't keep her eyes open. She was so wet now that you could hear the juices splashing as they met his dick. A few more strokes and he was going to bust.

They heard a knock at the door. They both jumped and covered themselves.

"Who is it?" Tiffany asked.

"I have to use the bathroom mommy," Neveah said.

"Ok baby here I come," Tiffany responded.

They hurried to get their clothes on, and when she finally opened the door Kobe was in the mirror brushing his teeth.

"Good morning sweetheart," said Kobe.

"Good morning daddy," Neveah repeated back.

Kobe left the bathroom with Tiffany. When Neveah was done, she came into the bedroom staring at both of them.

"What's wrong, Neveah?" King asked.

"Why were both of y'all using the bathroom at the same time?" asked Neveah. They looked at each other and laughed.

"We were both getting dressed and ready for our flight back home," Tiffany explained.

"Ok. Oh, and mom you forgot your underwear in the bathroom on the floor," Neveah added.

"Ok thank you. Now go wake up your brother and tell him it's time to get ready," said Tiffany.

Neveah walked away without even responding. Kobe looked at Tiffany and laughed even harder. "That girl is way too smart and aware," Tiffany mentioned.

"Well, that is a good thing though, right," Kobe asked rhetorically.

Once everyone was packed and ready to go, they went to a bagel shop and got breakfast. Kobe bought everyone bagels with eggs, cheese, and turkey with orange juice and hash browns. Adoree' finished his plate quickly and asked for more. He seemed to have been eating more but wasn't gaining weight much. Kobe told him to look at the menu for something else to eat. Adoree' scanned it.

"Dad, what's a croissant sandwich?" Adoree' asked.

Kobe and Tiffany both looked at him shocked that he could pronounce that. Kobe went ahead and ordered the sandwich with a glass of milk. A cab was waiting for them outside to head to what Tiffany and the kids thought was going to be the airport but instead they went to a very tall building. Kobe's friend, Shondell, came to meet them in the front.

"The Matthew's family, I haven't seen none of y'all since the little ones were still newborns. They're growing fast as hell. Adoree' you ready to play football like your old man?" Shondell asked.

"Yeah, I'm playing this summer. We starting to train after the New Year," Adoree' responded.

"Aww that's what's up. I know I'll see you out there one day. Y'all ready?" he asked.

"This doesn't look like the airport. Ready for what?" Tiffany asked.

"Follow me, he said as he began to walk toward the elevator.

They followed him to the top of the building where they saw a private jet. The kids started running toward it.

"Babe, what's this?" Tiffany asked. Kobe just smiled. "How in hell di…" Tiffany began to ask before he cut her off, assuring her that they were just taking a trip back to Maryland in style with it.

He grabbed her hand as they walked to the jet and boarded. They waved at Shondell who was watching them from the ground while they were taking flight. The pilot was a middle-aged African American male that instantly knew who Kobe was and asked for an autograph.

They arrived back to their city in no time. Tiffany went to the bathroom and then to bed shortly after. The kids watched tv in the living room. It was near 3:30 p.m. The time that conflicted with both of their favorite show's time. Neveah argued that she made it to the couch but Adoree' ran in and grabbed the remote before she could. Kobe overheard them going back and forth from the kitchen, so he intervened and told them to go in their rooms to watch tv. They were getting up to leave when Kobe stopped and asked them to sit back down for a moment.

"In four months it will be our 10-year anniversary. Do y'all know what an anniversary is?" asked Kobe.

"Isn't that something like when people are married for a year?" Adoree' asked in response.

"Yes, so for me and your mom this is year 10," he answered

"10 years? Dang that's a long time daddy," Neveah chimed in.

"Exactly, a longgggg time. Older than both of you. So, I want to do something very special for her. Something called renewing our vows. Who knows what vows are?" he asked.

"That's easy dad. A, E, I, O, U and sometimes Y," said Adoree'

"Haha, good guess but that's a different type of vowel. In a marriage, a vow is a promise or a pledge that the man and woman make before they get married. So, a vow renewal is re-promising the old vows and making new ones," Kobe explained.

"So, something like a pinky promise?" said Neveah.

"Just like a pinky promise," said Kobe.

The thought of remarrying his wife made him smile. He wanted it to be special and he knew the twins being a part of it would make it so. His love for her was so strong that he couldn't imagine it happening any other way so again he knew he was making the right decision.

Chapter 5

What's done in the dark must come to light

Pictures of Neveah and Adoree' were being posted all over the city. From newspapers to even the growing internet, they were stars in the making. Tiffany and Kobe decided to allow the twins to model for an agency that he was slightly familiar with. His sister. Christine, had other interests besides banking. She had a passion for children. Once she got married, she moved to Grand Rapids, Michigan with her husband where they soon after had a son. Christine hadn't been able to meet the twins since they were born but she saw a ton of pictures of them. The upcoming weekend would be when they would finally meet, and she would conduct a private photoshoot of them and of her son, Christian Jr; who was a year older than they were. Christine and Christian Sr. started the Bright Stars modeling agency a year prior to their son being born so when he was four months old, they began posting pictures of him. They hired several photographers and the agency ended up being really popular in that area.

Kobe was not excited to see Christine at all but since he would finally get the chance to meet his nephew, he accepted it. As adults they had a lot of disagreements from how their parents treated him. The way she saw it, Kobe should have just obeyed them. To add more pain, she shoved his career ending injury in his face, explaining to him that he should have finished college. Majority of his hatred towards her was that she didn't respect him. He considered her the golden child because she got whatever she wanted but in whatever she did whatever their parents wanted.

She went to college, managed her parents' finances, and visited them when they wanted her to. These bottled emotions brought out the best and worst of him. Him knowing that Christine was coming down encouraged him to get all the damages in the house repaired. Tiffany noticed the rise in Kobe's anxiety, and she tried to calm him. It took days but she was successful once she explained to him that he didn't have to prove himself to anyone, especially not her. Of course, he denied that he was doing such. Just a few days prior he took her and the kids to the mall and bought them all several new outfits. The kids needed something brand new to wear for the photoshoot anyway, but Kobe and Tiffany already had a lengthy wardrobe that still had tags on them.

Once Thursday rolled around, Kobe received a call from Christine that their plane would be arriving in a couple hours. The anxiety ate at him as he searched his pockets for a bail out; a Newport 100. This had been his go to ever since he retired from playing ball up until he and Isaac put the finesse move down.

It took for this moment to realize that the drugs were only a getaway to suppress his pain. Since life had been good lately, his pockets were empty. He sat there thinking about his childhood and his dream being taken away from him. Thirty minutes turned into an hour and before he knew it, he sprung forward for a quick fix. He drove down to the convenient store on Hyde street which was where they lived before buying their new home. He saw nothing but abandoned homes and drug dealers patrolling the block as a flashback when he pulled into the parking lot. When he stepped out, he smelled the aroma of the cigarette already in the air. Now he had to have it as he made his way to the store's entrance.

"Kobe Matthews," someone yelled from behind.

He quickly turned around to get a face to match the voice. It was Leslie, his ex-girlfriend. She was looking like a snack, wearing a red suit dress with a black pen on it that read, L. *Johnson for Mayor 02*. Her hair was long and jet black that looked good with her hazel eyes and coke bottled shape. Kobe instantly recognized her, but he didn't want it to seem so. He looked at her from head to toe, remembering everything he once did to that body. It was lust at sight again. So, he made a look of confusion as he began walking towards her.

"Hey, can I help you out with something?" Kobe asked.

She smiled. "Do you not remember me superstar?"

"Superstar?" he chuckled at the idea of that being relevant. "I'm no superstar. You look familiar. Where I know you from?" he asked.

"Wow, you're kidding right? Or maybe not because you did dump me back in 1986 while we were at a track meet. I remember it like it was yesterday," she said.

"Leslie Johnson? Damnnn girl! How are you? You don't look bad," Kobe said.

"Thank you, sir. You aren't looking too bad yourself. I'm well though. Just going around trying to do a little self-promotion," she responded.

That whole time, looking at her appetizing body he never once noticed the pin on her shirt until she mentioned that.

"Aw shit you're running for Mayor?" Kobe asked.

"Yeah. I thought you were staring at the pin on my shirt."

Naw, them titties, he thought to himself before saying,"Congratulations, I'm wishing you the best and sending my prayers."

"I appreciate it. I'll need it too because I'm the only female candidate, so you know how that is," she said.

"Oh, don't worry. You got this," he assured her.

"I'm going to take your word on that. Your twins are gorgeous. I saw them in the paper a few weeks ago. You have a beautiful family," said Leslie.

"Aww, thanks. So, what else is new?" he asked.

"Nothing really. I live in Glacier Hills. Alone. Well, me and my dog Sparkle. Oh, and I'm councilwoman still. That's honestly it," she said

"Oh yeah? I live in Glacier Hills too. I'm surprised I never saw you over there," he said.

"I stay on Slate St. Where you stay?" asked Leslie.

"Noble rd.," he responded.

"Oh ok. Well, you see why I'm here in the city right now. Why are you here?" she asked.

"On my way to pick up my sister and her family from the airport in a little bit. I was just sliding through the city to see what was going on. Haven't been here in a little while," said Kobe.

"That's good to hear. So how long you and sis been on good terms?" asked Leslie.

"Uhh, that's a long story," Kobe said as he shook his head.

"Ok ok. I see that nice car over there," she said in an attempt to change subjects.

"Oh, that's my wife's car. You know if imma be riding around in something colorful, it'll be red not yellow," Kobe joked.

"So be honest. Was it worth it?" she asked.

"Worth what? What you talkin' bout?" he asked puzzled.

"Your wife? Was she worth losing me? You know you just up and broke up with me with no explanation at all. Was it to be with her? Were you seeing her while we were together?" Leslie asked.

"Whoa whoa. Look, that was almost 15 years ago. It's irrelevant now. Just know that I loved you and you were a great girlfriend and person in general. But we had our time and obviously things didn't work out," he answered.

"No need to get all riled up, Mr. Matthews. I apologize, I just wanted some clarity that's all," she added.

"Well, there you have it. It was good seeing you, future Mayor of the city," Kobe fed back.

"Good seeing you to Kobe," she reciprocated in the same tone.

She handed Kobe a flyer before walking off. The surprising run in made him forget that he was going to buy cigarettes, so he just drove straight to the airport. He couldn't stop thinking about her the entire ride there.

"Mayor?" he said out loud.

Kobe didn't even know that Leslie was into politics. Her major was psychology when she was in college. To make his mind scatter even more, he thought about the question she asked him. He started thinking about how he did in fact cheat on her with Tiffany and how he talked to Tiffany about he and Leslie's every problem. He shrugged his shoulders at the idea of leaving her for Tiffany. I mean she was his wife now and he was happy that everything panned out the way that it did.

The airport was packed. Kobe walked near the restroom where it was a bench for him to sit down. He sat down and noticed his right shoestring was about to come loose so he tied it. He looked up and saw another face he hadn't seen in years. This time the faces came in a pair. He stood up and started walking toward them. He hadn't seen the two since his high school graduation, so he didn't even know what to say.

"Mom. Dad. What's up?" he said slowly.

"Son, so nice to see you. It's been forever. I've been hearing nothing but good things about you and your family. Your mom and I are very proud of you," said Kobe's father

"Yes son, very proud. I'm sorry it's been so long since we last saw each other. But we're here now," his mom joined in.

"Wow. I don't even know what to say. Y'all basically abandoned me and now y'all just try to pop back up like nothing ever happened. Really it's because Christine and her family are coming. That's some bullshit!" Kobe shouted.

"Aye now watch your mou…," his father said.

"Nah I ain't tryna hear that shit. I can't believe y'all," Kobe returned.

Kobe spotted Christine and her family approaching. She was cheesing hard. She truly was happy to see Kobe even though they hadn't gotten along much in the past.

"Wow, the whole Matthew's family altogether at once. I couldn't pray for a better day," Christine exclaimed. Kobe looked down at Christian Jr.

"Hey nephew, nice to meet you. And you must be Christian? Nice to meet you as well," Kobe said.

They shook hands as Christine hugged both parents. Everyone headed to Kobe's house shortly after. He had decided to postpone the tense conversation with his parents for a later time but deep down he felt some type of way about the ambush. He was only doing what he thought was right not only for him but for the sake of the children. Their family was very small, especially being that Tiffany only had her sister Jane and no one else. So, when they got to his home, he introduced everyone to each other. Adoree' and Christian Jr. instantly began interacting while Neveah did her usual and stayed to herself.

Once everyone was settled into their rooms and unpacked, Kobe's parents went home after announcing that they would be coming back tomorrow for breakfast. Christine went over to her brother and Tiffany in an attempt to catch up on things while Christian was out back playing with the boys.

"Hey Kobe. I just wanted to apologize for having mom and dad just pop up like that without warning you. I just wanted everyone to be together finally and I didn't know how you would respond If I had told you in advance," Kobe's sister intervened.

"You know, Christine, that's just like you to dictate things in your favor without anyone else's input. But I'm not even going to trip about it, but this shit has been going on for years. Decades rather. The fighting and going back and forth. It's time we move past that and be a real family. If not for us, then for the children," said Kobe.

Tiffany began nodding her head in agreeance and so did Christine.

"You know what, you're right, Kobe. I've been a poor sister to you and I'm finally seeing that. Sorry. I mean that," she said.

"Apology accepted Christine. Now let's have a drink, or two, or three," he responded.

They laughed.

Kobe pulled out three wine glasses and poured Château Pontet Canet Pauillac.

"So how did you guys meet?" Christine asked.

Tiffany and Kobe looked at each other and smiled. The attraction and intimacy of their first couple encounters was a thing to remember. Tiffany began telling their story while Kobe chipped in with a few details throughout. Christine marveled at their narration. Then she mentioned the photoshoot that was soon to happen. She asked how they thought it should go and they both shrugged their shoulders.

"What colors should they wear, baby?" Kobe asked.

"Should we let the kids decide?" Tiffany asked.

"How about we just let the kids choose what y'all think about that?" Christine asked in response. They both nodded.

"Well, I know that this shoot is for the kids but how about we all take a family picture," Tiffany added.

Christine looked at Kobe to see his reaction because she was on board with the idea. Kobe sat there stuck. It wasn't that he didn't like the idea. It was just something new to him. Even as a kid he couldn't remember him and his family taking pictures together. But just as he did the entire day, he sucked it up and went along.

"Of course we can do that," he said. The next morning, Tiffany woke up early to make breakfast. She had a banging headache from the four glasses of wine she drank the night before, so she swallowed two Motrin pills from the bathroom's medicine cabinet. They were expecting Mr. and Mrs. Matthews to be over by 9 a.m. Kobe, Tiffany, and the twins hadn't eaten breakfast as a family in a while because one or both parents would be rushing out to work. So, Jane usually came over to help here and there.

Today was Jane's day to open the salon but Tiffany decided to shut it down and invited Jane over to breakfast.

Adoree' and Christian Jr woke up arguing about who would win in a foot race. They were so loud that Tiffany heard them downstairs over the music she was playing. She yelled upstairs to Adoree' for him to lower his voice but Kobe had already taken care of it.

He told them to put their shoes on and meet him in the front of the house. As he was approaching the sidewalk, he noticed a woman jogging by, so he waited for her to pass by first. And when she did, their eyes met one another's.

"Hey Kobe. Ohhh, so this is where you live, huh?" Leslie asked.

He smiled and nodded yes. She asked if the two boys walking down the steps were his and he told her that it was his son and nephew. Leslie and the kids waved at each other before telling Kobe that she had to get back to her jog.

"On your mark, get set, go!" Kobe yelled as Christian Jr and Adoree' took off running.

It was a good race all the way until the end where Christian Jr pulled away with the victory. Adoree' got mad as he claimed that Christian Jr. had somehow cheated.

"He did not," Kobe said. He explained to Adoree' that to be a great athlete, you have to have good sportsmanship... "You'll get him next time son," Kobe added. He found humor in Adoree's facial expression after he lost the race because it reminded him of when he would react the same way when he lost as a kid.

After breakfast, Tiffany and Christine went to the mall to buy everyone's outfits for the shoot. The children decided on wearing black and gold. While they were out shopping, the rest of the family went to Kobe and Christine parents' house. The home had a discreet scent. The same one it had when Kobe lived there as a child. It had been almost 20 years since he had seen the home.

"Is my room still upstairs?" asked Kobe.

"Yes, it is son. Still looks the same. Go check it out," his dad responded.

Kobe told the kids to follow him as he went upstairs. The old bedroom now smelled like an attic. It still looked the same as it did when he lived there. He had posters of semi-nude women on his wall along with his high school freshmen jersey.

"Dad, why you like the number 8 so much?" Adoree' asked.

He took them down to the dining room where the china cabinet stood. Nearly one hundred trophies and medals filled the gigantic cabinet. Everyone else walked in the dining room as they showed the children and Christian Sr. the accolades that Kobe and Christine had accumulated throughout their childhoods. Christine was a bit of an athlete herself. She ran track and cheered all through high school. Besides her awards, the cabinet was mainly filled with Kobe's earnings. He nearly had a championship trophy from every year he played little league football and several MVP trophies.

The special cabinet also held a few autographed footballs and bobble heads from retired NFL players that he either met or watched play as a kid.

"Dad, I didn't know you boxed and ran track," said Neveah.

"Yes baby, I went to the Jr. Olympics for boxing and I broke the 100 and 200 meter dash at Linda B. Young middle school," Kobe replied. "It was my second year playing little league football and the coaches were passing out jerseys. I was an average player this year and the year before I was a scrub. So, he threw a jersey to me. I don't know how the number 8 ended up being left but it was, and the team captains were pissed that I had ended up with a single digit number. It was their attitudes that drove me. The doubt and unworthiness that they felt about me was what motivated me. Here's the result of that season. And the rest are the seasons that followed," Kobe shared.

He grabbed the most improved trophy from the bouquet of awards and handed it to Adoree' while pointing at the others which were MVP trophies. A few minutes later, Kobe's parents made lunch, and everyone ate together while Tiffany and Christine were still out shopping. At the table, Kobe brought up that he wanted to remarry Tiffany in the upcoming weeks and that he wanted to propose during the photoshoot since the whole family would be there. Kobe's parents were happy to be a part of the moment of seeing Kobe propose and in a wedding.

When Tiffany and Christine got back to the house, they noticed that no one was there. Christine called Christian Sr. but she didn't get a response and neither did Tiffany when she called Kobe. \

"Maybe they took the kids out to do something," Tiffany said.

"Well how about we do something fun?" Christine responded.

"Yeah? Like?" asked Tiffany.

"I hear there's a nice bar over near Crenshaw Rd. It's kind of a low-key bar, cheap food, and drinks," said Christine.

"I only ever go out with Kobe and we rarely go out," Tiffany said.

"Exactly girl, so let's go have some fun, just us, while the kids and the husbands are away," Christine said.

"Ok, I'll be ready in 30 minutes," Tiffany replied.

Meanwhile, the children and the guys were just leaving the jewelry store. They were helping Kobe ring shop. It took him a minute to find it, but when he did, he fell in love. The ring cost thirteen thousand plus tax and Kobe didn't hesitate to buy it because he knew that it was worth it. When they made it back home, both Christian Sr. and Kobe noticed that they had missed calls from their wives, so they called them back to find out that they were out having drinks. A few moments later, Kobe went to take out the trash. As he was turning around to go back inside, he heard a new familiar voice.

"Kobe, wait up," the voice said. He turned his body to notice Leslie standing there.

"Hey there. If I wasn't mistaken, I would think you are stalking me Ms. Mayor," Kobe humored.

"Haha, no silly. We just so happen to run into each other here and there. I mean we do live only a few blocks away from each other. What are you about to do anyway?" she asked.

"Uh, nothing I guess. Why what's up?" he asked.

"I want to show you something. Follow me," she said.

Knowing that he shouldn't, Kobe followed her anyway. As they walked through Leslie's front door, Kobe asked, "What is it that you have to show me?"

"Patience is key Kobe," Leslie said as she continued walking towards her bedroom with Kobe still following her.

At this point, Kobe was so confused at this mystery that she obviously wanted him to see so badly. As she opened the bedroom, she turned to Kobe and grabbed his arm for him to follow her to the bed. She sat down with her legs wide open, revealing her freshly shaved pussy that sat under her shorts. Kobe's eyes got big. He quickly snapped out of the idea he was having and thought to himself, *this bitch is crazy*. He turned toward the door and took two steps before Leslie stood to grab him by the shirt.

"What's the problem?" she asked.

"What's not the problem? You know I have a whole family around the corner," said Kobe.

"Well obviously I know that Kobe. But you're here. With me."

After that statement, Kobe stood there, at loss for words while they both staring each other in the eye. She grabbed Kobe's arm again and walked backwards to the bed. When she sat down, she rubbed Kobe's dick through his pants, took her other hand and licked two fingers before playing with her pussy. As she did this, she felt Kobe's dick grow harder and harder, nearly bursting through his Levi jeans. He looked up at the ceiling and thought about Tiffany. He hadn't cheated on her since their first year together. Tiffany found out about Kobe's affair and they almost broke up but managed to stay together with Kobe promising not to ever cheat again. Even with the sudden thought of Tiffany, Kobe couldn't fight the temptation of Leslie. She wasn't quite as sexy as Tiffany, nor did she have the sex appeal his wife, but Leslie was a gorgeous dark-skinned chick with a great body, not one that you could easily walk away from if you saw half naked.

Leslie pulled Kobe's dick out and started sucking it. She was so good at it and took it in so deep that Kobe thought to himself, *does this bitch have a gag reflex?* In only a few minutes, he felt like he was about to cum and that gave him satisfaction.

Yes, I cheated, but I only got head. Hell, Bill Clinton did too, he thought.

The satisfaction went away when Leslie stopped.

"Not just yet baby."

She laid backwards and pulled Kobe on top of her as they started kissing. He raised up and began peeling off Leslie's clothes. She didn't have on much, so they were off quickly. She helped him take off his shirt to reveal his cut up body.

"Damn!" Leslie said out loud.

Kobe smiled.

"This body looks the same as the 20-year-old body that I remember," she said.

As she used her hands, slowly examining Kobe's body, he then caressed her breasts with both hands and started kissing her neck slowly before making his way down to her inner thighs, causing her legs to shake uncontrollably. When he licked the top of her lips, and around her clit, she let out a moan of pleasure. It was a satisfaction that he didn't want to give her so after a few seconds, he stopped and turned her around on her knees. Her ass sat up in the air, providing an amazing view. He took both hands and gripped her ass then went inside her like he actually belonged. Leslie was so wet.

After only a few strokes, Kobe wasn't sure of how much longer he'd last. He had to close his eyes because the view of Leslie's ass bouncing back and forth on his pole was enough to make him erupt. Leslie played with her clit as Kobe was hitting from the back. She came once and was working on a second orgasm, so she moved up and signaled Kobe to lay on his back. She put her feet outside of Kobe's hips and began riding him. Kobe took one hand and grabbed one of her breasts and placed the other around her hip. After about five minutes, she turned around while his dick was still inside of her and rode Kobe from in reverse cowgirl position. Kobe couldn't believe that he hadn't cum yet. But that was about to end real soon as Leslie looked back at him.

Meanwhile, Christine was having fun of her own. She saw an old boyfriend that she dated in high school. They began drinking and as the drinks kept coming, their conversation became more intense.

"Chrissy, you talk a good game, but I remember in high school, you used to do a lot of running. And I ain't talking about track," Doug stated.

"Aha! Wow! I can't believe you're making a comparison of me now to almost twenty years ago," Christine fired back.

"I'm just saying, baby girl. Those are the last memories I have of you before your parents found out about us and made you stop seeing me," he recalled.

"Yeah, I was so sad when that happened. I didn't talk to them for days after that. But still, that's the past, D. It's 2001 now," she said.

"Sounds like you say you're a little more experienced and advanced now," Doug said with a head nod.

"Or a lot more," she said smiling.

The drinks continued coming. Before you knew it, both Christine and Tiffany were drunk as hell. The bar was about to close in twenty minutes so Doug asked Christine if she was going home with him. When asked, Christine immediately looked at Tiffany for her reaction. Tiffany gave her a face that read, 'are you serious?' Christine looked back at Doug.

"Wait a minute," she said, pulling Tiffany to the side. "Why the nasty face, Tiff?"

"Really Christine? You're married! We came here to grab a few drinks and have some fun. Not go home with a guy who couldn't even afford to buy you a drink," Tiffany reminded her.

"Exactly, we came here to have fun. Which is exactly what I'm trying to do. Plus, Christian hasn't even tried to have sex with me in months," Christine said, trying to validate the proposal.

"Well, none of that justifies you trying to go home with a guy from the bar. You can be using this time to talk to him," she replied.

"Listen. I've already made up my mind and I'm going to leave with him whether you're on board or not. So, are you going to go with me because I don't want to go alone?" she asked.

Tiffany paused for a moment then she looked at Christine. "I guess. Where does he live?"

Christine looked at Tiffany and smiled before saying, "I'll ask him."

The three arrived at Doug's house around 2:30 a.m. He lived in one of the worst neighborhoods in Baltimore. Doug's house was one of the few houses on the street that wasn't abandoned, but it still looked awful. The front stairs were beginning to cave in and the screen door was missing. When they first stepped into the house, you smelled nothing but a mixture of tobacco, rotten food, and old beer. Tiffany was pissed and Christine was pretty disappointed.

They followed Doug up the stairs where the bathroom and bedrooms were. Tiffany went to the bathroom as Christine and Doug made their ways into the bedroom. As she sat on the toilet, to get rid of the fluid she had been holding for hours, she wondered what the kids were at home doing and more importantly how Kobe was worried about her. She knew that her staying out late would make him suspicious, but she was only doing it to go with Christine at this guy's house. When she was done in the restroom, she walked out to the hallway. She wasn't sure which room Christine and Doug had gone into to know what room not to go into. The lights were off in every room, so she just decided to go into the first room she came across. The room smelled of burning marijuana and she heard a voice telling her to cut the light off. When she did, she saw Doug and Christine smoking. Doug held the blunt toward Tiffany's direction as an offer.

"Uh, no thanks," Tiffany replied.

"Come on, Tiff, just try it one time," Christine said.

"I have never done any drug before. I'm cool. Just not my thing," Tiffany responded.

"Well, you don't know if you like it until you try it," Christine proposed.

Tiffany said to herself, *fuck it, I'm already taking risks*. She walked over to grab the blunt from Doug's hand and took a puff. She started coughing and Doug and Christine started laughing.

"Here let me show you," said Christine. She grabbed the blunt from Tiffany and showed her how to take small puffs and to inhale just a tiny bit since it was her first time. She gave it back to Tiffany and she took another stab at it. This time she barely coughed.

They spent the next twenty minutes smoking and laughing. The effects of the weed began to balance out them being drunk and now high.

"I'll be right back," Tiffany said as she went to the bathroom to rinse out her mouth from the cigarillo taste.

She looked in the mirror and noticed how low and red her eyes were. When she went back to the room, she found Doug and Christine making out. And when Christine noticed Tiffany in the doorway, she told her to come over there. Once again Tiffany was hesitant at first, but she walked over. Christine leaned over and kissed Tiffany on the lips. Tiffany jumped back in surprise. Tiffany was surprised that Christine did that, but more surprised that her vagina had tingled from the kiss. Christine kissed Tiffany again and this time Tiffany kissed her back. They sat, kissing slowly and passionately as if they had both done this before.

In the midst of them kissing, Christine placed her hands on Tiffany's thigh and rubbed until she was under Tiffany's dress and onto the band of her thong. She slowly pulled them down to her knees and Tiffany pulled them off from there. Once they both got each other naked, they noticed that Doug had gotten himself undressed too. Though he didn't have much money and his house was a disaster, Doug's body was very much fit. He looked as if he worked out on a consistent basis and he was handsome. This made Tiffany hornier as she laid on her back while

Christine kneeled between her legs. As soon as she felt Christine's tongue touch her vagina, she moaned softly with her face toward the ceiling and off went the bedroom light.

***

Springing forward from the bed, Kobe rushed to the restroom and washed up before going back to the room and grabbing his clothes.

"Leaving already?" asked Leslie.

"I have to get home," he answered.

Leslie sighed. "Ok, well when will I see you again?"

"Never!" Kobe said aggressively, making his way to the door.

"That's it, no hug or nothing?" Leslie asked.

"I have to hurry home," he said as he slammed the front door.

He stormed onto the sidewalk with his head down, disappointed that he had fallen into his ex-girlfriend's trap. During the walk home, Kobe tried to think of a lie to tell Tiffany when she questioned his whereabouts.

I could just say I went to a late work meeting. No, that won't work. Shit, he thought to himself. Still in mid thought, he saw his wife and sister pulling into the driveway from a few houses down. As guilty as he felt, he still wondered why his wife would be coming home at 5:30 a.m.

"Babe, what's up?" he asked Tiffany.

"Hey handsome. I know it's late as hell, well early. Christine and I were out all night and we just kind of lost track of time. We had fun though. How was your night?" she explained.

"Well despite me being worried sick about you all. I had a decent night," he replied.

"I'm sorry, baby. I'll make it up to you, if you let me," she volunteered.

"I'm in need of that baby. You look a mess though so let's go in, get you cleaned up, and get some rest," said Kobe.

Damn that was easy. Too easy, Kobe thought to himself. But little did he know that his little secret wasn't the only one.

That next morning was the photo shoot. A big day for the whole family, especially Tiffany, who would be blind to the upcoming surprise. Kobe had everything well planned out, but it was just one thing that he was forgetting, and he knew it was important. So that morning, he pulled Christian Sr. to the side and told him to tell his wife about the proposal while the two of them got dressed. Christian Sr. assured him that he would, and Kobe felt relieved because he knew that Christine being the only one blind to the proposal besides Tiffany would make her feel some type of way. The shoot was scheduled for 10 a.m. Everyone was dressed by 9 a.m. and on their way to pick up Kobe's parents.

The photographer was a woman that got her hair done regularly at Tiffany's shop. She had conducted shoots of the twins before, but this was her first time doing a shoot of more than just two people. But after Christine gave her the layout of what the family wanted, she improvised and came up with some great poses. The last photo to be taken was of Kobe and Adoree.' While walking up in front of the camera, Kobe tripped over a prop and started holding his ankle. Tiffany and Neveah walked over to Kobe.

"What happened?" they both asked.

"That fucking box thing. I didn't see it when I turned around and tripped. Fuck this shit hurts," said Kobe. Tiffany lifted Kobe's pants leg to examine his ankle.

"Mommy! Mommy!" Neveah yelled.

"What baby?" Tiffany said and when she turned around to Neveah, Adoree' passed the ring to Kobe and he got up on one knee. He grabbed Tiffany's hand from behind to turn her back to him.

"Babe, you know I love you, right?" Kobe asked.

"Of course I do," she assured him.

"Well, it's been ten years baby. And I want to reassure you that I want to be with you forever. Will you marry me again?" he asked.

Tears came to her eyes from joy and from the unexpected gesture. From the corner of her eyes, she saw a flash from the photographer snapping a picture of the proposal. She looked over to her and smiled.

"Congrats," the photographer mouthed to Tiffany. She looked at her family; the kids first, her in laws next, and last was Christine. They hadn't said a word to each other since the night before.

She looked back at Kobe. "Yes baby."

The warehouse broke out in an applause. Tiffany was the happiest girl in the world and Kobe's proposal brought back memories of the day they first met.

"Well, the photos won't be ready for another week, babe. We should use her again at the wedding, which is next month, April 18th," Kobe warned her.

"Next month, Kobe?" she asked completely caught off guard.

"Don't worry about it. I have everything done already. All I need is for you to have your gorgeous ass there in a wedding dress and prepared to renew our vows," he replied.

"Ok, daddy. You got it," Tiffany said with a smile.

"Let's go celebrate. All of us. There's a new restaurant on Central Ave. and after that, we can go to the new bar near Crenshaw Rd. Cool?" he asked.

"Uh, let's check out the new restaurant. We can drink at home," she responded.

"Why not the bar? We haven't gone out together in forever," he questioned.

"I just want to enjoy this day with you and family babe," said Tiffany.

"Fasho," Kobe said.

***

The day of the wedding was a nice Spring evening. Kobe had sent out about 250 invites to the wedding and expected at least 175 of them to show. The location of the wedding was outside near a pond where the two had bought property previously.

Next to the pond was Tiffany's beauty salon that she had practically let Jane take over since she worked and spent all her free time with her family. Jane had been doing a wonderful job. The shop now was still doing as good as it had in the past. Jane did Tiffany's hair for the wedding that complemented her dress. Neveah was the flower girl. Adoree' and Christian Jr. were the ring bearers and Kobe's friend, Issac, and three others were the grooms while Zeus was his best man. As Kobe stood in front of Tiffany and said his vows, he evaluated his life up until that point. He felt accomplished and to top it all off, he was marrying his soulmate again. Adoree' and Christian Jr. gave the ring to Kobe once it was time.

"So glad the young King and Queen are able to be a part of this," he said to Tiffany.

When he grabbed her hand and smiled as he was putting the ring on her finger, he heard a gunshot sound from his right ear. The bullet flew right past Adoree's face, barely missing him to hit its intended target. Adoree' stood there with his mouth and eyes open as he heard people yelling and screaming in the background.

Chapter 6

Rise of a new era

"Let's go we have fifteen more minutes," the twins were told as they were packing the last of their things into the truck before they left.

It had only been three weeks since the funeral, but the family felt like they needed a fresh start. And with that being in mind, they were moving to New York. The problem with that was everything that they created would be left behind. The beauty salon was still up and running thanks to Jane. The home that they spent so much time and money remodeling would be sold for sixty percent less of what it was worth. More importantly, the family was being broken up again and the kids were leaving their friends behind. Adoree' and Neveah were sad about moving during the middle of a school year. Adoree' had only attended one school so he felt that starting at another school would be difficult.

His former school had a nice football, basketball, and track team and he was excited to try all three. But he would have to try at another school, and that school would be in New York City. At least he was already determined to do so. He told Neveah that whatever school they went to he wanted to be the best player there and he wanted Neveah to be the best cheerleader.

"Neveah, Adoree' are y'all ready?" the twins were asked as they looked at each other and headed toward the door.

The ride to New York was silent. Everyone was still taking in the tragic event that the family had endured the past few weeks. Leaving the only place that they've known for their entire lives didn't make it any better. Well maybe a new residence in a new state could be exactly what they needed, but it wouldn't help them to forget about the death of a loved one.

Up until they made it to the freeway, the twins stared out of the car looking at all of the Baltimore roads that they had never even seen before because they stayed in the suburbs for as long as they could remember.

The first thing the twins noticed about New York City was how busy the traffic was. Traffic was so packed that they were stopped at a traffic light for three minutes.

"Look at the kitty crossing the street with the people Adoree," said Neveah.

"That's not a cat, silly. That's a rat," Adoree' responded.

"Rat's aren't that big," she said.

"Well, they are in New York City. I hate it here already," said Adoree.'

When they finally made it home and got everything unpacked, Adoree' and Neveah went to go sit on the front porch. It was a different type of environment for them. Their new house wasn't in the hood, but it also wasn't the suburb. They saw kids outside playing, fighting, and walking around looking like they had nowhere to go. It was a Sunday evening, and they were supposed to start school the next morning, so after they played the video game for a few hours, they bathed and called it a night early.

The next morning, Neveah was awakened to the loud sounds of her alarm clock. She felt nervous and scared at the same time. She didn't know what to expect but she knew that she would have Adoree' by her side. With cold still in her eye, she knocked on Adoree's door. No answer. She knocked again but harder this time. Still no answer, so she just opened his door and woke him up.

"Whatttt?" he grunted.

"We have to get ready for school. It's 7:00," she shouted.

"Bus comes at 7:45 right?" he asked.

"7:30. Adoree,' hurry up," she demanded.

After they were dressed and waiting for the bus to come, Neveah looked at Adoree' and said, "I hope they have some good breakfast food because I'm starving."

As the bus pulled up, they both stepped on and it appeared to them that all the kids were staring at them. The kids were loud, some smelled, and at that moment they realized the difference from the kids that they went to school with in Maryland. What they didn't know was that the kids in Maryland parents were of a higher social class, but they couldn't really understand that anyway. Adoree' and Neveah kept quiet the whole ride to school. When the bus stopped, they were the last to get off.

Mary M. Louise was a K-8 school where most of the east side kids went. It was a miracle that the school lasted for as long being as poor and not successful as it was. The building looked about a hundred years old and the walls needed a new paint job. The floors were stained and damaged from water leaks. And the curriculum was so outdated simply because the school hadn't received new textbooks in five years. Luckily, the school year ended in mid-June and it was the first week of May. Neveah and Adoree' went to the principal's office to find out where their classroom was. The principal, Mrs. Johnson, was a middle-aged African American woman. She was lenient as she was from the hood and had been her whole life. Mrs. Johnson pulled up Neveah and Adoree's file.

"Wow, twins. I believe you two are the only set of twins here at Mary Louise. Did your parents not come today?" the principal asked.

"No ma'am. Do you know what classroom we're in?" Adoree asked.

"A mannered and eager young man. I like that. Ok, so Mr. Matthews you are in classroom 221 and Ms. Matthews, you are in classroom...221 as well," stated Mrs. Johnson.

"Wait. She's in the 5th grade Mrs. Johnson," Adoree' stated.

"Mhm, Neveah I see that you had been skipped two grades back at your old school. But our school policy requires that you will have to take a placement test to be placed back in that grade. So Green County school district in Maryland. What brings you here to New York City?" she asked.

"Just a fresh start I guess," he replied.

"Well welcome to Mary Louise and I hope you enjoy the rest of the short school year. Neveah, I will come and grab you around noon to test," Mrs. Johnson added.

Mrs. Johnson smiled as the twins walked away. Adoree' looked at Neveah and frowned.

"What?" Neveah asked.

"Why didn't you speak up for yourself?" he scorned her

"I don't know," she responded.

"Well just make sure you pass that placement test!" Adoree' demanded.

They made it to their classroom about twenty minutes after the start time. The classroom door read *Ms. Green*. She hadn't even began teaching yet when they walked in. Similar to the bus ride, the kids were loud, and they were throwing things around the classroom while the teacher just sat there. When Adoree' and Neveah got to the front of the class, the students got silent. Mrs. Johnson wasn't lying when she said she believed them to be the only set of twins in the whole school. At that moment they felt like the whole world was staring at them. They didn't like the feeling and they were eager to just get the day over with at this point.

"Good morning. I want everyone to welcome our two new students to our class. Neveah Queen Matthews and Adoree' King Matthews," the teacher said to the entire class. A group of boys in the classroom began laughing.

"Lamont, Jordan, and Ronald, how about you stand up and tell the classroom what's so funny," Ms. Green asked.

When the boys stood up, they all put their heads down. Then Ms. Green asked them to tell the class again and Jordan lifted his head.

"He's no king and she's no queen. They're both kids just like me," Jordan said.

"It's not nice to try and make fun of someone's name. Their parents named them Queen and King so that's exactly what they are. Now all three of you go and change your behavior cards to green," Ms. Green demands.

"But Mrs. Gr…" Lamont started.

"Now!" she yelled.

The behavior cards were a color system where the teacher identified a behavior problem from a student, they were to go down a color starting with blue and ending w/ red. The further down, the more trouble you got yourself in. Ronald, Lamont, and Jordan were just given a warning for that incident. Down another color would result in yellow, a time out, then down another color after that would result in a phone call home which was red.

At around 11:50 a.m., the kids were getting ready for lunch and it was about time for Neveah's placement test. Mrs. Johnson brought her to the office and gave her a bag lunch before starting. This was Neveah's only chance to prove that she belonged in a higher grade, two grades to be exact. So, when Mrs. Johnson handed over the test with the test booklet, she wished her luck and reminded her of the importance of the test.

As Neveah lifted her pencil to write her name, she thought about the moment her parents came home from her parent teacher conference meeting when she was in kindergarten and how happy that made them. The flashback caused a few tears to cloud her eyes. She thought about how fun it was to be classmates with Adoree.' Adoree' was funny and pretty popular at their school back in Maryland. With all those thoughts going through her head, she started her test.

Meanwhile, Adoree' was at lunch with his classmates. They all had to sit at the tables first before being called up to get in the line to eat. Adoree' found a seat at the end of the table where no one was sitting. Then a group of fifth grade girls came to sit near him. He sat there staring at his brand-new Jordans he'd never worn that his dad had bought for him just a few months prior. The clock on the wall displayed it was 12:36 p.m.

"Two more hours," he said to himself.

"Aren't you one of the twins here?" one of the girls asked. He nodded his head but didn't turn to look her way.

"I'm Destiny. This is Tameka, and this is Shaniece," said Destiny. Adoree' looked over and waved.

"So where is Neve… Neve…" Destiny attempted.

"My sister Neveah? She's taking a placement test," Adoree' replied.

"Oh, her name is pretty. What's your name?" she inquired.

"Adoree,'" he answered shyly.

"I like that too. That's different. So yall in Mrs. Green's or Mr. Smith's class?" she asked.

"Well, I'm in Mrs. Green's class. She'll be in one of the 5th grade classes. She skipped two grades," he explained.

"Damn. Two grades. She's smart. Y'all live close by?" asked Destiny.

"Not really sure, we just moved here yesterday from Maryland," he responded.

"Oh ok. I never been out of New York. You want to walk home together?" she asked.

"I have to catch the bus, or I'll be left."

"Ok well I'll catch the bus with you then I'll just walk home from there," she said.

"Yeah, meet me in the front of the school when the bell rings," Adoree' said.

As school was ending, Neveah and Adoree' met in the hallway before leaving. He asked her about the placement test, and she told him that she felt good about it. He told her that one of the girls he met at lunch would be getting on the bus with them. Neveah shrugged her shoulders. The siblings stood on the sidewalk and while waiting, Adoree' heard footsteps of someone running behind him. The footsteps sounded closer and closer, so he turned around and noticed the group of boys from his class.

"What's up pretty boy?" asked Lamont. Adoree' didn't answer and just looked at him.

"What you can't hear now? King," Lamont said, trying to be funny.

"What's your issue, bra? Look man, I don't want any problems," Adoree' finally responded as he put his arm around Neveah, and they walked a few feet away.

Lamont came up from behind and pushed Adoree.' Adoree' stumbled as his heart began to beat fast. He balled his fist and turned toward Lamont. Everything else just became a dark tunnel with Lamont being the only thing visible. He ran toward Lamont and tackled him. Then he punched him in the face several times before banging his head on the ground until Lamont's boys wrestled Adoree' off of him. The three of them together punched and kicked Adoree' while Neveah screamed and yelled for them to stop. But they just kept at it causing her to cry. Then out of nowhere, Destiny came and started pulling the boys off of

Adoree.' After all, three of them were on their feet the boys ran away.

"Are you ok?" Destiny asked.

"Yeah," Adoree' responded in pain.

"You're bruised up. We should get some ice on that. Come on, the bus here I think," she replied.

When they went to their house, Destiny put ice on Adoree's face. His eye and lip had swollen up pretty bad. He left Destiny in the kitchen while he went to his room to change out of the destroyed school clothes. As he was tying his shoes, he noticed that he had ruined them.

"Fuck!" he said aggressively to himself.

His parents had always taught him to take care of his shoes for appearance purposes. He took a few deep breaths to finally calm down. He had gotten so upset after the fight that his eyes were bloodshot red and the vein in his forehead looked like it was about to pop. In addition to him being upset after his first fist fight, he was nervous being around Destiny. He didn't understand why a fifth-grade girl wanted to hang out with a third grader. But he knew she was a pretty girl and he felt embarrassed that she had to help him when the boys were jumping him. While walking to the kitchen he heard a conversation being held between his sister and Destiny.

Damn, she doesn't usually talk to anyone she doesn't know, Adoree' thought to himself.

So, as he got close enough to hear them without being seen, he stopped to listen.

"Yeah, that's what Adoree' told me, was it easy or hard?" asked Destiny.

"It was actually really easy, but I failed on purpose. I want to be in class with my brother. He's funny," Neveah responded.

"You sure that's what you want? I think you have great advantage over most people," Destiny warned her.

"Yeah, I know, but I'll just finish school with Adoree.' I'm scared to go to fifth grade," she replied.

Then Adoree' walked into the kitchen and asked the two if they were hungry and they both said no.

"Actually, I should start heading home Adoree,'" said Destiny.

"Ok, I'll walk you there," he responded.

"I don't think that's a good idea. You won't know your way back. And you'll be by yourself," she said.

"Exactly, that's why I think I'm walking you back," said Adoree.' Adoree' knew that he was to come home after school and stay there. He also knew that he wasn't supposed to have company over without permission, but he didn't care.

"Stay here, Neveah," Adoree' demanded as he and Destiny walked out the house.

"I only live like ten minutes away. So, it's a short walk. Pay attention to the shortcut we take here so you can remember your way back. I wonder if my mom is back yet," Destiny said.

"What time was it?" he asked.

"It was like 3:30 I think. Sooo… your mom and dad at work?" she asked.

"Uh, yeah sort of. You like sports?" he asked.

"Nope. I like painting my nails, I like to braid, oh and I like jump roping."

"So why are your nails not painted right now?" he questioned.

Destiny laughed and then said, "I just forgot to do them, I guess. Why were you and those boys fighting? Neveah said you were beating him pretty bad. You like fighting?"

"Naw, first fight ever. The boy pushed me. I honestly don't know why. He said something in class too. But my paps always told me to defend myself," he replied.

"Dang, how did you get into it with people on your first day?" Destiny said laughing.

"I don't know," Adoree' responded with a shoulder shrug.

"Well, those boys are bad. I've watched them get into stuff all school year. Maybe they're just jealous of you and your sister," she stated.

"Why would they be jealous of us?" he questioned.

"Because both of you are good looking and everyone in class probably were staring at y'all when y'all walked in. People hate to see and hear people talk about someone in a good way and that's probably what the little girls in your class were doing. Stuff like, *'Oh my god, he's so cute. Look at his hair.'* Haha I bet that's how they were," she explained.

"Yeah yeah. Well, what can I say?" he joked.

"Oh, whatever boy. You alright. Oh, that was fast, that brown house is mine. Well Mr. Adoree.' Thank you for walking with me," said Destiny.

"Thank you for helping me earlier," he replied.

"No problem, you needed it. Oh wait, you asked if I liked sports. Do you?" she asked.

"I love football. I'm going to play on a team next year," Replied Adoree'

"Ok I'll have to go to some of the games. See you tomorrow Adoree.'" she concluded.

Destiny reached her arms out for a hug and when they did she kissed Adoree' on the cheek and went into her house. Adoree' started walking back with butterflies in his stomach. It was his first time having feelings for a girl. And the girl just so happened to be two years older than him. The walk back home felt like forever to him. He was pretty good at following directions, so he had no trouble remembering his way back.

"Aye youngblood!" a voice from across the street yelled. Adoree' looked over to where the voice coming from. It was a middle-aged male dressed in all Gucci apparel and draped in gold jewelry.

The man was driving an old school Cadillac with tinted windows and enormous rims. Adoree' was flabbergasted by the man. As dumbfounded as he was, he still managed to keep walking without responding. The man pulled up next to Adoree.'

"Aye youngster, I was riding past ya school earlier and I saw you beat that boy's ass. You got some good hands on you. And you seem polished. I go by D-Money. What they call you?" he said.

"Adoree'," he responded.

"Is that your real name?" D-Money asked.

"Yeah," Adoree' responded.

"You need a nickname youngster. Something that separates you from everyone else. Here, go buy yourself something nice," D-Money said before handing him a stack of twenty-dollar bills. "I'll see you around youngster," he concluded before speeding off.

"Thanks," Adoree' said in a low tone as he wasn't able to say it in time.

He stood there, staring at the money in confusion. He couldn't believe that just his second day in New York City was already turning into a movie. He was now holding the most amount of money he's ever had in his hands. He made it back to the house around 4:15 p.m. Walking through the door of his new home still hadn't become accustomed to him yet. He pulled out his key to unlock the door to find it. When he walked in and headed towards the steps, he was caught off guard from the back of a hand to his face. It was Tiffany who was pissed.

"What the fuck did I tell you to do when you got home from school? Come straight home and lock the doors, right? So where were you and why the hell was Neveah left here by herself?"

"Mom I'm sorry," he cried.

"Answer the damn question!" she shouted.

"I was walking my friend home. I didn't want to take Neveah because I didn't want her to get in trouble," he explained.

"Your friend? We just moved here yesterday; you don't have any friends. Now go to your room and don't come out until I tell you to!" she yelled.

Tiffany smacked Adoree' so hard that he fell to the ground. The whole time she was yelling at him she didn't even notice the bruises he had from the fight earlier that day. She hadn't heard about the fight yet because as soon as she got home and found Adoree' to not be there, she waited in the living room for him. After a few hours passed, she and Neveah went into Adoree's room. He was asleep. When they woke him up, he sat up to stretch. Tiffany noticed the bruising of his face and she knew it wasn't from her smacking him.

"What happened to your face, son?" she asked.

"I got into a fight at school," he mumbled.

"Why? What happened?" asked Tiffany.

"These boys from my class came up to me after school picking with me then one of them pushed me. So, I did what dad told me to do when someone puts their hands on me. I beat him up then they jumped me," Adoree' explained.

"Well, what happened in class to make the boys pick with you?" she questioned.

"Nothing. When the teacher introduced us…" he began.

"Us? Who is us?" she butted in.

"Neveah and me. The principal said she had to take a placement test before being put up to her grade. Their 'policy' she said," he broke down to her.

"Those motherfuckers! Ok finish," said Tiffany.

"Well as Ms. Green, our teacher, was introducing us, the boys laughed at our middle names and then got in trouble," he stated.

"Well, it sounds like those boys were jealous of yall. You are a king and your sister is a queen and that's why your dad and I named you the way we did. With that being said, next time just walk away. Neveah was the placement test easy?" she asked.

"Yes mom," Neveah said softly.

"So, tell me about your first day," Tiffany asked.

"It was… different. The kids are different, mom. I feel like everyone just stares at me," explained Neveah.

"What do you expect? You're a queen. And you're a king," she looked at Adoree' and said before continuing. "Plus, y'all are fraternal twins that actually look alike so people will always stare at y'all when y'all are together," she finished.

It was at that moment that Adoree' realized he could go by something else other than Adoree.' So, he thought of the guy driving the Cadillac earlier.

"Something that separates you from everyone else," he remembered. Then he thought about the last words he heard his dad say to his mom. The words played over and over in his head as Tiffany pulled out the photos from the photoshoot for them all to reminisce.

Chapter 7

All in the blood

Two weeks later, Adoree' had already become one of the most popular underclassmen in the school. The entire school had seen him fight and they were aware of Destiny's interest in him. With it only being two weeks of school left, he knew that he had to spend as much time with her as possible because all of the boys from his class to even some of the eighth graders wanted her. It was a Friday morning when the twins were getting dressed for school.

"So, your test scores should be back by now, right?" asked Adoree'

"I guess yeah," Neveah responded.

"So, when will you be in your right grade?" he asked.

"I don't know, King! Why so many questions this morning?" she barked.

"Because I'm mad at you. You failed that test on purpose and don't lie and say you didn't because I already know," he informed her.

"I…" she began.

"Whatever. Just tell mom that you failed, and you don't know how. Cuz she's gonna be pissed," he said.

Neveah stood there in silence trying to think about what she had done. Tiffany was running late for work so she knew that telling her now wouldn't be a good idea. She decided to wait until later. She heard the bus pull up while she was combing her hair. Her and Adoree' had curly jet-black hair that hung down to their backs. He usually kept his in braids while Neveah's was usually styled by Tiffany. But this particular day she didn't have it done. She ran outside to the bus with the comb still in her hand. Her eyes went to King, talking to some boys from their class. She went to sit next to him and laid her head on his shoulder.

"I don't like New York City, King," she said, sounding fed up.

"Give it some time," Adoree' responded. His attitude about moving had already taken a positive turn.

The bell sounded for school to start at 8 a.m. Destiny and King were still talking outside of his classroom. At 8:21, Ms. Green opened the classroom door to find King and Destiny laughing.

"Class begins at 8:00 Mr. Matthews," she said in a stern voice.

"I know, I was just coming in," he responded before waving goodbye to Destiny.

This was the third time this week he'd been tardy for class. Ms. Green allowed her students a fifteen-minute window to be present in the classroom, so she decided that a phone call home was needed. But since Tiffany wasn't home, she called her at the job to tell her. After a few minutes into the phone call, Tiffany asked to speak to Adoree.'

"Hello," Adoree' answered.

"So, I gotta stop doing what I have to do at work and take a phone call because you decided to go to class late, AGAIN? I'll see you when I get home."

King felt his stomach drop. He was terrified of what the statement meant, especially considering the back hand that he'd just received two weeks prior. With the sick to the stomach feeling he had, he went to his unassigned seat to find someone already there. He went to sit at the only open seat, directly in front of the teacher's desk. Throughout the entire day, Ms. Green called on Adoree' to answer questions about the lesson plan. He answered every last one correctly. Though he could be a class clown in which Ms. Green hadn't experienced him, he was also very intelligent and well above his educational level.

At 1:30 p.m., the class walked over to the gym for physical education. Entering the gym, King watched all the boys run onto the basketball court and Neveah watched the girls run to the double dutch circle. Back at their old school, gym classes were based on improving and testing on physical ability. Here at Mary Louise, the twins saw that they had more freedom to do what they wanted in class.

The girls taught Neveah how to jump rope and double dutch the whole class period. She was actually having fun with them. All the boys begged King to play basketball after he told them he never played before. He grabbed the ball and shot it with an unorthodox shooting form that resulted in an air ball.

After a few shots, they began playing a five-on-five game. The gym teacher, who was also the school's basketball coach, saw the game from the sideline. The basketball season had already ended, but he was recruiting for next year's season.

Coach Ivey overheard the kids discussing that King never played basketball before. But he wasn't seeing his inexperienced skill set. He was impressed by King's athletic ability. After the class, Coach Ivey walked over to King.

"Mr. Matthews or King, which one should I call you?" Coach Ivey asked.

"Either one is cool Mr. Ivey," King stated.

"Just call me Coach. I coach the basketball team. I know you're pretty young, but have you played an organized sport before?" he asked.

"I played football in the backyard," he answered.

"Haha, I meant for a team. But check this out. You got some potential and I think I can help you develop some skills. By any chance can you come up here to practice over the summer?" Coach asked.

"We just moved down here two weeks ago, so my mom is strict. You'll have to call her and ask. She's at work now so you should probably call later tonight or tomorrow," King responded.

"Do you think she'll let you out tomorrow?" he asked.

"Probably not," King admitted.

"Alright Matthews, get back to class."

King jogged to catch up with the other kids. He never thought about playing basketball, but the physical education teacher made him aware of his potential. His dad never mentioned anything about basketball to him, but he thought he'll give it a try. Later that day, when Tiffany made it home from work, King told her about the coach's interest in him playing.

She was happy to hear that King could potentially have a hobby for the upcoming summer. Her only worry was what Neveah would be doing. She thought about the placement test, so she called Neveah into the kitchen where she was cooking. Before Tiffany could even finish her question, Neveah just began crying and confessing.

"There's no way you failed that test. Neveah. You're way too smart and you said it was easy," Tiffany yelled.

"I….I didn't do well on purpose mom. I don't want to be in the 5th grade. I want to be in class with King," Neveah admitted.

Tiffany looked at Neveah in disbelief. Then she looked over at King remembering the phone call home that she received.

"What the hell has gotten into y'all kids," she said in a very calm voice.

"King, you want to play sports, but you can't even make it to class on time and Queen you won't even take advantage of the opportunities right in your face. I honestly don't get it. Both of you are so gifted at a young age. What would your father think?" Tiffany explained while shaking her head. "Queen, what are you gonna do over the summer?" she asked.

"I want to run track and go to summer camp," Queen replied.

"Summer camp? Run track where? Your school only has a boys' basketball team," Tiffany interrogated.

"I know but there's a rec right around the corner I heard. They have a summer camp with all types of activities and sports," she explained.

"I'll go down there this weekend and sign you and King up. How will you get to and from practice though?" she asked.

"I don't know. Coach Ivey should be calling you tomorrow," he replied.

"You definitely won't be going if you don't find a ride," she assured him.

A few weeks later, King went to his first basketball practice. It had previously been arranged that his coach would pick him up. But the day before at school, he told his coach that his mom will be dropping him off. So that morning, after his mom went to work, he and a classmate from down the street rode bikes up to the school. The

practice lasted for about an hour and a half before Coach
Ivey had to rush home.

"Y'all stay here and wait for your parents to arrive,"
he said after they pretended to call home.

"OK coach," the boys said.

"Let's go to Destiny's house. She said that they
were having a sleepover and her parents were gone for the
weekend. I think Peyton is there too," said King.

"We there," Anthony responded.

On the way there, they stopped at a gas station for
snacks and something to drink. The gas station was packed
with kids who were out enjoying the weather. As they were
placing their bikes on the kickstand, he noticed the old
school Cadillac from the day he walked Destiny home. He
tried to hurry and cycle out of the gas station's parking lot,
but D-Money yelled his name and signaled for him to come
here. King paused for a second then looked at Anthony.

"Come here with me real quick, bra," King insisted. They walked their bikes over to the car.

"Adoree,' what's up youngblood? Where y'all heading to?" D-Money asked.

"It's King now. And this my friend Ant. We heading over to my friend Destiny's house," King responded.

"A nickname. King, huh? I fucks with it," he said as he reached his hand into his glove compartment. "Shit y'all going to a bitch house, take these," he said while tossing King a pack of condoms and more money. "Y'all lil brothas be safe out here," he said before speeding off.

King and Ant stared at the pack of condoms not knowing what they were at first before reading the pack. When they looked back up, D-Money was pulling off. He gave half of the condoms to Anthony and put the rest in his gym bag.

"Who was that?" Anthony asked.

"Oh, that's just a friend of the family," Adoree' said.

He knew if he told Anthony that he didn't know who D-Money was or what he did, he'd probably freak out, so he just made up a lie before they finished the ride to Destiny's house.

"Hey King. I didn't know you were coming over. Where's my friend?" Destiny asked as she answered the front door.

"Who is your friend?" King asked.

"Queen silly. Why didn't you bring her?" Destiny asked.

"Well, I'm supposed to be at practice," he gestured with his fingers. "We got out early so I stopped by," he continued.

"Aw ok.. So how was it?" she asked.

"It was fun. I'm tired, oh this is Ant," King stated.

"Anthony. I know who he is. That's Ariana's little brother," she said.

Destiny and Arianna didn't get along very well. They hadn't been friends since second grade when Ariana told the whole class that Destiny still wet the bed.

"Let's go upstairs," said Destiny. She had three of her friends over for the sleepover. They were listening to music when they walked in.

"Heyyy Adoree," all three girls said at the same time.

"It's King. Only I can call him Adoree'," Destiny said smiling.

"I know but his name is just so sexy," one of the girls responded and all three of them laughed.

They spent the next several hours talking and listening to music before King realized what time it was. It was 3:40 p.m. and his mom got off work at 3:30 p.m. so he knew he had a short window to get home before she did.

For all she knew, Coach Ivey was supposed to be dropping him off around noonish. He gave Destiny a hug before he signaled to Anthony to leave. It usually took Tiffany fifteen minutes to get from her job to her house. King and Anthony cycled their bikes as fast as they could. They rode on the streets instead of the sidewalk. After crossing Martin Luther King Dr, the street around the corner from there, Anthony's dad spotted him on the bike. His dad slowed down and waited for him to get in front of the house before he pulled into the driveway.

"I thought practice was over at 12?" he asked.

Anthony turned around looking surprised. Usually, his parents didn't care about Anthony's whereabouts because he usually just played nearby in the neighborhood. But Anthony's last report card wasn't the best and he was paying for it.

"We do, dad. I was just down at Kings house playing the game," Anthony explained.

"Next time, you need to let one of us know that you're going somewhere. What if something happened to you. We wouldn't even know where you were," Anthony Sr. broke down to his son.

"Ok dad," he said.

"How was practice though?" he asked.

"Practice was fun. Ya boy gone be playing point guard this year," Anthony bragged.

By the time Anthony got to the front of his house, where his dad greeted him, King was already in his room. He emptied his bag on the floor to put his dirty clothes away when he noticed the stack of condoms. King grabbed the condoms and placed them into the top drawer of his nightstand then took his shoes off and laid down. So exhausted, he fell asleep in less than a minute.

The next Saturday was similar, except practice and afterwards King and Anthony just hung around in the neighborhood. They sat on the steps of an abandoned house while King secretly waited to see if D-Money would ride past. He was really interested to know what D-Money did and why he always spoke to him when he saw him. So out of curiosity he and Anthony rode down the street where he first saw D-Money. His car was parked in front of a purple house. King and Anthony heard two people arguing in the home. A few seconds later D-Money stormed out of the house and to his surprise he saw the two again.

"Put y'all bikes in the back and hop in," D-Money said. The boys quickly got inside the Cadillac. They rode in the car listening to Tupac for about twenty-five minutes before he pulled into a driveway and a Caucasian male approached the car.

"Get in," D-Money told the man. The man got in, looked in the back of the car and said,

"What you running a daycare now?"

"Dey family, bra. Relax," D-Money responded.

He went into his pocket and handed over a small bag of a white substance in exchange for a nice amount of money. King and Anthony looked at each other for a moment as the white man exited the car.

"King, hop in the front seat," said D-Money. After he did so, he pulled up to the nearest gas station and parked the car.

"Why you looking so nervous? You scared?" he asked.

"Scared of what?" he wondered.

"Did you see how fast that was? $1,500 in 30 minutes. This could be you. I think you got what it takes," D-Money stated.

"I never sold drugs before," King replied.

"Obviously. You don't just hop on a bike one day and know how to ride it. It takes practice young. Check this out. I've been having a lot on my plate lately. I get married in three months and my fiancé is having our baby sometime after that. What I'm saying is, I need someone to help me move some of this product. I'll take care of the big boy drugs and I'll just need someone to move the weed around. What you think?" asked D-Money.

"I don't know how. I never even saw weed besides on tv," King explained.

"Of course you don't. I'll show you everything you need to know," he assured King.

"I don't know man," he said.

"I'll give you a week to figure it out. Come back next Saturday. Same time," he said to King.

"Ok. Can we go get something to eat? I'm starving," King cried.

D-Money started laughing and pulled off. After they ate, they were taken back to their bikes. Before they rode off, D-Money said, "Think about what I said King," and that's exactly what he did for the entire week.

Every day he went to Ant's house and they discussed it. He was the only person he trusted to have the conversation with without being judged or just flat out against it. Also, if this was something that he decided to do, he wasn't going to be doing it alone. The next Saturday morning, King woke up both anxious and nervous at the same time. After he got dressed, he went to the backyard and grabbed his bike from under the porch. He had his bike there because his mom never bought him a bike, so she didn't even know he had one. The bike belongs to one of Anthony's cousins who never used it. He rode down to Anthony's house, then to practice.

Coach Ivey had the middle school players working out with the elementary players. They did an hour of conditioning and an hour of scrimmaging with two 10-minute breaks in between. This was the most physical activity that King and Anthony had ever done. Both were exhausted afterwards as they waited for the coach to pull off to grab their bikes. They rode out of the parking lot and into the street toward D-Money's house. D-Money was sitting in the driveway. He saw the two and smiled. He signaled for them to get in.

"My favorite two youngins, what's up?" asked D-Money,"

"Are you ever in the house? Seems like you're always in your car," said King.

"The money ain't gone make itself King. You gotta be a go-getter," he replied.

"So, I've thought about it all week. Me and Ant. We're ready man. Only one thing though, we get half of the profit," King proposed.

"Haha. Half, huh? How about this. I'll start you out at a third and if in a week you doin' yo thing, I'll raise you to half. Cool?" he countered.

"What's a third?" King wondered.

"I'm talking shit, bra. Half is yours," D-Money said.

So, for the next week, D-Money showed King and Ant the ends and outs of the weed game. He took them on buys, showed them how to bag the weed up, weighed it on a scale, and even how to stretch it and make it look like there's more there than there really is. King was able to get out of the house more because football practice started. Football is really what he wanted to do. He remembered all the stories that his dad told him about football and he even remembered playing in the backyard with him. Queen also started summer camp this upcoming week. Tiffany made King walk Queen to summer camp every morning since it was close and walk her back home. Soon after Tiffany got off work, she rode King down to football practice.

The first summer in New York was interesting, busy, and experimental all at once for the twins.

Chapter 8

One to remember

"Ten...nine....eight," the crowd shouted as the last few seconds of Kings middle school basketball game was coming down to a last second shot.

When the clock got to six seconds, King called for a timeout.

"King, what the fuck are you doing?" Coach Ivey yelled.

"Coach, that play you called isn't going to work. We've been shooting poorly from the three-point line all night. On the other hand, we've shot great free throws.

We're only down by 1 point so let's get to the basket and potentially draw a foul," he responded.

"He's right coach," Anthony and other players added right before the referee blew the whistle for the game to resume.

King looked over to the stands and saw his mom up on her feet smiling while he smiled back and went to inbound the ball. After he passed the ball, he ran baseline to the hoop and jumped as high he could to receive an alley-oop from Anthony. He caught the ball and slammed it into the hoop as time expired. The crowd stood in amazement. Even Coach Ivey stood there in awe as everyone rushed to King and his teammates to congratulate them on the win. Tiffany and Destiny hugged King at the same time.

"Where did y'all learn that play?" Coach asked.

"We practiced it in King's backyard all summer," Anthony replied.

"I had no idea you could dunk man. I knew you could jump but damn," said Coach Ivey.

"That was my first time. It was the adrenaline rush, coach. Wait, mom where's Queen?" King asked as he scanned the court.

"She stayed home, baby," Tiffany responded.

Queen had only been to one game all season. Any time she wasn't at track practice or doing homework, she was asleep. Track consumed a lot of her energy. She ran hard and it paid off because she was ranked as one of the top 100m in 200m dash runners in the city of New York. King knocked on his sister's door following the game. She yelled for him to come in while she was lying in bed listening to music on her MP3 player.

"What's up, slim?" asked King.

"Hey King. Everything cool?" replied Queen.

"Everything's fine. Just curious as to why my sister wasn't at my game. AGAIN!" King yelled.

"Oh shoot. Sorry. I forgot," Queen cried.

"Something you've been saying all year. I only have two games left before the playoffs. And if we don't win both, we won't make it," King explained.

"So, in other words, I need to be there, right?" she asked sarcastically.

"Well ultimately, that's up to you. Would I like for you to be there? Of course," he said.

"I'll be there. I promise," she assured him.

"When's your first meet this year?" he asked.

"My first indoor meet is in March," she responded.

"Running the 60 m dash again?" he continued,

"Probably so," said Queen.

When King left out, Queen's cell phone began to ring. It was her friend Tyra calling to see what she was up to. They decided on having a house party later that night at her house since Tiffany was going to visit Jane in Baltimore for the weekend before bringing her back to stay.

After Queen hung up the phone, she ran to King's room to ask him what he thought about throwing a party at the home. Tiffany already had party equipment stored away from a party that she hosted there for a friend's birthday party last year. All that was needed now was a DJ and promotion. So, when King was notified about the party, he got excited. Not just because of the party, but because his sister finally wanted to do something more than just sitting in the house. He called all of his friends at school and told them to let all of their friends know about the party and to be there at 8 p.m. Anthony was good at controlling the music and he liked to play with beats on his computer. Next, King called Destiny.

"Hello?" answered Destiny.

"Hey babe. Me and my sister throwing a party tonight. You're going to be there right?" he asked.

"I thought you were coming to my house. You know my mom has to work tonight," she asked.

"Yeah, just come to the party. It starts at 8 p.m.," he added.

"I'm coming. I'll be there a little late because I have to finish making the chicken that's in the oven. See you soon baby," she said before hanging up.

King and Queen started cleaning and decorating the house. Anthony brought his speakers from down the street and an extra set of lights.

"Aye, King looks like we got everything but the alcohol and weed," Ant said.

"Come on dude, you know I don't get down like that. If you want it, you grab it!" King responded.

Most of King's classmates and friends drank and smoke, but he actually listened to his mom when she said that it would stunt his growth and cause him to perform poorly in sports. But he didn't mind being around it. People started coming to the party just as fast as 8 o'clock did. The music was loud, food was good, and everyone was having fun. People were still congratulating King on his game winning dunk. They tried to ask him if he decided on a high school yet and he quickly rejected those conversations.

"Tonight is about having fun, no sports talk tonight guys," was what he kept telling them. Then he went to find Queen. She was in the living room dancing with Tyra. Tyra was always trying to get on with him and was trying to get Queen to set them up, but she always told her that he was taken. Destiny and Queen were still friends but weren't as close after she left Mary Louise and went to high school across town.

"Hey Adoree," Tyra said smiling.

King looked at both of them and asked them if they were having fun. They danced for two songs before Anthony came and pulled him to the side.

"Yo, who invited Ronald and nem?" Anthony asked.

"What?" King responded and he looked back to see them talking to a group of girls. He and Anthony walked over to the boys.

"Who invited y'all?" King asked calmly.

"Shit we just heard that there was a party here, so we came to check it out," Ronald responded.

"Yeah well, this my party so imma ask y'all to leave, man," Adoree' stated firmly.

"We not leaving, bra. We're here to party just like everybody else here is" Ronald said back.

"Imma ask y'all one more time t.."

Before King could finish his sentence, he caught a punch to the mouth by one of the boys. Everyone swarmed the fight. King stumbled backwards into a girl that was drunk; she didn't even know what was going on. Mostly everyone at the party was either friends with King or Queen or just people that knew them and were cool with them. So, Ronald and his boys were outnumbered. King didn't even get a chance to fire a punch back. A significant portion of the party chimed in with Anthony and other members from the hoop team in fucking up the unwanted guest. After getting the shit beat down their legs and stumped, they ran outside. All the girls including Queen walked up to King to see if he was all right. He had blood on his shirt that had dripped from his mouth.

"I'm fine," he exclaimed as he looked over in the doorway shaking his head. Destiny ran up to him.

"What happen, babe?" Destiny shouted to her boyfriend.

"Fucking Ronald nem came here uninvited," he mumbled.

"Let's go upstairs and get you cleaned up," she instructed.

The upstairs bathroom was next to King's room. Destiny grabbed a towel to wet with cold water and placed it on King's mouth.

"Seems like deja-vu, huh" she said jokingly, and they both started laughing as they went into King's room.

"At least it's a banging ass party," King looked at Destiny and said. She chuckled a little and stared him in his eyes. "What babe?" he asked confused.

"Nothing. Just looking at how handsome you are. Even with that fat ass lip," she responded with a smile.

She leaned in to kiss him. What was usually a routine peck on the lips, gradually turned into an erotic tongue fight. King felt his dick bulge through his Levi jeans. He pulled Destiny in closer, and closer until he eventually laid her on her back. She didn't have on much clothing, so he pulled down her leggings and aided her in taking off her shirt. Then he bent down to kiss her neck. All that was left on her was a gold necklace he had bought her for her birthday last month.

"You sure you ready?" he asked her softly directly in her ear.

She opened her eyes, looked up at him and nodded her head as she wrapped her arms around his neck and started to kiss him again. King quickly took off his clothes and reached over to his top drawer for a condom. When he turned back around, he saw Destiny staring at his dick with her mouth and eyes wide open. King was packing an enormous 13 inches and she couldn't even fathom it. He tried to put on the condom but struggled. Once he was finally able to get it over the head, it ripped.

"Shit," he muttered.

"It's not even lubricated, Adoree. How old is it?" she asked.

"I don't know, some years I guess," King responded.

"Years? We can't use that anyway bae. It's ok," Destiny said. They both laid back and stared at the ceiling until Destiny turned over and put her hand on King's chest.

"You're big as fuck," she said.

"I only weigh a hundred thirty-five pounds," King said back.

"I'm talking about your dick, silly," she said while rolling her eyes.

She slid her hand down his chest until she found what she was searching for and began stroking it until it was fully erect and throbbing in both of her hands. Destiny got up on her knees and put it in her mouth with her ass positioned perfectly in the air. Before she even took it down past the tip, she looked at King and smiled then turned back to his dick and kissed it all over.

King closed his eyes while Destiny sucked it. She eventually started to use both hands.

For a quick second, she looked up to see if he was looking at her, but he was stuck in enjoyment. Her left hand tightly squeezed both while her right hand glided up and down the shaft with the support of her saliva. The length of his dick was the biggest she had ever taken on, so she was trying to make sure she gave it her all. She kept sucking until she felt King lift up and say, "I'm boutta cum." Then she started sucking harder and faster until she felt a burst of cum shoot into her mouth. King never had a feeling so good in his entire life. After he came, Destiny continued sucking until King couldn't take it anymore and he grabbed his dick and pulled it away from her. He immediately laid backwards feeling drained and suddenly tired.

"Let's get back to the party," Destiny said with a slight smirk on her face.

When they got back downstairs the party was still lit even after people left following the fight.

"Aye, King, play our cut," Anthony yelled from across the living room.

"Naw man, they ain't ready yet," King laughed.

Anthony played it anyway. The beat came on bumping. Then King started rapping the first verse.

"Babe, is this you?" Destiny asked.

"Yeah," King replied while blushing a little. He looked around and saw people enjoying and dancing to his song, so he went over by Anthony.

"Bra, they fucking with this joint," King yelled with excitement.

"Yeah, it's our time now, bra. 9th grade next year!" Anthony yelled back.

"Man, I know. It's been a crazy ass Friday, bra," he said as he exhaled.

"Game winning dunk, people fucking with the track, and a banging ass party. You doing yo thang fasho!" he assured him.

"Hell yeah. Plus, man Destiny just sucked me DRY!" he replied.

"What? You finally hit that?" he shouted.

"Naw the fucking condom broke. Remember them condoms D gave us a while ago?" King asked.

Anthony busted out laughing before saying. "Man, you still got them? And you tried to use em? You crazy as fuck King," Anthony joked.

King started laughing too then said, "you know I did," King joked back.

"It's cool fam. Next time. Aye see if she a put me on with Peyton," he said.

"Man, you been tryna holla at her since elementary. All the girls in our class that be on yo heels," King said as he shook his head.

"It's just something bout her man. She gone be mine. Watch!" Anthony assured King.

"I believe you, bra," King nodded.

After the party, King saw Queen talking to a boy on the front porch. Like any brother would, he got close and listened to what they were saying. The boy asked if they could go to the movies next weekend and Queen said, "I don't know." He hid there until the boy left. Then he went to look for Destiny. She came through the front door as he was walking upstairs.

"So, you're still coming over my house tonight?" she asked him.

"I don't want to leave Queen here alone, especially after that party," he said.

"Of course not, babe. Both of you can come," Destiny said in a sassy tone.

"Alright," he said as he locked up the house before they got into Destiny's car and left.

***

The lights were on when they pulled up to her house. "I thought you said your mom had to work?" King asked, sounding confused.

"She do. I must have left the lights on," she replied.

King and Queen had both stayed the night over Destiny's house before, so Queen went straight to the extra bathroom and passed out. Meanwhile, Destiny told King to wait downstairs really quick. She had to re-light the candles and turn on her stereo to play the R&B cd she had specially made for King, then she called him upstairs. When he walked in her bedroom, he heard one of his favorite songs playing; *Let Me Hold You* by Bow Wow and Omarion. The candles were burning a sweet lavender scent; a scent that both he and Destiny mentioned to have liked before. He hadn't had sex before, but he knew what this scene meant. So, he sat at the end of the bed and took off his shoes while Destiny was in the bathroom doing whatever it is that females do before sex.

As he was putting his shoes under the bed, he noticed an empty condom wrapper under the bed. Then Destiny walked out of the bathroom with an all red robe draped in flowers and made of silk material.

"Damn," he whispered to himself. And quickly, the empty condom wrapper flew past his mind. Still fully clothed he stood to his feet and grabbed Destiny around the waist. She put her arms around his neck and from there they began to kiss passionately. King was so horny that the erection of his penis pressed up against her belly button.

"I love you, baby," Destiny said in a soft voice with her robe collapsing to the ground showing off her nice young body.

Next, she started taking off King's clothes aggressively. She was ready for it. Needed it; she felt like because she had waited for so long. After his boxer briefs were down, she got right down to her knees and put his love in her mouth. She bobbed her hair back and forth until her jaws hurt.

When she stood back to her feet, King laid her on her back and kissed her down from the middle of her chest to the bottom of her stomach where he felt her whole body jump and lift up slightly. He heard her moan softly then he went down lower and kissed her between both lips where the single jump became a repeated shake of her legs. He started kissing it deeper before taking his tongue and licking all around her clit. Her pussy continued to get wetter as her moans cried louder. King took his hands and slowly lifted her legs while still massaging her lips with his. Destiny's body tensed up when she was about to cum, but before she could King lifted up. She wiped her juice off his mouth with a fake smile on her face because her body was yearning for that orgasm. They stared at each other for a brief moment. They were ready to display their love for each other physically. Destiny reached on to her nightstand and grabbed a condom, one that wasn't old as shit. She tried to hand it to him to put on but thought about earlier and chuckled to herself.

"Never mind, I got it," she said. And when she went to roll it on his love her eyes were again captured by his size. She laid back down and waited for him to stick it in.

"Be gentle baby," Destiny whispered in King's ear while he tried to enter her delicate walls.

He was barely inside her, but he felt her starting to squeeze his back and breathe heavily. His baby strokes slowly became small strokes. Then the small strokes turned into longer strokes resulting in, "Adoree, yes, yes baby, mhm, mhm, mhmm…" from Destiny. After five minutes of stroking, King raised up while still inside of her and he put his hands around her neck. Her mouth opened and he heard a slight gag from her. Then he flipped her around on her stomach to kiss and lick her down her back. The kisses became bigger once he was on her booty. While still up on his knees, he stuck his love back in as she gasped louder this time. He leaned in a little and put his hands on her back while she bit down her lip to contain her moans. As he went deeper, she got wetter and started to gyrate her hips beneath him to intensify the moment. The more she moaned, the closer he was to cuming, but she didn't want him to just yet and neither did he, so he smacked her ass and instructed her to get on her knees. She did as told. He started stroking intensely while grabbing onto her hips. Then he started going faster…..deeper…. and harder. Damn near screaming and telling King to get this pussy, "your pussy" in her exact words.

"I love you. I'm loving that dick, daddy," she repeated.

And before you knew it, they both were shaking until he collapsed on her back. They laid there panting, out of breath, and gasping for air. But… it wasn't over yet since round two was yet to begin.

Chapter 9

Double Whammy

"Let me get a quarter?" a young man asked over the phone.

"Bet," King replied before he hung up.

He hurried to get dressed. His team had made it all the way through the playoffs and were playing in the championship against a school across town. Harry Truman Junior High School was one of the worst schools in the city from academic test scores, to student dropouts, and students getting juvenile cases. But they could play ball like a motherfucker. They hadn't lost a game all year, which landed them home court advantage in the championship game. Four years ago, Ronald and his crew transferred to Harry Truman when the principal threatened to tell the police about an incident; she suspected him to have done when a little boy was beat up badly in the bathroom.

This game wasn't just a championship, it was a rivalry between two young men who couldn't stand the sight of each other. Tiffany pulled up while King was still getting dressed. She blew the horn for him to come outside. In the car with her was Jane and her three-year-old son. Jane had decided to move to New York with Tiffany because the beauty salon was failing. In hindsight, business was booming in New York City. So, her and Tiffany thought it would be great to relocate, where she would allow King and Queen to help. When King was finally dressed with his gym bag in hand, he ran out to the car.

"Hi King," Adonis, Jane's son, said with a wave.

He responded with, "sup youngin,'" and gave him a high five as Tiffany sped off in a hurry so King could warm up.

Harry Truman's gymnasium was packed with loud boos directed toward King and his team. Queen and Destiny were already sitting in the bleachers waiting for the rest of the family. Both teams had begun their warmups. King's coaches and teammates were happy to see him. Prior to seeing his face, they weren't sure if he would make it since they had been calling his phone and texting but never got a response which wasn't like King at all. He was just busy trying to mentally prepare his mind for the biggest game of his career thus far.

He ran to his team's bench and quickly put on his number jersey. He ran onto the court and took a few shots before the buzzer sounded for the game to start. The players took their spots on the court for the opening tip-off and this was when he and Ronald eyes met each other. They were the only two players on the court who didn't shake hands. The tension in the air felt hectic as King's team got the first possession of the game.

Anthony brought the ball up to the court while the team's center Jamal came and set a pick for him. Once he reached the top of the three-point line, Anthony drove past his defender through an outlet pass to King for a three-pointer. The ball rimmed in and out. Ronald got the rebound and took it to the other end of the court where he then took a 3-pointer of his own that went in all net. The two went at it for about seven minutes straight until Coach Ivey took King out for a breather.

At half-time King's team was leading by only a single point. The energy in the locker room was unusual. At halftime, they were used to leading by at least six points. But little did they know, Ronald's team's typical energy was off in the locker room as well. Coach Ivey did as he always did and gave the pep talk to his team before going back onto the floor for the second half.

"King, come here," Coach Ivey yelled.

"What's up Coach?" he responded.

"Man, Ronald is killing Anthony on offense. You're going to have to guard him this half," he stated.

"Coach, Anthony is too short to guard my man," King explained.

"Just listen to me, son. You gotta take Ronald. Number 24 ain't done shit the whole first half," he responded.

King took a deep breath and ran back onto the court to take a few shots thinking, *of course that nigga ain't been doing shit all day. I've been checking him.* The second half started out the same as the first. Both teams traded baskets back and forth. King was able to slow Ronald down, but Anthony's man picked up the missing load. With every basket he scored on Anthony, King looked at his coach and shook his head. All the coach could do was shake it back. The third quarter flew by leaving the fourth quarter tense as the teams continued to keep trade lead changes. Eventually, someone had to take the lead.

During a timeout break, Coach Ivey told the team to run the same play that they ran when King had the game-winning dunk. Even the home crowd stood in amazement. The play was run successfully putting them up by 2 points with 9 seconds remaining in the game. Ronald's team took a timeout and drew up a play. Coach Ivey already knew who the ball was going to just like everyone else in the gym, so he told King to play tight defense without fouling. After the time out, Ronald got the ball and King pulled up tight to guard him. Ronald went left as a player on his team set a pick on King. King fought through the pick while listening to the crowd countdown. Four... three, and after fighting through the pick and getting back to Ronald, he jumped in the air to defend Ronald's shot only being about an inch from blocking it. When he came back to his feet, he looked over to the hoop as time expired and the ball hit the backboard bouncing to the front of the rim.

The crowd silenced as the ball seemed to have missed but rolled backwards and went in. Ronald jumped in the air throwing both fists in excitement. The crowd and bench players rushed onto the floor. King set there in disbelief. He held his head and put it down as he watched the tears sprinkle onto his sky-blue uniform shorts. Coach Ivey was the first to come over and give him a hug while King's family struggled, trying to maneuver through the celebrating crowd.

"You played an amazing game, son. You played great all season and sometimes games come down to the last shot and today we just so happened to have gotten the short end of the stick. Now come on and stand up. Let's go shake these bums' hands," Coach Ivey said in King's ear to be heard over the trumpeting crowd.

When King stood up, he saw his family all standing with open arms.

"You played a hell of a game," Jane said.

"Come on, King," Coach Ivey yelled.

King got to the back of the line to shake the other team's hand. He shook and shook all with a blank facial expression until he got to Ronald's hand and the expression turned into a frown. Ronald had his hand stuck out, but King just walked past toward the door where his family had walked over to.

"Aye hold up, bra!" Ronald yelled as King turned around. "You played a good ass game. I hit a lucky ass shot to be honest. You defended it well," Ronald sympathized.

"Yeah, same to you. Congrats on the championship," King responded.

"Thanks, bra. Shit man this lil beef we got going on should have been dead. It's old as fuck now. Plus, we bout to start high school man," he said.

King stood there quietly for a few seconds just taking it all in. He thought back to his first day of school in New York, to the incident at the house party, and then to the shot he just made over him. But he did consider that he was getting older and becoming a man so he knew that this would be a good step in that direction of growth.

"Yeah, you're right, bra. All this shit is old and petty as hell," Kind replied.

King stuck his hand as a confirmation of the truce and Ronald shook it as they both nodded their heads.

"Let's go, King!" Destiny yelled over the still crowded gymnasium.

He walked away feeling incomplete. A missed opportunity at his first championship. On his way out he heard people saying *good game,* and when he looked up to say thank you; he noticed that they were looking over his shoulder and speaking to Ronald. He and Ronald eyes met, and Ronald gave him a head nod as if he was saying farewell. As soon as he stepped onto the parking's lot pavement, he heard his phone vibrating in his gym bag seeing that he never turned the ringer back on from earlier.

"Aye, I just saw you leave out. You still got me on dat?" the caller said.

"Yeah, I forget all about you, bra. Meet me behind the school," King responded before hanging up. He told his family he'll be right back and jogged toward the school's back door where the boy who called was standing.

"What's up homie?" King asked the teenager.

"Shit just chillin.' I didn't see the whole game, but I heard you was doin' yo thang," he replied.

"Yeah. It was a good game. Now where do I know you from again?" he asked.

"We were in the same class last year. Mr. Kramer's class," the teen responded hesitantly.

"Oh yeah I remember. You transferred or something?" asked King.

"Naw man. I dropped out. Fuck school," he said with confidence.

"Yeah I feel you. You got the 90 dollars."

"I can get it for $80?" he bidded.

"Yeah, I got you this time" King replied.

It was late when the family got back home. They ate out for dinner at the new seafood restaurant a few blocks away. King was exhausted so he tried to lie down right after his shower, but Jane asked him to go to the store with her after Destiny went home. She usually brought Adonis with her when she went to run little errands but this time she asked Queen to watch him. King thought that was a little unusual.

They went to the nearest convenience store for a few miscellaneous things. There weren't many people in the store at the time. As they walked down the general purpose cleaning aisle, Jane picked up a bottle of Pine-Sol to check the price on it. She stared at it even after she saw how much it cost.

"So Adoree,' I've noticed you always keep a decent amount of money on you," Jane said

"Yeah, I save so that's why," King answered.

"Yeah, I understand that. So, after the game that you played very well in by the way, you jogged off after you took that phone call and left for a few minutes. Where'd you go?" she asked.

"Oh, I just went to holla at one of my friends," he replied.

"Oh really?" asked Jane.

"Yeah, what's up, why you ask that?" he questioned.

"Look, Adoree' or King I should say, I know what you're doing. 13-year-olds don't carry that much money or even save that much. I can't tell you what to do, but just be careful. And that's be careful with who you deal with and the police. You probably didn't know this but at one point in time before you were born, your dad sold drugs. Don't tell your mom I'm telling you this and I won't tell her about what you got going on. Deal?" Jane asked.

"Deal," he agreed.

As they continued to shop, King thought about what Jane had just told him. More so, the part about his dad selling drugs before he was born. It made him smile a little to think that he was following in his dad's footsteps no matter what it was that he was doing.

One month later, Mary Louise was holding their athletic banquet. All the players were able to bring their family and friends to see them get honored for their accolades to the team. King and Queen both wore their school colors in casual attire. Destiny brought her friend Peyton along since King kept asking her to hook her up with Anthony. And Jane dressed Adonis similar to King. Tiffany was grateful to see both of her children get the most valuable player trophy. She always knew King would play sports just from the enthusiasm he showed when he was younger playing with Kobe. But Queen's athletic nature surprised her. She ran track in elementary school, but she always came home complaining about all the running and she always had to convince her to stay on the team. So, seeing them get recognition for being the most valuable players was heartwarming to her.

Afterwards, she took both of them shopping. She told them to get what they wanted. Queen bought clothes from about five different stores. King already had a closet full of clothes, so he just bought some games and a new pair of Nike flip flops. Unlike Jane, Tiffany never recognized King's wealthiness for a youth. Probably because she worked so much and really only took off to attend the twins sporting events. She had a great relationship with both of them though. Obviously, King only told his mom what any other boy his age would tell her. But her and Queen were really like best friends. They discussed just about any and everything and they always held a girl's night at the house on various weekends. It was usually Tiffany and a few of her co-workers and a few of

Queen's friends and as of lately, Jane had been the newest addition. She brought a different type of fun to the group and she showed them how to do hair. Her and Tiffany tried to convince Queen to get paid for doing her friend's hair. Even though her mom was willing to give her anything she asked for, she knew it would be great for her to learn a new skill this early in her life while making a profit off of it.

Hours after the mall trip, Destiny went over to the Matthew's house to pick up King and Queen. She had planned on taking them to a bowling alley. On the way there, they stopped at a corner store for something to drink. Queen stayed in the car because she was sending an *important text* which is what she called it. At the front counter, when they were paying for the beverages, King was looking behind the counter at the cigarillos. Then he glanced at all the different condoms. Him and Destiny have been having sex nearly every night since their first time, but they hadn't in 3 days because she was on her period.

Even still, he had been meaning to buy condoms anyway. While still glancing through all the condoms, one brand in particular caught his attention. A red pack that read "cock sock" on them. The same brand of condoms as the one he saw under her bed the first time they had sex. He looked over at her as she was collecting the change back from her purchase. He started to say something then but decided not to. King had a better idea in mind. When they got back in the car, he claimed to have dropped something in the store and said, "Wait, I'll be right back."

King ran back into the store and bought a handful of infamous condoms. He walked back to the car slowly with the condoms in his pocket.

"Did you find it, babe?" Destiny asked.

"Hell yeah," he responded as he pulled the stack of condoms from his pocket and started flinging them at her one by one.

"What….The….Fuck...Are….These?" King asked with each fling of the condoms. His words came out raging with aggression.

"What are you talking about, Adoree?" she barked back.

"Oh, so you don't recognize these bright ass red fucking condoms, huh?" he shouted.

Destiny examined the condoms quickly and instantly caught on to what he was talking about. In just a few seconds, she had a face full of tears rolling down.

"Adoree' I'm sorry," she cried.

"Yeah, I bet," King said softly.

He looked in the backseat and gave Queen the *let's go* gesture while opening the car door. Destiny got out of the car behind him and tried to explain the situation, but King just ignored her. The corner store was only two blocks away from his house, so he and Queen walked back.

Queen was oblivious to what had just happened. She tried to talk to him, but his mind was so befuddled.

King went straight to his room and locked the door when he got home. He felt heartbroken. The only girl he had ever had feelings for had cheated on him. He felt betrayed and manipulated. Embarrassed even. After a few minutes went by, he laid down on his back to collect his thoughts until he heard a knock at the front door. King already knew who it was from by the sound of the knock. Destiny always knocked three times, paused, and then knocked three more times. But he didn't even care so he continued to let her knock. The repeated knock eventually woke up Tiffany, so she answered the door while King sat at the top of the stairwell to overhear what Destiny had to say.

"Destiny is everything okay? Why you crying?" Tiffany asked.

"Yes, Mrs. Matthews. I was trying to talk to Adoree' but he's ignoring me. We had a situation earlier and he's mad at me," she explained.

"Well, sweetheart, I can't force him to talk. And neither can you. You'll just have to wait until he's ready to talk, ok?" said Tiffany.

"Ok. Thank you. Let him know I stopped by," she said as she sniffled.

"Alright babe. Take care and stop crying," Tiffany said.

Tiffany went up to King's room after she shut and locked the door. King had quickly ran to his room and locked the door back. When Tiffany didn't get an answer after knocking twice, she called his name. He answered her quickly and came to open the door. Before she walked in, she looked over by Queen's room and saw her standing in her doorway looking curious. She shut the door behind her and sat on his bed.

"What's going on, son?" she asked.

King just looked at his mother with tears in his eyes prepared to fall.

"It's going to be hard to get over if you keep it bottled up. Whatever happened, that girl seemed desperate to talk. Things happen. Relationships aren't perfect," she explained.

"She cheated on me, mom. I found an empty condom wrapper under her bed!" he voiced.

"Wow. Well to be honest, I saw that coming. She's in high school, King. Meaning she's a little more advanced, mature, and probably hornier than you are. Don't get me wrong now, what she did was absolutely wrong on all levels. Do you think it's something that you could forget and forgive her for?" she asked.

"I'll never forget this," King replied.

"Can you forgive her? Is she worth trying to fix this to you?" she asked.

"I don't know," he said with uncertainty.

"Now you have something to think about. I'm sorry this has happened to you son. Think it through," said Tiffany.

Then she hugged and kissed him on the cheek. Queen was still standing in her doorway when she walked out of the room.

"He's alright," Tiffany assured her.

Destiny was basically in her room doing the same as King. Questions race through her mind like, 'should I call him? Or should I shoot him a text? Does he hate me?' King was her first love as well but unfortunately; he wasn't her first sexual experience. She knew she was wrong, and it was nothing she could do to change it. But her love for him was so strong that she was determined to fix it. She let the rest of the day fade out and she sent him a long text the next morning before school the text read:

Good morning my handsome. I know I'm prolly the last

person you want to talk to right now and I totally

understand. But I still want to tell you how sorry I am!

Baby, I fucked up. I never meant for it to happen. It just

did. Never in a million years did I not want you to be the

first person I had sex with. I've wanted to have sex with you

for a while now. About two years to be exact but you were

so young and when I did mention it a few times you just

kind of changed the subject. I'm not trying to justify

anything. I'm just telling you how this happened. I hope you

understand, somewhat. Please write me back and tell me

exactly how you feel about EVERYTHING. I love you so

much and I pray that we can work through this.

~SoCuteDestiny <3

Destiny checked her phone every minute to see if King had responded. By noon, she began to worry. Still no text or call. It felt like someone was squeezing her stomach. After her class came from lunch, she snuck out the back door and drove to Mary Louise school. When she got in the school's parking lot, she called King's phone. No answer so she called again and again and surprisingly, on the third try he answered.

"What?" King asked.

"I know you got my text message this morning. You could have at least wrote back. And don't answer the phone like that," Destiny barked.

"Man, what do you want?" King asked with frustration.

"I want to talk. Can you come outside?" she asked.

"Dude, are you serious?" he asked.

"Well, I'm not joking. Come on please," she begged.

"Here I come dude!" he said before hanging up the phone.

King wasn't participating in class anyway. He looked around before sneaking out the gyms back door that led to the parking lot. Destiny had already drove up near the back door. She watched him all the way until he got into the car and slammed the door.

"Damn, don't break the door," she said in a crackling voice from crying all morning. King just looked at her with disgust on his face. He had felt somewhat better from the talk with his mom last night.

"So, you don't have anything to say?" she asked.

"What is there to say?" he returned.

"Come on it has to be something. Do you accept my apology at least?" Destiny asked.

"I don't actually. If I had never found out on my own, you would have never said anything so you're only sorry because you got caught," he replied.

"Babe I was goi…" she began saying.

"Stop it. Stop lying. If you were going to tell me then you would have. So, who is this dude?" he demanded.

"You really want to know?" she asked.

"I didn't waste my breath to ask," he said.

"This guy at my school. He's a senior," she stated.

"So, is this your new boyfriend now or something?" he asked.

"No babe. You're my boyfriend if you still want to be," she assured him.

"Yeah, I don't know about all that," said King.

Destiny smiled and said, "well since we're both out of school let's go do something. Something fun."

"Like what?" he asked.

"I don't know. We'll figure something out," she told him.

Destiny drove back to her place first to change out of her school clothes. Then they went to a house that King was familiar with.

"What's here?" he asked.

"I'm about to pick up something," she responded.

"Naw, take me to my house real quick," King demanded.

Destiny didn't even ask why. She just drove him there. King ran in the house. He went to his closet and opened his safe. The safe was stuffed with money and weed. He grabbed enough weed for the two of them to smoke and a stack of money just in case. Then he went back to the car and told Destiny to drive to the store. Destiny did as she was told and pulled off. The car was loud of marijuana as soon as he stepped a foot in the car. She didn't want to go to the same store as yesterday, so she went to the drive-thru a few miles away.

"Let me get two white owls. Destiny you got a lighter right?" King asked.

"Yeah," Destiny replied before reaching into her armrest to grab it.

While she was driving to a safe place for them to smoke, King was rolling up. She knew that King didn't smoke or drink, so she was wondering how he knew how to roll. He noticed that Destiny kept glancing over at him so he laughed softly and said, "what you think cuz I don't smoke I can't roll?"

Destiny just shrugged her shoulders and raised her eyebrows. King was good at rolling blunts. D-Money taught him when he was in the third grade, and he's been doing it ever since. He used his rolling blunt skills as a way to enhance his hustle because some people in his age range, and mainly females, didn't know how to roll so they paid extra for a pre-rolled blunt. Before Destiny parked the car the blunt was lit. The sound of the tobacco paper sizzling was a confirmation to King that he had rolled the blunt to perfection. So, he let the seat all the way back and kicked his feet up on the dashboard and passed it to Destiny. Destiny grabbed the blunt and examined the neatness of it.

"Ok I see you did yo thang," she said.

In a matter of minutes, they were both high. So high that Destiny nipped the curb driving and they both laughed. They pretty much laughed all the way to downtown Manhattan where the ferries were. Neither of them has been on a ferry before so they decided to take it to Liberty, New Jersey to see the famous Statue of Liberty. It was a 10-minute wait before the next ferry arrived, so King and Destiny just sat and chatted. She couldn't believe that King was actually smoking. Everybody always knew King to refuse smoking.

Once when he was younger, he got caught smoking in the basement by Tiffany and she didn't even discipline him. She just explained to him that he shouldn't smoke because he played sports. Tiffany was a pretty laid-back, lenient parent. At times she could display her dominance over her children but that was rare. She knew that she had to be tough at times in order to replace their father's absence. But King and Queen were for the most part good, respectful kids who rarely got into trouble.

When the ferry was a couple minutes away Destiny spotted an older female walking with her young kid toward the ferry station, so she called her over.

"Hey sorry to bother you, but we were supposed to be meeting our parents here for a quick trip to Liberty City, but something came up and they couldn't make it. Is there any way…" explained Destiny.

"No problem. We were actually on our way there too. I'm Diane by the way and this is my son Raymel," Diane responded.

"Nice to meet you. I'm Destiny and this is my boyfrie… I mean brother Adoree'," Destiny stuttered.

Diane laughed and said, "It's okay. I understand. We better hurry before it leaves."

Luckily, these were the only four passengers boarding the ferry. Destiny almost had King where she wanted him. Not exactly alone but with very limited people around and doing something that would take the pressure off the incident from yesterday. She put her hands on his shoulders and began massaging them.

"You forgive me yet baby?" she snuck in. King lifted his head and smiled at her.

"You're very persistent. I like that. Let's just enjoy the moment for now though," King responded. Then he placed his arm around Destiny's legs while the two enjoyed the ride.

Chapter 10

Decision! Decisions!

August 27th, 2007 was the twins first day of high school. Queen was accepted into the best academic school in the New York City area. Her stellar grades allowed her the opportunity of a scholarship. Things had started going well with Tiffany and Jane's beauty salon as well. It had been up and running for about five months now, but business soared with the busy New York City population. Tiffany usually had Queen come up to the shop a few times a week so that she could learn various styles. King came up here and there also just to help keep the shop clean. He wasn't old enough to get his barber's license, so Tiffany didn't let him cut in the shop. But he cut hair under the table for his friends and whatever clientele they brought in. Queen was nervous for her first day of high school. She was quickly becoming the young woman that she wanted to be. Her high school was found about thirty-five minutes away or more with the busy New York City traffic. Jane usually opened the shop early on weekdays anyway, so she volunteered to take her to school.

"If you're ready, I'll teach you how to drive this summer," she said to Queen. Queen just nodded her head. She wasn't really paying attention to much of anything going on. Her mind was on her new school, the new students, and her being on a different side of town. Jane kept glancing over to her to make sure she was cool. She waited until she was near the school before she said anything else.

"What are you thinking about?" Jane asked.

"Oh, nothing I'm sorry. I didn't hear you. What did you say?" Queen asked to get back on track.

"Are you nervous about high school?" asked Jane.

"Not nervous. I just don't know what to expect. This cool isn't even a part of the New York City public school district. So, the curriculum is hard. What if the students don't like me?" she replied.

"Queen, you have never gotten a grade lower than a B in your life. You are one of the smartest people I know. Even smarter than your mom was at your age and everyone thought that she was a genius back in the day.

"Shhh, don't tell her I told you that," Jane said with a laugh then continued to talk after the car was parked in front of the school. "And don't worry about the students. Because whoever doesn't want to be your friend, is missing out."

Queen smiled at Jane then said, "thank you Auntie."

When Queen opened the door to get out the car, she saw a group of boys staring checking her out. Queen turned back to Jane, who was already smirking at her. The layout of the high school was nice. It had vending machines and the cafeteria offered a great selection of food. The majority population of the school were white or blacks who wished they were white. After Queen received her schedule and went to her first class, she checked her phone. She had two text messages from Shelton; the boy from the house party last year. The first text said, *Good morning Gorgeous, I hope your first day goes well*, and the second text said, *Hey Beautiful, I hope your day is going well so far. I can't wait to see you this weekend.*

Queen hadn't told anyone about her and Shelton talking. The two only text and spoke on the phone here and there but this weekend was supposed to be their first official date. Queen wrote back and told him that she liked the school so far and that she was sorry for text back so late. Though she hadn't seen Shelton much over the summer, she liked him. Shelton was a laid-back person. He was a one foot in, one foot out type of street guy. He sold drugs sometimes and partied a little, but he was low key, and no one knew of the things he dabbled in. He maintained decent grades and he was a star football player going into high school. Queen loved how good he was with his words. He always made funny jokes but knew exactly what to say and when to say it. She could tell him anything. Queen always told him that if he didn't play professional football that he should be a therapist or a lawyer as long as he stayed out of trouble.

Shelton made a promise to try so if his dreams never came true. He had done a one-year juvie bid when he was only eleven for stabbing his mother's boyfriend 7 times in the leg during an altercation between the boyfriend and his mother. His mother was a recovering crackhead and has now been sober ever since Shelton got convicted and sent away. Queen was eager and excited for the date. It would be her first real date with a boy. At lunch Queen got a salad. She wasn't really hungry yet. As she was paying for her food a student walked up behind her and spoke.

"Just a salad, no food?" he asked her. Queen was slightly startled so she turned around quickly.

"Yup. Just a salad. I'm not really hungry," she said.

"Have you eaten already today or something? Well besides breakfast?" he asked.

"Nah. This is it," she said with a smile on her face.

"Oh, how rude am I. I'm TJ. You know us black folks have to stick together in here," said TJ.

"Boy I know your mom didn't name you TJ. Now what is your real name?" she asked.

"Ok ok. It's Terrance. Yeah, I know. It sounds all nerdy and shit so that's why I just go by TJ," he explained.

"Well, Mr. Terrance my name is Neveah. And I mean you here at this school, so you have to be nerdy right?" she joked.

TJ broke out laughing and said, "not necessarily. What class do you have after this?" he asked.

"Um… chemistry I believe. How about you?" Queen asked.

"Chemistry? In room 113?" he replied.

"Hm.. Let me check," she said before pulling her schedule from her folder. "Yup, Mr. Heckler room 113," she stated.

"Well, I guess we might as well eat lunch then walk to 113 together," TJ finished.

They found a spot at the table where only a few students were sitting. TJ teased her once more about her salad while he ate his pasta. The two sat and talked for the whole thirty-minute lunch period. They seemed to have a lot of things in common. Queen was a twin and so was TJ, but he had an identical twin brother. Another thing in common was they both ran track. TJ was a long-distance runner while Queen was a sprinter. Both of them realized that their middle schools had competed against each other just last year.

After school ended, they met back up. Queen and TJ walk down the hallway out to the parking lot.

"You need a ride home?" he asked.

She looked up at his tall 6-foot Slender body and asked if he drove. TJ drove his ex-girlfriend's old car sometimes. He drove illegally. He wasn't old enough for a driver's license, but he had decent driving skills. TJ had been in a couple of close car accidents and he was pulled over a few times. But luckily, his dad's girlfriend was a police officer, so he used her name to get out of those predicaments.

"Yeah, I don't have a license, but I drive my dad's car sometimes," TJ responded.

"I ain't trying to die now. You know what you doing?" Queen asked just to be clear.

"Don't worry, I got this under control Nevaeh," he assured her as they both got into the car.

He turned the volume up a little to hear the Jay-Z song that he had been playing earlier, he asked her who her favorite rapper was, and she told him that she didn't listen to rap music that much. She mainly listens to R&B and some pop music, so she asked him to turn on the radio and to her surprise it was an old TLC song playing. Queen sung along Softly. As talented of a person she was, her singing sucked. TJ gave her the disgusted face which did nothing but made her sing louder. When he got to her street, she made him park a few houses down.

"This yo spot?" he asked, and she told him no while pointing down to her house. "So why you tell me to park here?" he asked her.

"Because. Don't worry about it," Queen said slowly. TJ recognized the house, but he couldn't remember where he'd seen it. He didn't mention it to her though. What he did do was ask her for her number.

"Why would you need my number if you'll see me in class Monday through Friday?" she questioned.

"Maybe I want to talk to you Monday through Sunday," he proposed.

"Well, what if I don't?" she asked jokingly. "Nah but I kind of have something going on with someone already," she continued.

"A boyfriend?" he asked.

"No, just a good friend at the moment. I'm sorry if I led you on," she said while looking him right in the eye. *But he is cute as fuck*, she thought to herself.

"Oh, naw I understand. I'll see you tomorrow," TJ responded.

"See you tomorrow. Thanks for the ride," said Queen.

She got out of the car and walked down to her home. She had butterflies in her stomach. She wanted to give him her number, but she felt that it would be wrong to Shelton. When she got into the house, no one was there so she went to her room and filled out her planner according to her syllabus. Afterwards, Queen napped for a short period before everyone got home. She was excited to see her mom to tell her all about her day. But she must have forgotten that her mom worked at the hospital and at the salon tonight. Jane was working late at the salon as well and King had football practice. So out of boredom, Queen called Shelton when she woke up. He was at home playing the video game that he paused to talk to her. They spoke on the phone for almost an hour talking about everything on their minds.

Shelton had a short practice today because his first game was the next day right after school. He was a little too advanced for the freshman team and not quite ready for varsity, so he was named the starting quarterback for the junior varsity team that hadn't won over 5 games in almost 4 years. Queen agreed to try and make it to the game if she could find a ride up there. His school was about 20 minutes away from her house.

After the call ended, she thought about who could take her to the game since no one knew about them. When

King got back from practice, she asked him if he knew where Martin Luther King High School. King knew who went to that school and that their first game was tomorrow. But just to act oblivious, he asked her why she wanted to know and if she was thinking about going there. She said she just wanted to know and went back in the kitchen. King laughed to himself. He found it funny that Queen thought she was keeping a secret from everyone and more specifically from him since they were so close.

Queen searched through contacts to find someone she can ask for a ride who wouldn't ask a thousand questions while doing so. The name D-Money popped up. Over the past few years, D-Money became acquainted with the family. They knew him as King's mentor and had no idea of his various roles in King's life. They all met one hot summer day when Tiffany and Queen were sitting on the porch. D Money had brought King back from what she believed to have just been basketball practice but really, he had taken King to meet his plug afterwards. Queen remembered their first interaction like it was yesterday because she saw her mom basically flirting.

D-Money waved at Tiffany and Queen when he first pulled in front of the house. When King got out of the car, Tiffany yelled to him.

"Tell your mentor to come here so I can meet him."

At first glance the D-Money didn't appear to her as a mentor. Tiffany thought he was dressed in hood rich clothing. By this time, D-Money had switched from the Cadillac to an all-2005 black Ford Mustang.

"Hi, how are you? I'm King's mother and this is his twin sister," said Tiffany.

"Mrs. Matthews nice to me…" he replied.

"Miss Matthews. M-I-S-S," Tiffany spelled out.

"Oh. I'm sorry. I didn't know. Very nice to meet you though. You've been doing a very nice job at raising King.

He's a wonderful kid and I'm pretty sure that his twin sister is also," D-Money responded.

"Thank you. You seem to be mentoring well also. I appreciate that and the help you do with picking him up and dropping him off," Tiffany responded as King walked into the house to get dinner ready.

"It's my pleasure. I do what I can," he said.

"So, what is it that you do to afford a car like that?" she asked.

"The same thing you do to afford the one you have," he said referring to the yellow Mercedes Benz in the driveway.

"Oh, that car is older than me." She smiled.

"Nah, but I work for a law firm in lower Manhattan. I've been working there since 94'," he responded.

"That's pretty cool," she replied.

"How about yourself?" he asked

"Oh, I'm just a RN at North Shore University Hospital. We were just waiting for King to get back for dinner. Would you like to join us?" she asked.

"Oh, I would love to, but I have to hurry back home to my pregnant wife before she kills me. Maybe next time Miss Matthews," he said slowly.

"Oh good. Congrats on the little one. I'm sure I'll be seeing you around," said Tiffany.

Queen gave D-Money a call. When he answered he was doing some work on his computer for the car lot he had just opened. He could leave the lot at any time tomorrow he told her. So, her ride to Shelton's game was confirmed. Following the phone call, she quickly texted Shelton to let him know she was going. Afterwards, she thought of the memory that led her to call D-Money. She called King to the kitchen.

"I'm worried about mom Adoree'," Queen stated.

She brought up how she remembered their mom flirting with D-Money, but how she never brought home or spoke of a man since their dad passed away. King dreaded the conversation about her mom and another man that wasn't their dad. He told Queen that she thinks too hard and she should just focus on herself. She rolled her eyes and went up to her room.

After school, the next day Queen waited outside for D money to pull up. Her and TJ didn't speak but did wave at each other. It was the awkward feeling between two people who like each other but are afraid to speak because they don't know how the other feels about them. She assumed that TJ would be upset about yesterday and he thought that she categorized him in the friend zone. When Queen got in the car, D-Money didn't pull off right away. He wanted to know who this guy was that she was so thirsty to see run up and down a field. Queen assured him that Shelton was a good dude. He believed her. His relationship with her wasn't as strong as the one he and King shared but it was solid. D-Money trusted her enough to babysit both of his children from time to time.

Martin Luther King stadium was packed, and it wasn't even everyone there who would be. The varsity had a night game a few hours after this one ended. Queen felt out of place. She didn't know anyone here and Shelton forgot to tell her what jersey number he wore so at first, she couldn't spot him out of the 30 players on the team. That was until she remembered that he said he played quarterback and she noticed long dreadlocks. "Lucky Number 7," she said out loud to herself. Shelton was on the sideline throwing the football back and forth with the coach.

The game started late like most of them did. After it ended, Shelton shook hands with the other team while looking into stands to see if Queen made it. He didn't see her so he started walking to the locker room until he heard someone say, "number 7," so he stopped and before he could turn all the way around, he saw her.

"I see you found a ride. Were you here the whole game?" he asked her while they hugged each other.

They stood and talked for about 30 seconds until Shelton told her that he would be right back out. While she waited, she went to the concession stand and grabbed some nachos and water. She turned and took a look at the field and saw the track. She wondered if she and her new team would have any track meets there. Back in the locker room, the coach gave his post speech, and the game ball was given to Shelton. He had two passing and one rushing touchdown. Once he took off his cleats, and put on some shorts, he walked back outside. Queen was sitting at one of the tables eating.

"You hungry?" asked Queen.

"Yeah, I can use something to eat and drink. I didn't bring any mo…" he answered.

"Don't worry about it. I got you," she cut him off to say.

"Thank you. And thanks for coming. How was school today?" Shelton asked.

"School was cool. Dude you played great. You can definitely get a scholarship to a big school," she replied.

"Haha. Slow down shawty. I still got three years. I have to come to one of your track meets now. When is the first one?" he asked.

"I don't even know. When I find out, you'll be the first one that knows," she assured him.

"But wouldn't you be the first one that knows?" he asked jokingly.

"Oh hush smarty pants. Let's get you some food," she responded.

After they ate, Shelton asked her to stay and watch the next game with him. But her ride was supposed to be there in the next 5 minutes, so she texted D-Money to let him know that she was staying till around 9 p.m. With just a little over an hour before the game, Shelton and Queen went inside of Martin Luther King schoolhouse. There was no one inside besides the varsity team who was in the basement. They went inside of his physical science room where Shelton found a folder of answer keys labeled with each assignment on it. Shelton didn't know if he could use them, but he copied them word for word and folded the papers into his pockets while Queen was flipping through one of the textbooks trying to see how their curriculum differed from her school.

She was really deep into the book when she felt a hand touch her butt. She quickly jumped and turned around. Shelton was smiling and very up close.

"What are you doing?" she asked.

"I just wanted to see how it felt," he said.

"Actually, that was rude as fuck. I'm ready to go," she told him.

She headed towards the door and said she heard voices coming from the hallway. Her and Shelton quickly hid when the sound of the voices got closer. After the voices passed the classroom that they were in, Shelton peeked out the door to see what it was. He couldn't believe what he was seeing. One of his classmates was touching and feeling all over his math teacher in the doorway of another classroom.

"What the fuck!" he mistakenly said out loud.

Queen asked what it was that he saw, and he just told her it was nothing and he looked back to apologize for touching her ass the way he did. She told him it was cool and headed toward the door again to leave. When they got back outside, there was only about a half hour until the game started. Shelton knew that Queen wouldn't be allowed to sit on the bench with him, so they went and solidified their front row seats. Queen looked over at Shelton and said, "don't do that again!" and he knew from the way that she said it, she was serious.

The next day at school was different. TJ came up and spoke to Queen while she was putting her book bag in her locker. He told her that she looked beautiful and she tried to hide her blushing, but she couldn't. She thought in her head that TJ looked good himself. He was wearing a brown Polo Ralph Lauren shirt with the tan logo. He wore a pair of cargo shorts that matched both the shirt and shoes he was wearing. He had a fresh haircut showing off his waves that were in a 360-degree synchronization. Shelton had a tiny bit of hair on his chin and thin mustache with hazel eyes and an earring in both ears. *Damn, why is this boy so gorgeous?* she thought in her head after every word exited his mouth.

"You good?" he asked her.

"Oh yeah," she responded as she got out of the daze she was in. He asked another question. This time about how her night ended, and she told him about the game she attended. He told her that he knew, and she asked how he knew.

"Because I saw you there with your little boyfriend," he told her. Queen was surprised. She didn't say anything but her facial expression told it all. "Yeah, my dad girlfriend's son plays varsity for Martin Luther King. It was a pretty decent game, right?" he asked.

"It was a good game but that isn't my boyfriend. I told you that on Monday," Queen exclaimed.

"I know, I was just messing with you. We better get to class before it's too late," TJ said in a hurried voice as he put his hand on Queen's shoulder and walked away.

Queen butterflies in her stomach once again. And now, she couldn't get TJ off her mind. She was damn near infatuated with him, but she was still willing to give Shelton a shot. Even after she felt somewhat violated by him the night before. Her mind was in limbo, but she wasn't at all straying away from the future tension. That weekend her and Shelton went skating. They both enjoyed themselves but afterwards when Queen got back home, all she could think about was TJ. Like what he was doing at home, what he was wearing, and more importantly, if he was thinking about her too. She knew that TJ liked her just from the few conversations they had. But still, she was curious about him and was willing to do whatever to figure him out even if it meant playing hard to get.

Chapter 11

Weather the storm

The school year was just about over. King had an okay freshmen football season. He was undersized and he didn't really like the vibe of the team. Since he had moved to New York, he and his family lived in urban neighborhoods, but his high school was in the suburban area. It was an all boys school designed to get teenage boys out of the ghetto neighborhoods, help build integrity, and realize their self-worth. Well, that's what the goal of the school was. They in fact developed a lot of athletes as well as convicts. King was used to being around girls in school. So, he wasn't very talkative while he was in there. He didn't make any friends. Anthony and a few other classmates from his middle school went there as well so they formed the small circle and only hung out with each other.

Basketball season was going well and King was doing good. But the school's track coach, who was also a linkage coordinator at the school, wanted him to take a stab at running this year. He wasn't sure if he wanted to. Queen had recently finished the indoor track season and now she was gearing up for the outdoor season, so she tried to convince King to run too. After a few weeks of thinking about it, he made his decision and that involved him doing both at the same time. He would practice basketball Monday, Wednesday, and Friday and the remaining days besides Sunday he would attend track practice. King looked at the two sports as a way of redemption for his not-so-good football season.

Football was his favorite sport, but he wasn't quite the size for it. At 5'3" and one-hundred and twenty-eight pounds, he was undersized for all sports really, but especially football. Also, he and Queen now had something in common besides being smart and being twins. One thing

King didn't have to worry about in school was female drama. He had a bunch of other girls at different schools that he spoke to, but nothing more than that. He was still in love with Destiny despite their rocky relationship. King was willing to stick around but deep down he wanted out. He never really felt that their relationship would be the same after finding the condom under the bed last year.

One day, Tiffany told him that their dad cheated on her once early on in their relationship.

"I was able to forgive him and move past it. But honestly, I never forgot. Your father and I were inseparable but sometimes people make mistakes. I never told anyone this, but I once cheated on your father too. Though he never found out, I still felt like shit about it. Even more so after he passed away. It's your decision son. Do what you feel is right in your heart," Tiffany told King in the same conversation.

King stared at her as she greeted her next client before starting their hair. He knew that what she was saying was real because she took a short break in between clients to have the conversation with him.

April 18th, 2008 was King's first ever track meet, but it was the team's sixth. He was set to run the 200m and 400m dash. Ironically, his team was running against Queen's school, Michael Reese High School. The girls' team ran the day before and Queen finished first in the 100m and 2nd and the 200m dash. She was ranked as the second fastest female freshman in New York City and that ranking was based on her performances from the past indoor track season. King attended every one of her meets while taking mental notes. Her advice to King was to drink plenty of water the morning of the track meet and not to overwhelm himself. Her method of staying calm before the start of the event was to close her eyes and take deep breaths while stretching. It took a long time but by now

Queen had started hanging with a group of girls from school. The girls stayed trying to hook up with King, but Queen never allowed it. She mostly got jealous when they flirted with him in front of her even though she was used to it. "That's a conflict of interest," she would always tell them.

The meet was set to begin at 3 p.m. so King and his team had to leave school early to travel to the school. A lot of the boys on his team were loud and did a lot of horse playing so King put his headphones on to tune everyone out. His playlist consisted of Lil Wayne, Soulja Boy, and Young Jeezy, three of the hottest rappers at the time. Once the team arrived at Michael Reese's track, King was so nervous he went straight into the bathroom. His stomach ached of a pain that made him believe he needed to use the bathroom but once he sat on the toilet, he found out it was just gas. While continuing to listen to the music, King left the bathroom and joined the team for the warm-up lap and stretches. He went straight to the end of the calisthenic line as he was sort of an outsider on the team. It wasn't that no one knew him. It was more so that he chose not to interact with people.

There was about twenty-five minutes left before the meet started when one of the runners tapped him on his shoulder. King quickly took off his headphones. He didn't want to be bothered until the meet began. So, he yelled what to the boy that tapped him.

"Aye chill, bra. Somebody want you at the gate," he responded. King turned toward the gate. It was Tiffany and little Adonis.

"Jane is gonna be bringing Queen as soon as she gets off," Tiffany yelled. She wanted to be there early for King's first meet. They waved to each other then he continued his warm-up routine.

"Runners prepare for the 200m dash!" a man yelled.

King's heart began to race. He was so nervous that he felt his hands sweating. When he took off his tracksuit, he felt as if the whole crowd was watching him. He jogged over to the start line where one of his teammates were waiting there, holding the sprint block for him. He jumped in the air and brought his knees to his chest. When he got in his running stance, he looked down at his rosary that Kobe once gave him as a child, and he kissed it. As he was putting his feet on the running block, he heard a gun go off. He flinched backwards first then took off. The flashback of his dad delayed his take off about two tenth of a second slower than other participants. But as a short-legged runner he had a fast takeoff. He was quickly able to catch up with the other runners within the first 20 meters. It wasn't windy outside, but he ran so fast that he felt wind hitting his face.

"Arms, King. Breathe, breathe," he heard his coach yelling from the field. By 50m into the race, he had taken the lead. Tiffany was clapping in excitement.

"Go go go!" she hollered.

With only about ten minutes left in the race, the runners at second and third place closed the gap and before the race ended, they passed King up. King put his hands on his head and looked in the air in an attempt to catch his breath. He was pissed that he gave up the lead the way he did. His coach walked up to him and told him that he had to finish the race better the next time. King didn't even know what to say. He just looked at him and nodded. Tiffany couldn't believe it either. She thought he had that first place sealed tight.

King walked over to the bench where his team was. There was one more heat of runners for the 200m dash. He paced back and forth as the runners prepared.

"Shit!" he yelled.

King went out of his way to kick over the tub of Gatorade. His coach was embarrassed and though he knew he was frustrated, he made him pick up the tub. There was a heat of runners for the 400m dash waiting to run before King's heat came up. The 400 meter was a different run pace compared to the 100 and 200m. In this race, the runners usually sprinted full speed for two quarters of the race and then sprint at about seventy-five percent of your maximum speed for the other two quarters. When it was time for him to run, he was placed in the eighth lane. Lane eight was the farthest one away from the rest of the runners. But to make up in the distance, the runner's starting place was ahead of everyone else. King flinched again when he heard the gunfire. He took off running at a decent pace. When he got to the second hundred meter, he sprinted his faster and followed that routine all the way through the race resulting in a fourth-place finish.

After the meet ended, King walked over to his family. He was disappointed in himself. Queen told him that he did good for his first meet.

"I came in dead last my first meet, brother," she added.

King didn't care about that remark. He was a winner, and he knew nothing but that. Once he was able to get back to his phone, he texted Destiny and asked if she had forgotten what today was. Destiny called him as soon as she got the text.

"Oh my God, I'm sorry, Adoree.' I totally forgot. When is the next one?" she asked with sympathy.

King didn't even respond. He held the phone for a few seconds and then hung up. She kept calling back and he kept ignoring it until he finally just turned off his phone. When he got home, he grabbed some clean clothes from his room and took a shower. He stood under the water for an half hour before getting out and laying in his bed. All he wanted to completely clear his mind but all he could hear was music and loud conversation coming from Queen's bedroom where she and her friends were. This had become a normal thing but by King being agitated, he went downstairs looking for his mom to complain until he got to the bottom step and remembered that she had gone into the shop tonight.

King quickly stormed back upstairs and knocked on Queen's door. Sierra, one of Queen's friends, opened the door with the biggest smile on her face when she saw that it was him.

"Hey King," she said excitedly as she stepped out of the room and closed the door.

"What's up, Sierra? You know I don't usually disturb y'all. But I have the worst headache right now. Can y'all just cut the music down a little and talk in slightly lower voices, please?" cried King.

"Okay I got you. Everything ok? You seem a little down ever since the track meet. You did good," said Sierra.

"Yeah I'm fine. It's just been a looong day ya know," he stated.

"We can talk about it. Where can we go sit?" she asked while looking in the direction of King's room.

He gestured his head for her to come on. As concerned as Sierra was about King's well-being, she also wanted him inside of her. Sierra was one of the quiet freshmens at Michael Reese High School. Like the rest of the girls Queen hung out with, she was a virgin. But she was practically in love with King. His good looks are what attracted her to him, but it was the way he carried himself that she loved most. She wasn't really interested in any of the boys at her school and by her being round King so much, she felt that he was the one for her despite him being in a relationship already.

He walked into his room and Sierra followed. They sat on the edge of his bed and King laid backwards after sighing.

"So what's going on, King?" she asked.

"Today has just been a lot. From the date all the way until my shitty ass performance at the meet," he replied.

"The date?" she asked confused.

"Yeah, Queen ain't never tell you?" he asked.

"Tell me what King?" she asked sounding even more confused.

"Our dad was shot right in front of us at the vow renewal ceremony 6 years ago today."

"Oh wow. Yeah she definitely never told me about that. She told me he passed away when y'all were younger and left it at that. I'm sorry King. I had no idea," she sympathized.

"Naw, it's cool. The gunfire at the meet just kind of brought back memories and it threw me off a little," he explained.

"I can see how that could have bothered you. Are you okay though? Anything I can do to help?" she asked.

"I'm fine. You can't brin…," he started to say until Queen walked in the doorway.

"Uh un. What's going on in here? Sierra, I told you that my brother is off limits."

"Queen, shut up. We're just talkin.' You always insinuating shit," he shouted.

"How dare you talk to me like that. You're just mad cuz I'm better than you on the track," she boasted.

"What? See you trippin.'" he fired back.

King stood up and slammed the door right in Queen's face. He walked back over to the bed angry as he plopped down. He laid on his back again. This time, Sierra laid back with him.

"I don't know why Queen be tripping over you like that. She knows that you're cute as fuck."

"Thanks," he said after he laughed a little.

"Oh yeah all the girls at our school are obsessed over you. We all talk about how fine you are, but I just think you are so different," she responded.

"Yeah well, they don't make them like me no more," he joked.

"Oh whatever," replied Sierra.

"I'm just saying. Where's your boyfriend at anyway?" asked King.

"Boyfriend? Don't have one of those. Where's your girlfriend at is the real question. Why isn't she ever here? I only saw her like twice," Sierra responded.

"Yeah man. It's complicated. She's the only girl I've ever been with. I don't know if that means anything but yeah."

"Of course, it does. It means that it's time to move on. Queen told me what happened last year," she said.

"Oh, did she? Well yeah. It happened," said King.

"So, it's time that you move on to something different. Something better actually," she bragged.

"I can show you," Sierra answered with confidence.

Sierra leaned in and put her hands on King's face. She moved in closer and tried to kiss him, but he quickly moved his head. They stared at each other for a few seconds then King grabbed her shirt to pull her towards him. Sierra's heart was damn near beating out of her chest. She felt a throbbing sensation coming from the midsection of her pants. This feeling was a mixture of being anxious and nervous both in one. King could tell she was a virgin. When he kissed her, she didn't really know how to kiss back. She kept holding her hands up not knowing what to do with them. Her body wasn't matured like a lot of females her age were. She had tiny breasts and hadn't developed any curves yet. But in this moment, King didn't even care about that. Neither did he care about Sierra being friends with his sister, especially after Queen had just barged in his room making assumptions. But it was fair game because Sierra didn't care about him having a girlfriend.

In her mind, she had what most girls wanted but couldn't have, well just in this moment at least. She was willing to do whatever he wanted. She felt the hairs on the back of her neck lift up as King began taking off her clothes. She made sure to cover herself with his bedsheet once they were off. The room was slightly chili because King kept the AC on, so she used that in defense to mask how shy she was.

Next, King stood up and took off his shirt. There was a little definition to his body, but he wasn't that big. It was enough to turn Sierra on as she sat closer to the edge of the bed to get a better view of him getting undressed. The mini strip show was great until King took off his boxer briefs and revealed his package. Her whole demeanor changed as she went from nervous and curious, too afraid especially when he began walking towards her. He stood there with his erection pointing directly in her face so that she would have no choice but to grab. She did so with just one hand, but it was too much meat for her small hand. She then grabbed it with both and lifted it up to examine.

Within minutes of King shutting the door on Queen, Sierra was sitting with King's dick in her mouth. She tried to take half of it down but kept failing. She had success at taking down maybe four inches. Once she was feeling confident, King grabbed the back of her head and started stroking her mouth. Sierra gag and gagged until she almost threw up. She had tears in both eyes causing her eyeshadow to smear. He pushed her on her back and lifted her legs. Sierra was terrified of what was about to happen next; her walls were fragile like fiberglass. Before he even stuck it in her she took in a deep breath in an effort to prepare herself. But it was too late for preparation, as he pulled her body closer and put the tip in. Sierra's whole body jumped as if she had been tased. She let out a loud moan and King was able to get in a little farther. When he was able to stroke regularly, they switched positions. King sat on the edge of the bed and instructed her to get on top. While she was riding him, he slightly tilted her body back and played with her clit, causing her to get wetter. She held her head back to enjoy the tingling sensation that she was experiencing for the first time. Then she laid on him while he gripped her butt cheeks.

Aw shit, he thought to himself because he felt that nutting sensation approaching.

King pushed her off and laid on her stomach. This was obviously his favorite position considering the fact that he only completed six and a half strokes before quickly pulling out. He grabbed it and held it tight at the top while grabbing Sierra with the opposite hand and turning her body towards him. She opened her mouth wide to take it all in. But to her surprise, King released his load all over her face with the first blast going directly into her eye, causing her to close both of them and squint like she was walking through a terrible snow blizzard.

She took the towel from King's dresser to wipe her face as she had been satisfied. It wasn't what she thought her first time would be like, but it was with the right person she convinced herself. King quickly put back on his clothes and when Sierra was fully dressed, he opened his door and walked toward the bathroom while noticing Queen who had walked up to the doorway of her room.

"What's wrong with you?" she asked.

King ignored her and kept walking toward the bathroom. Queen felt disrespected so she grabbed his shoulder, but he yanked away and closed the door in her face. Now she was furious. She busted the bathroom door open and started yelling.

"WHAT IS YOUR FUCKING PROBLEM?" she roared while Sierra stood in the doorway appearing to be overwhelmed.

"Nothing dude. I wish you would stop following me though," he said.

"I'm just trying to talk to my brother and understand why him and my gullible ass friend can't respect me. You know I don't want you fucking with any of my friends. Sorry if I came at you wrong but you know better Adoree'!" she responded.

"Look Nevaeh, I can't help that your friends like me. But Sierra and I were just talkin. I was venting to her that's all. Now that comment you made about me being mad that you're a better track runner to me was kind of unnecessary. But you were just in your feelings, so I get it," King stated.

Queen then looked over at Sierra, who was on her way to her bedroom to grab her belongings. She followed her in there and shut the door. Sierra wouldn't even make eye contact. She had the guilty conscious and their other friend, Cassidy, didn't make it any better with the complete silence in the room.

"Bitch, you know better," Queen said to Sierra. She continued putting her folders and notebooks into her book bag.

"Aye hoe, I know you hear me talking to you," Queen with aggression.

"Alright now. Watch your mouth when you're talking to me. You can't be mad that your brother is fine as fuck. Like he just told you, we were just talkin' like regular people do. Matter of fact, I don't even know why I'm explaining myself to you. I'm grown as fuck. I'll lock the door on my way out," Sierra spit back.

"Yeah, you do that. Little whore!" Queen yelled.

Sierra and Cassidy had gotten a ride from Jane after school to King's track meet. So, they didn't have a ride back home. Queen was so mad that she didn't even care how they got home. She slammed her bedroom door behind the two. They lived closer to their school across town, so King volunteered to take them home. He didn't really care for either of them, but he felt so bad, he walked down the street to grab Anthony mother's car he sometimes used when she wasn't around.

Anthony was sleeping on the couch when he got there. The front door was unlocked as usual. He had been doing drugs and drinking a lot ever since his mom and dad separated. Everyone around him could see how it affected him. Some days he didn't even shower or brush his teeth. King hated to see him like this. King sometimes thought at least he still had a father to combat the sympathy he felt for him.

"Anthony, get up!" King yelled loudly.

Anthony continued sleeping. King yelled again before roughly shaking him on the shoulder. Anthony looked up, still halfway asleep. He mumbled something but King couldn't make out the words.

"I'm bouta grab the whip, son," King said.

He went to Anthony's room and grabbed his blanket to cover him with after taking off his shoes and laying him on the couch. He walked to the kitchen, where Anthony's mom kept the car keys and grabbed them before pulling back up to his house. Sierra and Cassidy were sitting on the porch waiting for him. Sierra sat in the front seat while Cassidy got in the backseat. They were both grinning.

"What y'all smiling at?" he asked and they both said nothing.

He knew that Sierra had told Cassidy that they had just had sex.

This lil thirsty bitch, he thought to himself.

Besides the conversation about how to get to their homes, the car ride was quiet. King drove very cautiously knowing that he didn't have a temporary driver's license, let alone a real one. He had set his phone on a cup holder when he first got in the car and didn't even notice when Sierra grabbed it. She had stored her number in his contacts. She was dropped off first because she lived the closest. Cassidy stayed in the backseat.

"Bye King," Sierra said when she got out of the car. Cassidy stayed maybe a mile away. When she got out of the car, she didn't say anything but a soft, "thanks,"

King laughed to himself and yelled. "Have a good night."

"Bye Adoree!'" she yelled back.

After King dropped the car off, and walked back home, he checked his phone. There was a text from Sierra. He stared at his phone confused. The text said, *thanks for the ride bae*. He didn't even reply. He figured Sierra would cling to him after he dicked her down. Queen was upstairs still with her bedroom door closed. He knocked on her door but didn't get an answer right away though he heard her talking on the phone. He stood there continuing to knock until she opened it.

"What's up?" Queen asked.

"Just wanted to apologize about earlier. We're better than that. And we definitely can't let anyone come in between us," King replied.

"I apologize as well. And yeah, we are better than that. Thanks for taking them home too. I felt bad after y'all left out," she admitted.

King laughed and asked, "yeah so how's school?"

"It's all right. I got an A on my chemistry exam. But how are you and Destiny? I see she didn't come to your meet today. What's up with that?" she asked.

"Man..." King dragged as he let out a deep breath. "We are not the best right now. She said that she forgot about the meet. I don't know. I'm kind of over her. Over the whole relationship really," he explained.

"Well, if you do decide to part ways. I'm sure you'll find a pretty, nice, and smart girl. I still don't know why all the girls like you, you're not even cute" she said while laughing.

"Yeah whatever. I'm about to go to bed. I'll holler at you in the morning. Good night, love you," finished King.

King walked in his room that smelled of sex. He sat on his bed and felt his phone vibrate. It was another text from Sierra saying, *so you just hit & quit huh?*

King shook his head. *This bitch tripping*, he thought. He texted back saying that she didn't even give him time to respond and that the ride was no problem. He asked her if she thought Cassidy would tell Queen about them two and she told him that she didn't tell her.

"She's lying. Why else would Cassidy be acting like that if she didn't know?" he asked himself.

King's track team didn't practice again until Saturday, but his last basketball game was the upcoming

Friday. His legs were still sore from the last meet. In basketball, he started junior varsity and got very minimum playing time on the varsity team. He probably would get more playing time if he was a few inches taller. The junior varsity team had already lost their city championship game. The varsity team hadn't played well enough to make the playoffs. The coaches wanted the seniors to play the entire game as a farewell to their high school basketball careers. King woke up Friday morning with the worst leg stiffness. By him starting to run track midway through the season, he only had a week to prepare for the upcoming meet and his track coach worked him hard.

He walked to the bathroom as if he was just learning to walk again. He didn't feel like getting on the bus, so he went to get the car from Anthony's house. He had forgotten to put gas in from the last trip, so he headed to the gas station before school. School had already started an hour ago, so King was trying to rush. When he almost spilled his coffee coming out the gas station door, he heard someone say to slow down. It was Jane who was stopping for cigarettes on her way back from dropping off Queen.

"Hey Auntie," he said.

"Running late again I see. And you're still driving with no license after I said not to. Now what if I told Tiffany?" she asked.

"Auntie, you know how far away my school is. Give me a break," he said.

"Yeah, alright boy. Be careful. I seem to tell you that a lot these days," she said to him then went into the gas station.

King hurried back to the car and headed to school. Before he could even make it off the street, Jane called his cell phone.

"Hey King. I forgot to ask you, but do you want to take a little road trip with me this weekend to Baltimore. My best friend is getting married. You don't have to go to the wedding. I just don't want to drive all alone. And Queen is already going to like Kentucky or something for a track meet. Otherwise, I would have asked her. What you think?" she asked

King sat silent on the phone for a moment. He hadn't been to Baltimore, or even in Maryland since they moved 6 years ago. The shooting, fun memories with his dad, and thoughts of his mother being happy all flashed through his mind. It gave his body chills, and he was all in a daze.

"Hello, King, King you still there?" Jane asked.

"Yeah, my bad. Yeah, I'll go. Are we leaving today? Because I have a game at 3," King finally responded.

"Okay cool and yeah, we'll leave right after. Text me everything you want me to pack and I'll bring it with me to the game. Is it a home game?" she asked.

"Yeah, we're home. I'll text it to you. Talk to you later. I have to be careful, remember?" he said sarcastically before Jane chuckled and hung up.

King didn't arrive at school until the end of second period. He couldn't believe that Anthony made it to class today, let alone before he did. Anthony looked terrible. You could tell he hadn't really been taking care of himself. His hair needed a cut, he needed more sleep, and his beard was patchy. King didn't have a beard. He had what people considered a baby face unlike his dad who had a full beard since the age of 16.

Second period was algebra. He was excelling in this class just as he did it all the other ones. Tiffany always told him and Queen that school should be their first priority and that everything else should come second. Even sports since she knew how much he loved them. King smiled when he saw Anthony across the room. Anthony signaled for him to come over.

"Let me guess, you drove the car here?" Anthony asked

"Yeah, how you know?" replied King.

"Cuz I know that you wouldn't have come if you had to catch the late bus that runs every hour. Oh and I see the keys boa," he explained.

King chuckled and said, "you already know. I locked the door for you too. You need to get that together. I'm glad to see you back in class," King responded.

"Yeah, my mom woke me up before work this morning. She said I looked bad the other night when she came in from work. I don't even remember getting my cover and laying down before I passed out. Shit I don't even remember passing out," Anthony said.

"That was me, bra. I used the car that night too. Oh, let me tell you, bra. I fucked Sierra!" King said with excitement.

"Who?" questioned Anthony.

"Sierra; Queens friend. One of the girls that's always over the house," Explained King

"Ohhhh, the thick one?" he asked for verification.

"Naw, the skinny one. The thick one is Cassidy," he stated.

"Oh yeah, man what? Queen allowed that? You know how she be cock blocking for her friends," Anthony said.

"Man bra, I hit in my room. She was thirsty as fuck. Her shit was wet too. Shid, wetter than Destiny's to be honest," said King

"Damn ok. I'm proud of you, yo scary ass haha. Shit I got to see what's up with Cassidy now. Her pretty ass," responded Anthony.

"Man, you still ain't hit Peyton yet?" King asked.

"Nope, she be playing. I know she feeling me but she fuck with some do at her school. Son probably a lame anyway," he said.

King and Anthony didn't notice how loud they were talking until they stopped and saw a few of their classmates eavesdropping. They had a test today. Anthony hadn't been to class in almost a week, so he wasn't prepared. King was aware of that so before the tests were passed out, he looked at Anthony and said, "I got you, bro."

It took him no longer than ten minutes to finish. When he was done, he and Anthony skipped the last ten minutes of class and went to the gym. They each grabbed a basketball and took some shots. Anthony was a little rusty. He hadn't shot a basketball since the team's last junior varsity game and it showed as he threw up several air balls.

"Ant, you dressing today for the last varsity game?" King asked.

"Shit, if coach lets me. You know I ain't been here in forever," Anthony responded

Well, we won't get a chance to play any way, King thought to himself. They shot around until it was time for their next class. King remembered that he had to text Jane what he needed her to pack.

Once school ended King, and Anthony went back to the gym, all the seniors were dressed for the game already. King grabbed his jersey from the coach's office while Anthony sat in and talked to the coach. The coach was grilling Anthony. King laughed as he hurried out of there to get dressed and join the layup line. The gym filled up fast with fans who were mostly family and friends of the seniors. King told his family not to come so the only person he was expecting was Jane. She showed up a little after it started. King was sitting on the bench. He didn't like being at the varsity games. He didn't play much plus he didn't get to wear his favorite jersey number because one of the seniors wore it. So as usual, he just sat and watched. His team was leading by six points. The game was going good until an unexpected injury occurred. The team's leading scorer for the past two years had went up for a dunk and landed wrong on his ankle after being fouled. You can feel the empathy from the crowd as a loud "awww" echoed through the gym. The game was delayed for twenty minutes while the medical staff carted the fresh 18-year-old off the court. The coach looked over to the bench. His eyes glanced at King, but then passed him.

"Bam Bam you're up!" Coach yelled.

Bam Bam was a senior on the team who didn't play at all. But he came to every practice and sometimes he helped the coach come up with new schemes. He had good basketball IQ, but his skill level wasn't the best. His first three plays in the game he made costly mistakes. The coach was red hot. He slammed his clipboard on the ground and took a time-out. He needed this game. His coaching job was on the line, but he wanted this game more so for his seniors that were playing in their last high school game. Coach glanced at the bench again.

Bam Bam has to slide, the coach thought himself. He glanced at King for a moment and again his eyes went past them, but this time they went back in his direction.

"King, come here," he said. The coach left the huddle and walked King over to the water fountain. "Your team needs you more than ever right now. We're down only by a point though. Can you handle this?" Coach asked sounding very concerned.

King looked up and nodded his head. He jogged toward the huddle as the time-out was nearly over. "I was born ready, Coach."

When the players stepped back on the court, one of the seniors put his arm around King's shoulder and told him not to fuck this up. King didn't even respond to him; his focus was on the task at hand. When the ball was inbounded to him, he jogged up the court and threw an assist to the senior that had just put his arm around his shoulder then looked at him and winked. The team went back up by one point. Both teams started off the second half slow.

By the fourth quarter, King had fourteen points and eleven assists. His teammates, the coach, and all the fans were impressed by the way the freshman was performing in the varsity game. Jane cheered King on, she didn't even expect to see him play. The seniors finished their last game with a victory. The final score was 71-63. All the seniors showed their gratitude with hugs and handshakes. The coach looked at him.

"Next year is yours," his coach said.

King smiled and waved at Jane before running to the locker room where the team concluded the season and he showered. Afterwards, he went back into the gym and made his way to where the exit door where Jane was waiting. There was still people in the gym waiting around and talking. King noticed a group of girls from his elementary school. One of the girls was Amara; a dark-skinned girl, who transferred in the fifth grade. She looked different. He almost didn't recognize her.

The girls began waving as he got closer, so he stopped and chatted for a moment. Each of the girls engaged in conversation except Amara but King noticed that she wouldn't take her eyes off him and neither did he. He told them that he was in a rush and he wished he could stay and chat, so he invited them all to the next track meet which was next Saturday here at the school before he headed back over to Jane. She held the door open for King and they walked to the car.

"Boy, if you play like this next year, you're going to get some early scholarship offers," Jane assured him.

"Yeah, I know. You know if you get tired of driving I can help out some," King suggested.

"Em hm. I'll think about that. So, how's destiny?" she asked.

"She cool," King said non chalet.

"I haven't saw her lately. Y'all still together?" she asked.

"I guess so," he responded.

"Not to sound even more cliche but you better be careful with those little girls. I saw you flirting back there," Jane said.

"I was just making conversation auntie. I know them from my old school," King said with a slight laugh.

"Yeah, I hear you. Let's go get some food so we can hit the road. It's like a little over 3 hours," Jane said.

After eating his food, and stopping to use the bathroom, King fell right asleep. He was exhausted. He felt great about the game and he kept replaying the words of his coach saying *next year is yours* before he fell asleep. Jane had chosen a bad time to travel as traffic was busy for the first two and a half hours causing them to be off schedule a little. When he woke up, he saw how dark it was outside, so he checked his phone for the time. It was 8:48 p.m.

"I thought we would be there by now, Auntie," he said.

Jane told him that they will be there soon and that they will be going to her best friend's house for a second before going to the hotel. He hadn't met any of Jane's friends before, but he figured if she was traveling to another state for a wedding, it had to be her close childhood friend. They arrived at 9:17 p.m. Her best friend stayed in the hood. There was a house party and people still hanging outside on the street she stayed on. The screen door was closed but the front door was wide open. Jane knocked in a girl with the red plastic cup in her hand answered. She was obviously drunk as she slurred every word.

"Hey, Jane, right?" she asked. Jane said yeah before her and King entered.

The music was loud, and it was all females there. When they got into the living room, they saw a man who was wearing nothing but very tight underwear that looked like panties King thought. The man was dancing over a woman who was sitting down staring up at him. You could tell she was drunk because she couldn't stop smiling and when she saw Jane she stumbled trying to stand up.

"Janeee. Hey best friend," she yelled over the music.

They hugged for a long time and then she looked over at King.

"And who is this little cutie?" she asked.

"Oh, this is my nephew Adoree.' He accompanied me on my ride here," Jane said to her best friend.

"Wait, is this Tiff's son? One of the twins?" she asked.

"Yeah," Jane replied.

"Oh my God. He's so big now. Where is the sister?" she asked.

"She had something to do Chelsea. Listen though, why didn't you tell me you were having a bachelorette party?" Jane asked.

"I guess I forgot," Chelsea said.

"Well, I'm about to take him to the hotel and I'll be back," Jane said.

"You don't have to leave, Auntie. Just give me the keys. I have GPS on my phone. What's the address?" King pitched.

"Boy, I'm not letting you dri…," said Jane.

"Girl, let him. You already late. Let's turn up!" Chelsea yelled.

Jane thought about it for a moment. She didn't feel comfortable giving him her keys to drive, especially not in a city he wasn't familiar with. But the excitement of seeing her old friend took over. She hadn't taken a drink in a long time. In fact, her last time drinking was with her best friend several years prior. Plus, it was her best friend's bachelorette party. With that in mind, she handed King the keys, gave him the name of the hotel, and told him to drive carefully.

"Use your GPS, turn signals, and drive the speed limit. Oh, and don't forget to cut on your lights," she said to him sounding serious as a heart attack.

King grabbed the keys and headed back toward the front door. As he was about to exit, another woman was entering. Their eyes met for a brief moment, leaving King with a weird feeling. When he opened the screen door, he turned around curious to whom the woman was just to find that she had turned to check him out as well. But they continued to walk, and King hopped into Jane's 2004 Pontiac Grand Prix and started it.

"Lights," he said to himself as a reminder to turn them on.

He entered the hotel's address into the GPS and headed that way. When he pulled up, he remembered that he wasn't old enough to check into the hotel by himself. He quickly called Jane. She didn't answer the first time, so he called again, and she picked up.

"Auntie, I can't check into the hotel. I'm not eighteen," he told her.

"Oh fuck, I forgot. I'm on my way," Jane said.

It took her thirty minutes to get there. She had been drinking and she didn't have her car, so she found one of the women there that was sober to drive her. King got out of the car when he saw Jane and the other woman walking into the hotel. Both of them turned and looked at the door when they heard it open. Again, King and the other women's eyes met; the same woman from Chelsea's house.

"Who the hell is this woman?" he whispered under his breath.

As he walked up, he quickly rotated his eyes to Jane trying his hardest not to look at her again. Even still, he felt her looking at him through his peripheral even as Jane was checking him in.

"All right I'll see you in the morning, King," Jane said before they left.

The next morning, Jane came into the hotel hungover. Her hair was a mess and her clothes looked sweated out and she reeked of alcohol. King woke up when she came in. She got in the shower. King woke up to a text from both Destiny and Sierra. He didn't text either of them back. When Jane came out the bathroom, he asked her what time the wedding started. She told him 2 p.m. Then he told her that he wanted to go, and she asked if he was sure.

"Yeah, why not. I don't have nothing else to do. I need a suit though," he said.

Jane had to go pick up her bridesmaid's dress from the shop anyway, so she figured she'd take him to get a suit while they were out. The bridal shop opened at 8 a.m. King already had a fresh haircut. A bald fade with waves was what he rocked for the past year since he had grown tired of his hair. He wanted to try a different look, so he had also gone and gotten his ears pierced and put in very small gold hoops that went great with his gold fossil watch. All he needed now was a tailored suit. So that's what he and Jane went and got. King reached in his pocket to pay for it, but Jane stopped him.

"Boy, save your money," she said as she swiped her debit card for the payment.

***

"Okay so behave yourself and make sure you stand and clap after they kiss. I'm going to be away, next to the other brides," stated Jane.

"Okay, I got you. So, is that woman that brought you over here last night a bridesmaid as well?" King asked anxiously.

"Yep," replied Jane.

The wedding's location wasn't far from the hotel. They went to meet up with Chelsea. Chelsea introduced King to her soon-to-be husband. He recognized King instantly.

"Little Adoree', how are you man? You don't remember me, do you?" he asked.

King stood there clueless without saying a word.

"I figured you wouldn't. I was a friend of your dad's back in the day. I haven't saw you since you were about two years old. You look the same though. Come on let's let the ladies get ready. I'm not even supposed to be seeing her until the wedding," he said with a smile on his face as King followed him to the other side of the building.

The wedding was being held outside since it was a beautiful day in April. It was a nice ceremony. It brought back memories from a wedding he had attended six years ago in the same city. King's father was on his mind even more being that there was someone there outside of his family that mentioned him. The reception followed the wedding in the same venue. King overheard Jane talking to Chelsea about how great the wine was, so he snuck and tried some. It wasn't long before he was buzzed and sitting alone. That was until the woman kept finding him and locking eyes, walked past. It probably was the alcohol that encouraged him to follow her. She must have known he would follow because she quickly turned to him after a few steps.

"You following me? I could have sworn I just saw you sitting down," said the woman.

"Nah, I was just heading back to my aunt," King made up.

"Oh okay. King, right?" she asked.

"Yeah, how you know?" he asked.

"I heard your aunt say it. So how is it out there in New York?" she continued.

"It's cool there. Different from here but it's cool," he replied.

"So, you like weddings or you just came to this one so your aunt wouldn't be alone?" she fished.

"Maybe I came to see you," he answered.

The woman laughed and asked, "boy, how old are you like 13?"

"Old enough to notice that you've been staring at me which probably means that you find me somewhat attractive," he assumed.

"What if I just like your haircut or something?" she said with a big smile.

"That could be the case. Only you know though so yeah. Oh, and I'm 14," he replied.

"Soo… young. Well Mr. King, it was nice seeing you. I have to get back to the reception," the woman said as she stood up.

The woman gave King a look that said she was looking forward to seeing him again. King went back to where he was sitting prior to the exchange and stayed there until it was time to go. Everyone said their goodbyes and congratulated the newlyweds. King looked around for the woman while Jane and Chelsea hugged but she wasn't nowhere around.

"Must have left already," King mumbled.

"You said what?" Jane asked.

"Oh nothing, I was talking to myself," King responded as they headed to the parking lot.

When they got to the car, Jane asked King what he wanted to do for the rest of the day. He had no idea, the only thing on his mind was that woman. He could tell she was older, in her thirties at least he thought just because she hung out with Chelsea who was in her forties. Despite her crowd, King thought she could maybe even be in her late twenties.

"I don't know, auntie. I don't know what it is to do out here. It's up to you," he said. James brought up that someone at the reception mentioned that there was a barbecue at Lewis' Park in the city.

"Want to check it out?" Jane asked.

The inside of King's body lit up at the possibility of seeing the woman again. After they changed their clothes, they headed to Lewis' Park. There were a lot of people there, mainly adults. Jane saw a bunch of her old friends and King saw two teenagers who he attended school with when he lived here. They stood around and talked while King kept his eyes wandering for the woman. He was surprised that he hadn't seen her yet. They stayed there until the sun went down and it was near dark outside. But still no sight of the woman. Jane had been drinking again so she had King drive. He had already sobered up from the wine earlier.

Jane woke up the next morning; she was hungover and felt like shit, but she spent time with old friends who she hadn't seen in years. They both showered before packing their bags to leave around noon. Jane still felt horrible, so King started the drive back to New York. Usually, King enjoyed driving with the music playing, but his mind was occupied on the mystery woman whose name he didn't even know; her face, her voice, her body was all he could think about.

The next week of school dragged with practice state tests. He worked his ass off the entire week except the day before the meet. His coach saw how hard he was practicing. King was leading the pack in majority of the workouts and he was even being more of a leader. His coach told him that this would all pay off this week at the meet. Saturday's track meet was an early one. Again, his family came to support but Queen didn't bring any of her friends this time. She must have learned her lesson from the last meet.

The gun sounded for the 200m dash and King paced himself perfectly around the track's first curve. Once he was on the first hundred-meter straight away, he ran hard but smooth at the same time. He finished in second place. He stretched and got ready for his next and final race. He heard a girl call his name. He looked up and remembered that he told the girls from his elementary school to come watch him run. But only one of them showed and favorably it was the only one he wanted to see.

"Good luck!" she yelled, and King waved at her with a huge Kool-Aid smile on his face until his coach told him to focus.

When the gun sounded for the 400-meter dash, King set a nice pace for all the runners as he led the pack. By the last curve, he had slowed down a little and by the last 100 meters he had given up the lead. By the final 50-meter mark, King's facial expression had changed. He looked locked in and determined. He began to take quicker but longer strides in perfect sync with his arm movement. With only twenty meters left, he regained the lead and it appeared as if he was gliding to the finish line. After the race he heard a loud voice announce a new city record over the intercom. As tired as King was, his eyes lit up and the leader board showed the time in which he completed the race.

"Fifty seconds!" he screamed to his coach who came and hugged him.

"I told you it would pay off," the coach assured him.

King was excited and so was his family. After the meeting ended, he ran over to hug them. Tiffany squeezed him hard, causing King to laugh.

"Set the city record though? I'm the goat," he said.

"The goat? Why not like a cheetah or something?" Tiffany questioned.

King laughed again. "Noooo. The GOAT. It stands for greatest of all time," King said.

"Ohh. Boy you know I'm old. I'm not familiar with all that slang you young folks use," his mom clarified, while noticing King's attention had gone somewhere else.

He saw Amara standing nearby wearing short shorts and a red tank top, his favorite color. He told his family to wait up and he walked over to her.

"I didn't think you'd come," King said.

"Well, I'm here," she said smiling.

"So, what's up? How you been? It's been a long time. Where you go to school at now?" King asked.

"Nothing just school and music. That's all I do. I go to Martin Luther King. And yeah, it has been a long time. I always knew you would be good at sports. That's all you talked about in school," she said shaking her head.

"Yeah ya know. Gotta love those sports. But you grew up I see. Not that little snotty nose fifth grader nomo," he said jokingly.

"Oh whatever. I see you grow up too. Well, you still look the same. All the girls used to crush over you and I secretly did too," she said.

"Really. I never knew. I rarely remember you saying even two words to me," he recalled.

"Well, I was shy duhhhhh," she responded.

"So, what you doing tonight. It's Saturday?" he asked.

"Um, I don't have anything planned. Why what's up?" she pitched back.

"We should kick it. Catch up. Where you live?" he asked.

"On Clark St. by the laundromat," she replied.

"Ok Ok, I know where you are. My phone is in my bag over there so take my number and hit me up when you get home alright? It's 347-521-7611," he said.

"Okay wait," she said as she grabbed her phone from her pocket.

"What is it again?" she asked.

King repeated his number to her and turned to walk away. "Good job today Adoree'," Amara said.

"Thanks," King replied.

Chapter 12

10 toes and two feet

It was the week of required graduation tests for all tenth graders. Each student had two full hours to complete each of the forty-five-minute questioned test. There were students who you worried about passing but then you had students like King and Queen who were expected to pass with flying colors on their first attempt. And just to reassure it, Tiffany reminded them of the importance of the test in addition to the support that they receive from their school's staff.

"I want you both in the house by 8 o'clock tonight and in bed by 10 PM so that you're ready for tomorrow," Tiffany demanded when she overheard King on the phone laughing Sunday night.

King continued his phone call after laughing some more when Tiffany made the statement. Queen walked in King's doorway as they both stared at each other before busting out laughing.

"A curfew?" Queen asked sarcastically.

King just shrugged his shoulders and told the person on the phone that he'd call them back. He was supposed to be meeting up with D-Money in a few hours. He didn't know what the meeting was going to be about because he hadn't spoken to D-Money in almost a year and cringed at the thought of hearing his name ever since Queen told him about the encounter between him and his mother. It wasn't that he felt a certain way toward D-Money. He had been so busy that they hadn't found time to kick it.

So maybe he just wants to catch up, he thought to himself while he got dressed to head his way.

Queen planned on staying home and studying. She called someone who she thought could also use a study session before testing began. Destiny was now a senior in high school, but she only passed four of the five tests. She just couldn't seem to pass the science test, so Queen was hoping to help change that.

"I'll be there soon," Destiny said before she hung up the phone and grabbed her car keys.

She really needed to pass this test. Her mom had now been in ICU for four days due to a heart attack. As a result, Destiny spent the last three days in a hospital bed holding her mother's hand until she told her to go home and get ready for the important test.

"I got this, now you go get that," she told Destiny the night before.

As she pulled up to the house, she noticed King walking out the front door. Her heart sped up uncontrollably as she parked the car and stepped out. Her and King hadn't spoken since New Year's Day which was two months ago. His stomach tightened when he saw Destiny. She was wearing one of his hoodies she had taken from him years ago. She had freshly styled box braids and her edges were laid perfectly. King stood at the top of the porch staring at Destiny as she walked toward the house with her head down.

"Hey, what's up?" King asked as he tried to greet his first love.

Destiny quickly lifted her head at the sound of King's voice. The words coming from his mouth didn't even matter. It was his presence just standing there over her as she stood at the bottom of the steps as the rain drops drizzled down onto her.

"Hey Adoree,'" Destiny said.

"Everything ok? It's always something when you call me that," he said.

Destiny smiled.

"Yeah everything cool. Haven't spoken to you in a while. Is everything ok with you?" she asked.

"Well, another day down. What can I say?" he said.

"You're definitely right about that. I'm just about to study with Queen for this test next week. Are you ready for them?" she asked.

"Yeah, I guess," he replied.

"Well, you don't sound too sure about that. Where you headed?" asked Destiny.

"Oh, I just gotta go handle something real quick. I'll holla at you," he answered.

"Ok see ya!" said Destiny.

Queen was scrolling through her social media page on her laptop when Destiny walked in her room. She instantly complimented Destiny on her hair. Destiny rolled her eyes and said, "thanks to you, girl. You've gotten really good."

"Thanks girl. I try," Queen responded, and they began to study.

They took a few breaks often to talk, mainly about passing the test, college, things of that sort. But they had a discussion about boys, and it was like Destiny couldn't wait for this to come up in conversation. She asked Queen question after question about King seeing other girls. She didn't mention anything about the girls she saw King having dealings with. Her and Destiny were good friends, but her and King were blood. Her loyalty lies with him so as she listened to Destiny ramble on and on about how she loved King, she laughed in her head.

After a few minutes, she looked at Destiny and told her it was time to get back to studying. Destiny said, "Ok wait, what do you think I should do, Queen. I don't want to be trying to make things right if he's uninterested. I'm not trying to be out here looking dumb. You feel me girl?" Queen looked at her with her mouth slightly open because she didn't know how to respond. Well really she did, but she didn't want to hurt her feelings.

"I don't know, Des. You should follow your heart and do what you feel is right and make him realize what he's missing. That's the only advice I have girl," Queen expressed.

Destiny took a moment to take in what Queen said to her while she sat there looking down at her notebook. She never responded back but instead started flipping through her notes before they resumed their studying.

***

King placed his bike on a kickstand in the walkway of D-Money's house and knocked on the door before hearing his voice telling him to come in. D-Money's house was always presentable for company. Over the years he and his wife put a lot of money into remodeling of the home. The downstairs had brand new hardwood floors and the upstairs was all carpet beside the bathroom that had two sinks and an enclosed shower. The kitchen was decorated with brown granite countertops that match the rooms color scheme.

"Aye King, I got some new wine I want you to try," he said to King.

King accepted the offer and followed D-Money into the kitchen.

"Man, I want a house like this when I graduate," King said calmly.

"Nah fuck that. You want a mansion. Dream big, live big, young brotha. I hear you were damn near a starter on varsity this season," D-Money responded. King smiled with his nearly perfect teeth. Then he nodded his head and smacked D-Money's hand that he had held out.

"See King, that's called growth. Last year you was almost in tears about yo freshman season. Now look, mental and physical growth. How tall are you now?" D-Money asked.

"Like 5'8-5'9," he guessed.

"Damn boy, you done grown about 6 or 7 inches, right?" D-Money evaluated.

"Yup, and I gained about 40 pounds," King added.

"Aw shit. You'll be NFL size in no time," he assured him.

"For sure. So, what's been new with you, OG?" asked King.

"Aw same ole shit, lil bra. Maintaining. You know Jr. a be starting third grade next year and lil Giovanni starts preschool next year. Crazy ain't it?" he asked.

"Hell naw. That's crazy. I gotta kick it with them this summer," said King.

"Yeah fasho. Look though King. It's time we talk business," D-Money said.

King's heart began to beat fast. At this point, he believed that D-Money just wanted to see what was going on with him, but after his last statement he wondered where the conversation was headed. Last semester, King didn't make money as he usually did in the summer because it was 2008 now and everyone was selling weed. He thought maybe D-Money would mention that, but he didn't know. He looked at D-Money following the statement and swallowed the spit in his mouth trying to anticipate what was next.

"So, I know you're not even close to one of the boys in the hood that's booming the pack. Plus, you been selling that shit forever now. You ready to move on?" he asked King.

King's heartbeat even faster now. *Move on to what?* he thought to himself. He was aware of the penalties that came with selling weed. But the penalties for drugs that D-Money sold were harsher.

"Of course I am. I've been waiting for you to say the word," King lied.

"My boy. Ok let's go hit one of my licks then we gone go to the trap and imma show you the ins and outs," he assured King.

They got in D-Money's all white Tahoe and drove to Sycamore Rd. which was the apartment buildings that D's client lived in.

The woman got into the car appearing anxious. She was a Caucasian woman with long blonde hair. Her face was red, and she hadn't changed her clothes all weekend. She left out the house for one reason and one reason only; to receive her daily medicine.

"Hey Tim," the female junkie said.

"What's up, Heather. The usual?" D-Money asked.

"You already know," she replied.

Heather handed the money over and D handed her a tiny piece of a clear bag with an off-white colored substance in it. She got out with her hands in her hoodie pocket, hood over her head, and head down as she walked back into the apartment building. The Tahoe didn't pull off right away. D sat and scoped out his surroundings before taking his foot off the brake pedal. King looked over at D and noticed that he had his left hand under his shirt but inside his pants. Besides the one time with Anthony, D had never taken him on a sale and that was when he was younger. Now a little older and more aware King saw how serious D-Money was with the whole transaction, even before and afterwards.

"Why did she call you, Tim?" King asked.

"I don't want her to know my name nor my alias. You know what an alias is?" he responded.

"I heard of it before. What is it again?" he asked.

"A nickname basically or a street name. That's what the police refer to it as. If she's a snitch, then she can't tell them my name and maybe they'll go around looking for a Tim," D-Money explained.

"Ohh ok. That's smart," King responded.

"Yeah, this ain't weed, lil bra. This the real deal," said D-Money.

"I see. So is that why you holding on to that gun under yo shirt?" he noticed.

"Kinda. This business is dangerous. People get antsy all the time and try to rob you and will even kill you over this shit. It gets real so you gotta always be prepared for the worst," answered D-Money.

King just nodded his head as the truck pulled out of the parking lot. When they got into the trap house, King sat on the floor in the corner while D went to gather stuff up.

As he sat there, he checked his phone. He had a text and a missed call from Amara. He smiled slightly at the thought of her. They had been talking ever since she came to his track meet last year but nothing serious. He liked Amara but she had a boyfriend that she had been with for almost two years.

Her boyfriend, Elijah, was the only son of two wealthy parents. Even still, Elijah went to school in the hood because he stayed getting kicked out of charter schools. She loved Elijah but she didn't feel that he was the one for her. They didn't have a lot in common plus she caught him cheating several times, even still Amara stayed with Elijah. But as of lately she's been entertaining King. The text from Amara read, *answer the phone big head, I gotta tell you something.*

King was just about to press the button on his phone to call her back, but D-Money came back in the room and told him to come here so he put his phone back in his pocket. D-Money laid down a bunch of empty baggies, a scale, and a bigger bag of the same off-white colored substance that he saw him hand to the junkie, on the table. Then he left the room again and came back in with five handguns and a bunch of bullets.

"Pick one," he instructed King. King scanned each one and of course he grabbed the biggest one. It was an all-black Glock. 40 pistol. Then he reached beside it and grabbed its clip.

"Glock 40. Ever used one?" he asked.

"Never," King replied.

"Well, I'll have to show you soon. You might have to use it one day son," he said.

"Uhh, I doubt it," he said with uncertainty.

"Alright now. Ok so this shit right here is heroin. AKA dog food, it goes for $250 a gram. It's pretty simple to eyeball. This is how a gram would look," D-Money explained.

D-Money's phone rang. He let it ring and finished talking, but whoever it was called back so he looked at the number and recognized it. It was one of his best customers who shopped often. He quickly answered then told King to take another quick trip with him. They got into the truck and drove to the man's spot that wasn't too far from the trap. When they pulled up and parked, D-Money called the man back, but he didn't answer. So, he sat there and waited. After a few minutes he saw the man walking up to the car. He was walking toward the driver door which D-Money thought was odd and he was wearing all black so that made him even more suspicious.

"Timmy, what's up," the man said sounding more excited than usual.

King was looking around and saw how dark it had gotten so quickly outside. Then he thought about the fake curfew his mom made up earlier. The man tried to hand over the money through the driver's door.

"Man, hop in," D-Money said.

The man pulled his hand back and turned to the backseat door to get inside. He must hadn't noticed King sitting in the passenger seat because when he got in the car, he smacked D-Money over the head with his gun and told him to hand over everything. King had quickly shimmied down in the seat. The man told D-Money to get out of the car while pointing the gun at him. D did as he was told and got out with his hands in the air. The truck was still running. King looked through the passenger window and saw another man dressed in all black running over but again, this man didn't see him either.

When he got past, the truck King reached in his hoodie pocket and pulled out the glock 40 and the clip that he had chosen from the gang of guns earlier. He had never used a gun, but he'd seen them used on tv plenty of times, so he improvised on putting the clip in that was already loaded and he cocked the slide back just like the people on tv did. He pointed the gun through the driver door that had been left open and he fire three shots. Both men took off running and one of them fell while the other turned back and returned fire as D-Money ran toward the Tahoe.

"Back seat!" King yelled while he climbed behind the wheel of the truck and pulled off before D could even get his body fully inside.

***

It was now 9:21 p.m. and Destiny was getting her belongings ready to return home. She had hopes of seeing King once he returned home but it was beginning to get late and she wanted to be up early so that she could meet the science tutor at the library. Queen walked her down to the door where they hugged, and Destiny wished her luck on the test. As she turned to open the front door, she heard someone opening the screen door, so she quickly opened it. At first glance she was in shock. King was standing in front of her covered in blood.

"Oh my god, what happened?" both girls asked in unison almost sounding like they practiced the same script.

"Nothing," King said softly. You could hear the draining emotions in his voice. His eyes were hot red from crying; his hands and shirt looked like a murder scene. He didn't want to talk. Just want to get cleaned up and go to bed.

"Adoree,' what the fuck! Are you ok?" Queen asked while raising her voice a little.

"Shhh. Where's mom?" he asked.

"She fell asleep not too long ago. I told her you were in your room watching tv," she responded.

"Ok. Man, I was with D-Money and he got shot. I drove him to the hospital and sat with him for like an hour. The doctors told me I should go home and get rest," he said.

"Oh god. Where did he get shot? Where were y'all and what were y'all doing?" Queen interrogated.

"Queen, why do you always ask me a hundred questions. We'll talk tomorrow. Just don't tell mom please...ok?" he cried.

"Ok," she replied.

Destiny was still standing there stuck in shock.

"I'm ok, Des," King assured her as he stared at her waiting for her to snap out of it.

"Were you leaving?" he asked.

"Oh yeah," Destiny responded.

After she left, King went upstairs to shower quietly before laying down. As he laid there, he stared at the wall. He tried to fall asleep for hours, but he couldn't. He couldn't believe what had happened earlier. He remembered that he needed to call Amara back. And when he picked up the phone to do so, he saw another missed call from her. King called and put the phone on speaker. Amara answered with a raspy voice. King assumed it was because she was asleep when he called.

:My bad. I had a crazy day man. How was your day?" he asked.

"Uhhhhh... it was terrible," she complained.

"Why, what happened?" he asked.

"I don't want to talk about it over the phone. Can you come over after school tomorrow?" she asked.

"Is it serious? I can come over right now," he replied.

"King, we have testing tomorrow," Amara stated.

"I'm not thinking about that test. I know I got that, and I know you do as well. But you know if you need someone to talk to, I got you," he notified her.

"You know what, you're right. Are you driving? You know my mom would kill me if I had a boy over this late," responded Amara.

"Yeah, I'm on the way," he said before hanging up.

King still had the Tahoe from earlier. He went to Queen's room to tell her that he was leaving out again.

Queen jumped out of the bed when he told her. After the way he came in the house a moment ago she was worried.

He can't even tell me what happened, and he wants to leave the house again, she thought to herself. She had to tell him how she felt.

"Adoree, where are you going at 12:15 at night? We have important testing tomorrow. You already came in here with blood all over you. What's going on with you? You ok?" she exclaimed.

King responded with a short, "I'm cool," and left the room.

Queen shook her head and laid back in bed. King knew where Amara lived because he dropped her off a few times after they hung out. He got to Clark St. in under 10 minutes and called Amara to tell her to come out and she did so while tiptoeing past her mom's bedroom and out of the front door. King had the biggest smile on his face when she got into the car. Amara was happy to see him too.

"What's up?" asked King.

"Today has been crazy. So, me and Elijah got into a fight early today and...," she began.

"Wait, wait, wait. So, you called me over to tell me about your boyfriend problems?" he stopped her to ask.

Amara began laughing then said, "Listen, you told me if I need someone to talk to, you got me. Right?" she quoted.

King laughed back and said, "naw go ahead. I just thought something serious happened," he responded.

"Well anyway, so yeah, we got into an argument about him flirting with the damn waitress right in my face. I ended up telling him that he was a piece of shit and I called him a bitch ass nigga and next thing you know this motherfucker reached across the table and smacked me in the face in front of everyone. It got super quiet. I was so embarrassed. I walked out of there and of course he followed me. I made him take me home and we got in another fight outside of my house. This time he punched me in my stomach hard as fuck. I was crying for like an hour," she narrated.

"Damn what the hell. He shouldn't have put his hands on you like that," he stated.

"Exactly, I'm done with his ass," she assured him.

"Are you really?" he said softly.

Amara looked down when she thought about the question. It was a good question and a lot for her to think about later because right now King was there for her.

"Thanks for coming" she said softly.

King grabbed her hand and said, "no problem, I told you I got you."

"So how was your day? You said it was crazy," Amara said.

"Nah, it was alright, it's better now," King responded with a slight grin on his face.

"And why is that?" she asked.

"I think you know why," King said back.

Seeing Amara was the best part of the day for him.

It felt good knowing that Amara was comfortable venting to him. It was one thing that attracted him to her. King's dick was fully awake in his pants by now. He placed his hands on her thigh and began to rub it. She was wearing a pair of grey leggings and a track jacket with her all-black house slippers. When she felt King's hand on her thigh, her first instinct was to resist it but the soft and gentleness of his rubs convinced her otherwise. So, she grabbed King's hand and helped him with rubbing her pussy through the leggings at first to show him how she liked it until she felt that he was ready to finish on his own. When she stopped, her body tensed up and she moaned with pleasure. King reached over to pull the jacket over her head so that he could get to her titties. He was so horny at this point that he didn't even care about the cars driving past on the street where he was parked. Amara was also super horny. Her complicated situation with her boyfriend made her even more horny with being uncertain about where their relationship lied.

As King sucked her breasts, she put her arm around his head and let the seat back for more comfortability. When he was done with her breasts, he helped her take off her pants before standing up as best as he could while she took off his. She could see his dick print through his sweats.

Next, he sat down completely naked in the driver's seat and grabbed the back of Amara's head as a gesture for her to give him head. She started sucking it so good that King mumbled some unknown words under his breath. Amara heard him but she kept sucking like her life depended on it. King looked over and saw her ass sitting up in the air and he felt a sudden tingling sensation through his penis. He reached over to grab that ass and when he did, he squeezed it and smacked it softly a few times. Soon after,

Amara sat up to slide down on King's pole. Her pussy was tight, but it was so wet that it practically slid right in. She bounced up and down repeatedly while King laid back and enjoyed, only coming up to lick her nipples.

Eventually the two made their way to the backseat where Amara bent over giving King the same view from moments ago. King kneeled down to feast on her drenched vagina while she bounced back and forth on his face. He licked her pussy from the top to the bottom once more then he sat back up to fuck her from behind. Again, Amara bounced back and forth but much faster this time. As much pain as she was enduring from King's blessing, it was pleasurable causing her to scream and moan. King didn't last much longer. His last stroke he went in as deep as he could and his cum shot all in her, tagging her walls like graffiti. King fell over to his side while Amara lied there flat on her stomach. The inside of the Tahoe was silent with the only noise being made was deep, quick breathing from the two trying to catch their breaths.

"Did you cum in me, King?" Amara asked in an exhausted voice.

King looked over in her direction and placed his hand on her butt cheek and rubbed.

"I did," he responded nonchalantly. Amara lifted her head from the seat and turned over to King, shaking her head.

***

Queen arrived at school the next day for breakfast a little earlier than usual. She saw TJ sitting at the table with his friends, so she signaled for him to come over to her. TJ took another bite of the scrambled eggs and tossed the rest in the trash on his way over to her.

"Oh, you can speak now, huh? I texted you last night," he made her aware.

"TJ, I was asleep by then. You ready for this math test?" asked Queen.

"As ready as I'm going to be. You?" he replied.

"Yeah, I've studied all weekend. So, let me tell you about my brother last night," she began.

She told him about how King came into the house last night covered in blood then how he left back out that night. She told TJ that she was worried, and he told her that she should sit and talk to him about it once they got home. Queen agreed. She hugged TJ and they both walked to the auditorium where they would be testing. Queen and TJ weren't in a relationship, but they had gotten really close over the past year. He knew that she was still involved with Shelton, but he didn't care. In his eyes, he and Queen were just good friends that once liked each other. Or at least that's what he wanted to believe. He loved the sight of that girl and he got butterflies every time he saw her and so did she.

A year had gone by, but it still wasn't easy for Queen to shy away from Shelton's selective word play and long dreads. With TJ, she felt that they could be great best friends though she wanted more. With Shelton, she felt that she was what he needed to keep his life on a narrow course. Right before the test began, Queen looked across the room at TJ and mouthed 'good luck' to him. TJ smiled and mouthed it back as they both picked up their pencils to begin.

They were given two hours to complete the test. TJ finished in all of fifty minutes before going back to make sure he had all the answers bubbled in. When he looked around, he noticed everyone still testing so he put his head down for a quick nap. Ten minutes later, Queen finished her test. She had been holding her bladder since the test began so she raised her hand to get the test supervisor's attention. No one was allowed to leave or enter the classroom ten minutes after the test began but the supervisor was familiar with Queen and how well she excelled in the classroom, so she did her a favor and let her go to the restroom.

"Don't take too long," the supervisor instructed while Queen walked out the door.

When she cleaned off the toilet seat before sitting on it, she pulled out her phone that she was supposed to turn in to the supervisor before the test began. Shelton had texted her wishing her luck on the exam and told her to practice hard later on. She texted back thanks.

When she finished peeing, she went back to the classroom and saw TJ asleep and she shook her head. After school, TJ dropped her off in front of the house. As she was opening the door to get out of the car, TJ leaned over and planted a kiss on her cheek. Queen was completely caught off guard by the gesture. She paused for a minute then looked at TJ with a slight smile and said, "see you tomorrow, Terrance," while she proceeded with going toward her home.

TJ laughed and yelled, "don't call me that, Neveah," before waiting to make sure she got in the house and pulling off.

Her mom was off from work today, so she called for her once she got inside. She heard a sudden movement from upstairs, but she thought nothing of it. She made her way up the steps and Tiffany came out of the room half dressed.

"Hey girl. No practice today?" she asked.

"No, every two days this week because of testing. Ma, where are your clothes?" asked Queen.

"Oh, I was getting dressed. How was the test?" Tiffany responded.

"Dressed for what? Why are you blocking the door? Your acting weird, ma," Queen said.

Queen went to her bedroom and shut the door. She chuckled a little to herself. *Mom is finally getting some. I wonder if its D-Money,* she thought to herself, but the thought quickly vanished when she remembered that D-Money was happily married with kids. It made her think about possibly having kids one day.

Tiffany always told her how painful pushing out two babies back to back were so that made her second guess it. As she was thinking, she stared out of her bedroom window that pointed toward the side house.

"Wait till Adoree' hears this," she said quietly then as she was turning around, she saw someone running from the driveway. She didn't get a chance to catch the face, but she thought that the person running looked like he was doing something he had no business doing. The person running had dreads and she only knew one person with those.

Naw that can't be him, she thought.

Queen quickly ran downstairs. Tiffany was standing in front of the side door as if she was looking out of it until Queen showed up. She had on some shorts and a tank top with just socks.

"What's wrong, Queen?" Tiffany asked sounding concerned.

"Nothing, I was just coming down to look for something to eat," Queen responded.

"I'm tripping. My mom would never do that. But maybe the person she was just fucking had dreads. Or maybe that person with dreads wasn't even running from our house. Could have hopped a fence or something," Queen pondered on.

There had been an increase in house break-ins over the past year, so she thought maybe the man with dreads had just broken in a house and was running away. She knew that her and her mother's bond was too strong for her to go behind her back like that so that idea quickly went away. She was just happy of the possibility that her mom was getting some.

After school, King skipped practice. He told his coach that he had to visit his uncle in the hospital who had been shot the night before. Coach was understanding of the situation and he told him to come to practice the next day prepared to run hard. He was still torn about what happened with D-Money. The person who had been there for him since he moved to the city. Someone who had seen the potential in him without knowing him. The doctors said that D-Money would make it. He had been shot in the back and the bullet came out through his stomach. The bullet was less than a centimeter from hitting his spinal cord the doctor said.

"Mr. Morgan is a very lucky man. He's going to be in lots of pain for, well there's no timetable on that. He won't be able to walk for a few days or a week or so. We're going to keep him for a few more days," King overheard the doctor telling Mrs. Morgan when he walked into the hospital room.

When D-Money's wife noticed King, she gave him the biggest hug. She was happy to see him. She knew that King was the last person she knew to be with her husband last night. D-Money's second emergency surgery ended a little over an hour ago and she still hadn't gotten a chance to talk to her husband. And with King now standing in front of her, she wanted some answers.

"King, I'm glad you're okay. You guys have testing this week, right? I hope this incident didn't affect you today," Mrs. Morgan said.

"I'm fine Kim. I'm sorry about what happened to D last night," he responded.

"What exactly happened, King?" she asked.

"D and I was going to drop something off to some guy and next thi…," He begin explaining.

"Drop what off?" she questioned.

"I honestly don't know. He just asked me to ride with him real quick. But when we got there, the dude got in the truck and tried to rob him. He made D get out of the truck and then some other dude came up and tried to help the guy rob him. They both had guns, I had a gun on me too and I shot at them and they both ran. One of the dudes shot back and I guess that's when he hit D in the back as he was running toward the truck," King explained.

"Oh my God. I can't believe that. King I'm sorry you were involved in this. But I have a question. You have so much going for you in life. Why are you carrying guns around?" asked Mrs. Morgan.

King just stood there lost for words. He didn't want to tell Mrs. Morgan that he had gotten the gun from D prior to the shooting. It would just make things worse. But he hated the idea that Mrs. Morgan thought he carried around guns. The state of New York didn't allow anyone to carry a gun. You aren't even allowed to get a carry and concealed weapon permit. King knew the penalties that came with carrying a concealed weapon and he knew that Mrs. Morgan did as well. Still lost for words King shook his head and shrugged his shoulders.

"You know better, King. I trust that you will stop whatever it is you're doing. Or it's two places you'll end up. Here," she said as she pointed at D-Money on the hospital bed. "Or in the grave. And I know you don't want either of those," she said.

"You right, Kim. I'll get it together," he assured her.

They sat there for maybe another 20 minutes until D-Money opened his eyes. Mrs. Morgan stood up first and walked toward him. The meds had worn off so he was in pain and he could barely move. He looked over and saw an IV and colostomy bag attached to him. Mrs. Morgan grabbed his hand.

"Hey baby. I'm here," she said. He looked up at her and smiled. He was happy to see her.

He looked over at King and remembered him being the one who took him to the hospital. He signaled for King to come over and when he did, he dapped him up.

"Thank you," D-Money said in a painful voice. King nodded his head and joked about the ride to the hospital last night trying to make light of the situation.

"Ohhh, ohh, hurry up King. It hurts," King reenacted sarcastically.

D-Money tried to laugh but his back and stomach hurt even more from the slightest movement. Mrs. Morgan laughed as well, then she changed the subject, asking King how his mom and sister was. After telling them that they were fine, he asked D-Money not to mention the situation to his mom. D balled up his fits and lifted it up as an ok gesture. King stayed there for a few more minutes before heading home.

When he got home, he parked the Tahoe down the street so his mom wouldn't know he was driving it. Her and

Queen were both in their rooms with the door closed so he didn't even bother them. He took off his book bag to grab his water bottle that he carried around with him everywhere. Then he sat on his bed. He felt his phone ring while he was in the hospital, but he just ignored it. When he thought about it, he figured it was Amara calling to talk about the test, so he pulled his phone from his pocket and when he opened it, he saw a missed call from Sierra. He called her back.

"Hello," Sierra answered.

"What's up, Sierra," he replied.

"Nothing, just chilling at home. How was that test today?"

"It was easy wasn't it?" he asked.

"Yeah, it was. What you over there doing?" she asked.

"Nothing just got in. I was at the hospital with my OG. He got shot last night," King responded.

"Where did he get shot at?" Sierra questioned.

"In the back. The bullet came out of his stomach," he said.

"No, I mean like where at, location wise?" she asked.

"Oh um, like by Ford Avenue," said King.

"Hol up! I think I heard about that. Was it two dudes trying to rob your friend?" she asked.

"Yeah. Where you hear about that at?" he asked.

"So, I guess your friend that got shot is like Cassidy's uncle or something. She said that his wife called and told her this morning," explained Sierra.

"Damn, that's crazy. I didn't know that," he said.

"Yeah, your friend is old," she said laughing.

"Yeah, he's like my mentor," King replied.

"Ohh I see. So, what you doing tonight?" she asked.

"Shit, I don't even know. You?" he returned.

"Oh I would love that," said Sierr.

"Huh?" he asked confused.

"You said you're doing me tonight and I said I would love that," she assured him.

King laughed then told Sierra that he would come over later tonight before hanging up the phone. They have hooked up on random occasions over the past year. It was nothing more than sex. Though Sierra wanted more, she was content with what they have. She knew that King had a ton of girls that wanted him, so she was just happy to be one of them that he actually entertained. For King, it was just convenient pussy that he could get whenever he wanted it.

The next morning, Queen called Jane to make sure that she was still coming. Jane was usually on time but today she was already thirty minutes late so Queen called her. She told Queen that she was up with Adonis all night who was sick and had an ear infection. She told her that she was almost there, and she had picked her up some breakfast since she would miss the one that the school offered. When she got into the car she looked back and saw Adonis sleeping in the backseat. He had dried up snot near the bottom of his nose.

"Aw, poor baby," Queen said as she reached back and touched his head before turning back around and eating her food.

When she got to school, TJ appeared to have been waiting for her. He gave her a nasty look, so she gave one back in return but hers came with a push.

"Boy don't look at me like that," Queen said.

"You late. Now come on," he responded as they walked to the auditorium to take the math test.

When school was over, TJ asked Queen if she wanted to go get some ice cream at one of the new ice cream spots near his house. Queen agreed and they drove there.

"You gonna get your license this year?" TJ asked.

"I don't know. It will be easier to get around if I learn, I guess. And my mom told me that she'll give us her Benz since she bought a new car. But I don't know how to drive," Queen explained.

"Learning to drive is the easy part. I'll teach you. You can't get your license until December anyway, so you got like what? Nine months," he asked.

"Ok cool. Thank you," she said.

"Fasho. Oh shit, don't you got practice today?" he asked.

"Yeah, but I forgot my spikes at the house. Can you swing by my house real quick?" she asked.

"Yeah, after we finish this," he replied.

When they pulled in front of the house, Queen noticed her mom's car in the driveway.

Damn two weekdays off in a row? That's unusual, she thought to herself as she used her key to open the front door.

She could hear the loud music from the porch. She walked in and looked around, but didn't see anyone. So, she followed the sound of the music into the kitchen and what she saw next brought immediate tears to her eyes. Tiffany was bent over on the stove with her face planted between her arms while Shelton was fucking her hard from behind. They were so engaged that they didn't even notice Queen standing there until she flipped the light switch on. They stopped and tried to grab their clothes. Queen turned and ran back to the car and told TJ to pull off. TJ wasted no time.

"Where we going?" he asked her and she said just to take her somewhere that was quiet and peaceful.

The only place he could think of during this time of day was his house since his dad didn't care about him having company.

Plus, he's probably at work anyway, TJ thought to himself.

TJ's dad was a small business owner of a landscaping company. So, he made decent money, enough money for them to live in the suburbs. Queen was silent the whole ride and kept shaking her head when TJ asked her what the problem was. She didn't speak again until right before they walked in the house and that was to ask if TJ lived there. TJ's thought was right. His dad wasn't home, and neither was his dad's girlfriend. They went straight to his room as Queen surveyed the house all the way up the stairs. TJ had recently moved his room from the second floor to the attic for more space. He had a whole furniture set up there with the pool table, computer desktop, and a mini fridge. Queen sat down on the couch as soon as she got up the steps while TJ grabbed two beers from the fridge. He cracked them open and handed her one. She shook her head no and he asked her to just try it. "It helps ease your mind," he said.

Queen grabbed the beer to take a sip and she nearly

spit it out. But from the way she was feeling, she was

willing to continue drinking. Next, TJ lit an unfinished

blunt from the night before and passed it to Queen. She

looked at it for a moment before grabbing it. She had tried

smoking before but couldn't get past the smoke. This time

she took two short puffs and passed it back to TJ and they

continued this until it was gone. For the first time ever,

Queen was high. And as weird as it felt to her, it also felt

good. She wasn't even thinking about what she had walked

into at home. TJ was high as well, but he smoked more so

than Queen did, so he obviously had a higher tolerance. He

sat next to her on the couch with his phone in his hand and

didn't even notice Queen looking over at him.

Eventually she pulled out her phone and she saw

exactly what she didn't want to see. The name "Shelton"

and "Mom" on the front of her phone. They had both tried

calling multiple times. *I wonder if they were still together when they tried calling?* Queen thought. She hurried and put her phone away and picked up the beer from the coffee table and tried to chug it down. She got maybe a quarter of the can down before putting the can back on the table and looking at Shelton again who was still occupied by his phone. Whatever he was doing on there made him laugh and Queen wondered if he was texting another girl.

Well I can't be mad at him, I'm the one who's been playing games, she thought.

She stared at him harder, examining every inch of him from the brush waves in his head to the Air Jordan shoes on his feet.

"Lord, why is this boy so fine?" she mumbled under her breath which caused TJ to look over still with a smile on his face. He didn't hear what she mumbled but he knew she said something.

"You alright, how you feeling?" he asked.

"I'm good" she said with a slight smile.

"Wanna talk about it now?" asked TJ.

Queen just sat there and Shook her head no.

"Ok," TJ responded.

He grabbed the remote from the table and turned it to a movie that he had already watched. Queen pretended to watch it for a few minutes, but she couldn't get into it. She had other plans in mind. She looked over at TJ, who was watching a movie, so she inched over closer to him until her shoulder was slightly touching his. TJ put his arm around her and slowly rubbed her side. She then put her legs upon TJ's lap, and she turned to face him. She stared at how sexy his lips were as he licked them. And at that moment she couldn't hide her hormones anymore. She inched over even closer and met TJ's lips with hers. They kissed for a moment then the next thing you know, both of them were naked. TJ reached his hand under the couch pillow and grabbed the condom.

"Oh you do this a lot, huh?" Queen asked jokingly.

TJ just laughed and shook his head. Then he signaled for her to go into the bedroom. He had a huge king size bed decorated with gold and black bedding. On his walls were multiple pictures of him, and his dad and others were of famous athletes and a seminude photo of Mariah Carey. Queen barely noticed any of it, Not even the noise of the fish tank that wasn't too far from the bed.

She went in the room and sat straight on the bed to put the comforter around her as she waited for TJ to approach her. He wasted no time as he laid her on her back and began kissing her. He felt his dick stiffen against his thick comforter while he rubbed her sides. He kissed her on the neck then licked her all the way down to her vagina where he stopped and kissed it. He had never eaten pussy before, so he didn't do anything further than that. Queen was ready for the dick, so she grabbed the back of TJ's arms and pulled him closer. He had already put on the condom, so he grabbed his dick with his right hand and put it in the mouth of her vagina. Queen's whole body tensed up.

"Damn, I ain't even in yet," he whispered.

Queen looked at him like he was crazy then he tried to push it in further. Queen was wet but they weren't making any progress. Her walls were so tight that TJ couldn't believe that there was an opening. He pulled back and tried again. Still couldn't get anywhere. But he did get it in a little further, so he tried to baby stroke his way in. After a few seconds Queen pushed herself up by using his shoulders as resistance. After minutes of trying, they still made no progress. TJ finally gave up and rolled over. In a way he was embarrassed but more so disappointed. He heard his father call his name. They both quickly jumped up to put the comforter over them as they heard his dad walking up the steps. When he came into the room, they pretended to be asleep.

"Son, you hungry?.... Boy I know you ain't sleep. I have some pizza down in the kitchen," Terrance Sr said.

"Thanks dad," TJ responded.

"So, who's the pretty girl?" he asked.

"This is my friend Queen," TJ replied.

"Hey Ms. Queen. Nice to meet you. Well, if I knew y'all were up here doing the nasty I would have stayed downstairs. Y'all get dressed and come eat when y'all get a chance," he said.

Queen gave TJ a fearful look.

"Don't worry. My dad is cool," he said to her as they both got up to get dressed.

When they got to the kitchen, his dad had the food already prepared. So, he told them to have a seat. As they ate, Queen and TJ's dad got to know each other while TJ barely spoke. He just sat there and thought of his next encounter with Queen. He still didn't know what upset her earlier, but now he knew that it had to be something dealing with Shelton. He still had the image of Queen's naked body in his head. She wasn't super thick, but she was slim thick, and she had nice curves. She was a fair height for a female with cute dimples on her face. TJ knew that if he had any chance of making Queen his girlfriend, the time was now.

Once it got late, TJ's dad told him to get Queen home safely. He took the side streets home to avoid police and the many traffic lights. During the drive, TJ asked Queen if she was ready for the social studies test tomorrow. She told him that she was and that she was sorry about earlier.

"Sorry for what?" asked TJ.

"Because we couldn't have sex because of me," she replied.

"It wasn't your fault. It will be better next time," he stated.

"Next time huh? So you just know you going to get some more of this huh?" she asked.

"I do," he replied with confidence.

"I see," she responded.

"So, I don't know what happened earlier when you ran out of your house but whenever you're ready to tell me, I'll be here," he said.

"Thank you, TJ. I promise I'll tell you after school tomorrow," she said.

"Okay cool. I hope you have a good night. See you tomorrow beautiful," he said.

"Goodnight," Queen responded.

She felt good knowing that TJ was being patient with her. She walked up to the front door of her home with butterflies until she thought of what happened the last time she walked into her house. It was almost midnight. King and Tiffany were sitting in the living room on the couch. When Tiffany saw Queen, she told King to go upstairs. King walked past Queen and shook his head at her. Queen tried to follow behind him, but Tiffany stopped her and told her to have a seat. The betrayal that she felt was so intensified that she didn't even want to sit at the same couch as her, so she sat on the loveseat with her head down. It was quiet at first until Tiffany broke the ice.

"You have every right to hate me right now. I was dead wrong. No excuses," Tiffany explained.

Queen didn't answer.

"Say something," Tiffany yelled.

Queen maintained her silence.

"I'm sorry baby. I didn't even know you knew him," she said.

"You know what, I don't even care. It is what it is," Queen said.

Queen got up and walked upstairs. Tiffany called her but she couldn't even imagine how she was feeling at that moment. She went straight into her room and slammed the door after her, but King caught it. When she didn't hear it close, she turned around then King closed the door. He asked what happened and Queen just broke down in tears. King wrapped his arms around her for a tight hug.

"It's okay sis, I got you," King said softly.

When she stopped crying, she began telling King the story of what happened. King couldn't believe what he was hearing. He even chuckled a little at the thought of his mom having sexual relations with someone.

"So was it an older or younger guy?" King asked.

"It was a boy that I know. His name is Shelton, you might know him. He goes to MLK. You know em?" she asked.

"Uh, nah. Never heard of him. So he's what our age?" King asked.

"Yup," Queen responded.

Queen was surprised that King didn't question her about this guy. He wanted to remain to her as someone who didn't know Shelton. But he truly didn't know about TJ. He and Shelton weren't friends, so he didn't feel that he owed him anything, but he expected him to have more respect for Queen. King was in rage, but he couldn't show it in front of her. When he left Queen's room, he went downstairs where his mom was still sitting on the couch. He walked past her and shook his head all the way until he got on the porch. He sat down on the swing for a couple minutes then Tiffany came out and sat next to him. She tried to explain herself, but King just kept mentioning the fact that the boy was a kid, and she knew it. Tiffany claimed that Shelton lied about his age, saying that he was 21 years old. Shelton probably could have passed for 21. He had a beard that wasn't full, but most boys his age didn't have one and neither did all the twenty-year-olds. Also, he was tall and had long dreadlocks. King believed his mom. He wasn't old enough to understand that adults were sometimes attracted to younger adults and teenagers, but he knew that he hadn't seen his mom with a man besides his dad, so he tried to sympathize for her. Their conversation ended when King got a phone call and Tiffany went back into the home.

"Come in and get some rest after that call ends. Goodnight, I love you," she said before leaving. The phone call was from D-Money.

"Lil bra, what's up?" D-Money asked.

"What's up OG? You cool?" King asked.

"Come on now, you know a bullet can't stop a real gangsta," he replied.

"Yeah fasho," King agreed.

"Yeah, I should be getting out Friday morning. Come to the trap after school or practice," he said.

"Alright bet," responded King.

***

Jane was late again picking up Queen for school. TJ waited for her again and they both smiled when they saw each other. They hugged and then went to testing. After the test, she went to track practice since she hadn't been the day before and she didn't want to be home. King went to basketball practice. He started playing guard for the varsity team and he was leading his team to one of the best starts in school history. They were undefeated and trying to solidify their spots as the number one seed for the state playoffs, a place the varsity team had never been before.

After practice, King went outside to the Tahoe that he was still driving around. It was about 5:30 p.m. He drove to Amara's house and they went to a movie that lasted for a little over an hour. The time was now 8:06 p.m., once he dropped Amara off back home, he drove to a house on Thomas Rd. He drove past the home to see if there were any cars in the driveway before parking several houses down. He reached in the backseat and grabbed a black hoodie and black jeans. He grabbed a pair of black gloves from a gym bag.

Lastly, King grabbed something from under the seat before he got out of the truck that was still running and walked toward the home. He knew that what he was about to do next was wrong, but it felt right. His heart was beating so fast that he could see his pulse through his hand. He tried to take a few deep breaths, but it only made his heartbeat faster. When he got on the porch, he hesitated before knocking, but then he remembered how upset he was. He knocked three times and he heard a voice say who is it, but King didn't answer. Then he heard the person opening the door. His heartbeat even faster and he frowned. When the door cracked open, King blacked out and the person who answered looked like they had just seen a ghost.

Chapter 13
Flew the coup

Entire body covered in a damp sweat and he had an uncontrollable shake, King was nervous but in the same instance he felt that he did what had to be done. He sat in Sierra's bed quietly as she repeatedly tried to find out what was wrong with him. He tried to act normal, but she knew he wasn't being himself. Usually when they met up, King was very outgoing, and he wasn't at all shy about getting down to sex. So, when he sat there quietly, she assumed that he no longer wanted dealings with her. Once she laid down and tried to go to sleep, King headed home. He knew that Tiffany and Queen couldn't have heard about what happened just yet, so he didn't have to worry about that. Luckily, they both were asleep.

King went straight to his room and showered. He had already changed his clothes at Sierra's, and he burned them on the way home. When he finally laid in bed, he couldn't do anything but keep replaying what happened earlier over and over again. He couldn't sleep. It was a gut feeling you get when you've done wrong but fed a deep desire as well.

D-Money and King met up Friday night at the trap and they were happy to see each other. Hell, they were happy to be alive.

"So how's my truck running, you know the one that you kidnapped?" asked D-Money.

"Yeah man, it's running good," replied King.

"My gift to you. You need to get ya license ASAP," he warned him.

"December 12th, I'll take my test. I start driving school next month and I'll get my temps in June," said King.

"Alright bet. So, I got word on dem niggas who tried to jack me," D-Money brought up.

"Oh yeah?" asked King.

"Yeah, I ain't even know you popped ole dude. They said he got shot in the leg twice," D-Money explained.

"Damn I ain't know either," King said trying not to smile.

"So, look I got to go handle dat! You down?" he asked. "Let's get it" King assured him. "Alight tonight it's going down then," stated D-Money

King got the same feeling that he had the night he was standing on the porch on Thomas Rd.

It had to be done, he said to himself.

For the next thirty-minutes, the two went over the plan for the night. D-Money wanted things to go smoothly without a tussle because he wasn't physically able to and he didn't want to force King into a situation like that. Also, he didn't want this to be linked back to King at all. For all he knew, King had never done anything like this before.

"All right, I'll call you at around 7:30 ish," D-Money said to King.

He nodded his head and hopped in the Tahoe toward home. It was a decent March day outside and had been raining for over a week. He heard the living room's TV from his front porch. He assumed that they were there watching a movie or something. When he walked in, Tiffany and Queen were sitting on the couch watching the local news channel.

"A 15-year-old was shot and killed in the front doorway of his home Wednesday night. The black male was identified as Shelton Ivory, a rising football star and New York City's Martin Luther King High School. The family will hold a candlelight for his passing tonight at Ruckers Park; 8 P.M."

Tiffany and King watched Queen cry for the third day in a row. They felt bad for her even knowing that they had something to do with her pain. Tiffany went over

Queen and she told her that she'll go to the vigil with her. She looked up and asked King if he'd come to support also. He wanted to be there for, but he knew the guilt would eat at him during the entire service. In addition, he had plans for tonight anyway and it didn't involve anything positive happening in the community.

"I can't, I have a basketball game tonight, remember?" he asked Tiffany.

Tiffany looked confused. She didn't remember him mentioning anything about a basketball game, but she just went along with it since she couldn't attend the game anyway. Queen got a phone call from TJ, so she excused herself from the living room and went to her room. She had already told him about the event between Shelton and her mom. He was calling to see if that was the boy she was talking about. When she confirmed it, TJ thought it was odd that he was murdered a few days after the incident happened. He asked her if she thought it was odd and it did make her think about it. She later asked TJ if he would go with her and he agreed. Going to the candlelight with her mom was something she didn't want to do.

King received a phone call from D-Money 15 minutes earlier than expected. That worked out for Queen because she didn't want King to see TJ Pulling up to pick her up. She told Tiffany that she would rather go with a friend and Tiffany understood. King left out the house minutes after his phone call ended. He headed back to the trap where he met up with D-money. When he walked in, he saw several assault rifles lying on the ground with lots of bullets and clips. He thought the room looked like a scene from a movie. He didn't know what it was, but it excited him knowing that D trusted him enough to help take care of this situation. Watching D-Money load of the weapons dressed in all-black gave him an adrenaline rush. D-Money looked up at King with a black and brown AK-47 in his hands and tossed it to him.

"You ready?" D asked. King put the AK in his right hand.

"Been ready," and he wasn't lying.

Though this wasn't his normal lifestyle, King felt some type of way about the two men trying to rob and nearly paralyzed his "mentor," So before D-Money ever brought up taking care of them, he was wondering how he would get back at them. D had the whole scoop on where the men were staying and how often they moved. It helped them that the candlelight was tonight because instead of local police patrolling the neighborhood, they were staying put at Rucker's Park. One of the men always left his spot around 8:15 - 8:30 ish to go to his girlfriend's house and his homie rarely left at night.

D-Money and King pulled a few houses down from where they stayed. Both dressed in all black, they put their ski masks on and jogged to the homes back door. It had a motion light that cut on when they got on the porch. D-

Money grabbed the doorknob quietly to see if it was open. They caught a break because they were able to get in without making noise. They heard noise coming from a TV as they surveyed the downstairs. No one was down there. So, they quietly went upstairs. Only one room was active. The others were empty. D-Money got close to the door to see what he could hear coming from the room. He whispered to King.

"Man, I hear some hoes and niggas in here," King looked at D-Money confused.

He didn't get what he was trying to say.

"What we going to do now man?" D-Money whispered, sounding nervous. King told D to move out the way and he kicked the door down.

"Everybody get the fuck down," he yelled.

They watched as all the bodies scrambled to the ground. The two men seemed to be more scared than the females were. They were shaking and begging them to just take whatever they wanted. D grabbed one of the girls and told her to take him to the stash. She did exactly so while sporting nothing but a bra and panties.

As they left the room King made sure that the others didn't move even the slightest bit. When he thought one of the men moved, he kicked him in the head and pressed the gun to the back of it to warn him that he wasn't playing. His adrenaline wouldn't allow him to stop pacing around the room quickly.

D-Money returned with the girl and the gym bag. He pushed the girl down with the others and said, "let's go" to King. While they were leaving the room, King stopped and aimed the AK-47 in the room. As D-Money took his first step down the stairs, he heard the shots from the AK-47 sounding off. The fire was rapid and nonstop. Bullets pierced all four of their bodies sounding like blows to a pillow. He shot fearlessly. D-Money ran back to King.

"Man, what the fuck, let's go," D-Money hollered. They ran out the back door and into the Tahoe as fast as they could.

"Bra, what the fuck is wrong with you?" D-Money yelled. "What?" he asked.

"Man, that wasn't in the fucking plan. That was hot as fuck," he continued.

"Man, you asked me if I was ready and I showed up. Just keep driving," King demanded.

D-Money didn't respond, he continued to drive.

He was pissed, but he had to get them somewhere safe before he told him how he felt. He didn't want to leave any trace, so they did as planned and drove to a nearby city where an old friend of his lived. They burned their clothes and shoes and got rid of the weapons. They weren't at the friend's house for long before D-Money emptied the gym bag onto the stained carpet. Stacks of money rap with rubber bands and some with hair ties poured from the bag.

King's eyes raised up with amazement. He hadn't counted it yet, but he could tell that it was more money than he'd ever had. There were also bags of heroin and coke that poured from the gym bag. He thought to himself how quickly D-Money had filled the bag and made it back to the room.

"Real OG," he mumbled under his breath as D-Money looked at him and turned back to finish unloading the bag.

Before heading out, they gave a few stacks to the friend. D-Money drove the same shortcut back to New York City that he did on the way here. Not too many words were exchanged on the ride home as both were filled with opposite emotions. King was ecstatic about the situation where as D-Money didn't like how it ended at all. He knew that the killing would be a big storyline for the city and the NYPD wouldn't stop investigating until they got a conviction. This left him worried for the next few days. Weeks and months even.

***

Summer 2009 started off great for King and Queen. Her and TJ made their relationship official and so did King and Amara. The difference was that Queen was being faithful. Before they got together TJ decided to tell Queen about his then relationship with his ex-girlfriend. She informed them that she didn't feel comfortable with them being in touch, so he ceased it. He returned her car to her and began to use one of his dad's cars which he was given permission since he had his license. Queen was still hurt about Shelton being murdered and it didn't help that the police still had no suspect nor a lead into the investigation. In New York City, someone getting murdered by a gun was a more serious crime since guns were outlawed to all regular citizens. But just the presence of TJ helped to occupy her mind. They were very supportive of one another as they attended each other's sporting events and he started teaching her to drive. She sometimes drove him to work and picked him up from practice. Her track performances had been so good over the past couple years that she received three offers from big universities to be a part of their team. Tiffany was beyond happy for her, but not so much with King because she finally realized that he was selling drugs.

A few weeks ago, when she was changing the lightbulb in his closet, she noticed that one of the ceiling tiles appeared to have been altered a little. She slid the square shaped tile over and a stack of money dropped down onto her head. So, she waved her hand around up there and grabbed a bunch of money and drugs. She couldn't believe it. When King arrived home later that day, all of his belongings were packed up. Tiffany told him that he couldn't live there anymore if he wanted to sell drugs. She finally told him that his dad sold and used drugs before they were born. And with that, King had to find elsewhere to live.

He moved in with Jane; someone who already knew what King did and her only rule was that he didn't deal out of the house. King also helped with bills and necessities around the home. He went to Tiffany's every Sunday for family dinner. Seeing King content with being away from home hurt Tiffany because she didn't want to see him falling off any more than he already had. He had only passed three of the five graduation tests and he was set to retake the other two this summer; one of the tests was science which was also one that Destiny failed again in March. It would be their first time seeing each other since she last saw King covered in D-Money's blood.

She knew that their relationship was done at that point, but it still hurt her to see him move on with someone else as she heard about him and his new girlfriend that she remembered going to school with. Destiny was unable to walk the stage with her fellow classmates so seeing King

taking the test over again in the summer made her feel

ashamed. She couldn't understand how someone as smart

as King could have failed the test. All she could remember

was seeing him with blood all over him and she wondered

if that had anything to do with his performance the week of

testing. Later on, today King had to go and get packed up

for football camp with his team in Baltimore, Maryland.

Chapter 14

I'm ready

"You sure you ready to do this?" he asked her as he placed his face between her legs.

He stuck his tongue in and moved his head from side to side so that his lips gently rubbed past hers. He could hear her panting like she had just finished running a marathon and she couldn't help it. She thought her soul was being snatched away. He raised up and tried to stick it in but with no condom this time. She had been telling TJ that she was ready for this moment for the past weeks. But this time it was working. She was so wet that he barely had any problems getting in. It felt so good that they stayed in the same position the entire time and when he came, he came hard. It looked like someone had poured out a bottle of lotion on her stomach. After they cleaned it up, they lay there and cuddled before resuming later in the night.

Around 6 a.m. King received a call from Rikers Island.

"To accept this call from Darius Morgan, press 1. To refuse this call, press 2," the ITC operating voice said.

King sprang forward and his hotel bed where he was having a great sleep after a great performance at the Nike all-american football camp. His skills had captured the attention of several big name universities scouts with one of those schools being Michigan and another Morgan State, both his parents' alma mater. He quickly pressed one on his cell phone's keypad and waited 10 seconds for the call to process.

"Hey, bra what's up?" said D-Money.

"What's up man. What the hell you doing in there?" King asked.

"They talking about my truck was seen driving to and from a murder. Some boy named Shelton Ivory. I don't even know this motherfucker. Plus, I was in the hospital at the time," D-Money explained.

"Man what! How they even get an arrest warrant to do that?" asked King.

"I don't know but I got Joseph on that. I need you to hold down the fort until I'm back. You got me?" he asked.

"You know I do," said King.

"Bet, imma hit chu back later."

Joseph was a Jewish lawyer that the wealthy drug dealers in the hood used, most of them had him on payroll. Even D-Money though he had never been in trouble, he knew to always be prepared.

King felt his stomach drop after he heard D-Money mention Shelton's name. He felt bad that D-Money was a suspect but even worse that the investigation was close to him. He looked across the hotel's room and saw his teammate that he was rooming with still asleep. So, he called Amara. Amara was half asleep when she answered. He never called that early, so she became really curious when she didn't hear him say much on the phone. She asked him what was wrong but King assured her that everything was okay. That was until King told her about D-money. When he told her exactly what D told him she told him that he was going to be okay and that he should be released from county jail soon.

After they hung up, they both went back to sleep. In a few hours King and his team had to get prepared for day two of the camp where the team would be competing in a 7 on 7 drill versus a popular high school from Tallahassee, Florida. Today King would have the opportunity to showcase his position capabilities. He would be converting from a cornerback to a strong safety which suited him well considering that he grew a ton since beginning his freshman season.

Yesterday, his 40-yard was clocked at a 4.38 and that's what mainly raised a lot of eyebrows to college recruiters and scouts. King's desire to play football extended to more than just a game. It was a lifestyle and he wanted to do it for the rest of his life. After they ate at a breakfast spot near the hotel, they headed to the field. King sported an all-black towel with the number eight written in gold to go along with his team's color. The camp's outerwear was sponsored by Nike, so he wore his brand new all black vapor cleats to go along. The shirt and pants also had his number on it in addition to his last name being on his shirt. He wore his name and number proudly on him as it was a representation of his father. A man was well-known and respected in this town.

King was the only player on the field that wore a headband and wristbands. His coach wanted the team to be uniform, but he was very aware of King flashy tendencies. Ever heard of the saying; *look good, play good?* Well, it was obviously true. At least King made everyone believe so.

"King let's go. Get the team warmed up," coach said to his star player as the team did so.

After the drill, an Ohio State recruiter came to speak to King. He told him about the team interest in him and asked if he had decided on a school yet. King told him he was keeping his options open before hurrying off to get on the team's bus. Coach had promised to take everyone to a buffet before heading back to NYC. When they got there, it was closer to 4 p.m. King had sat at the back of the bus with the quarterback talking about football, girls, and other shit that teenagers discussed amongst themselves. Harry, the team's starting quarterback, had his way with females. He had slept with over thirty girls just this year and he just turned seventeen a week prior. He advised King to stay out of relationships and to just fuck all the hoes. King just sat back and laughed for nearly the whole ride. He was a lady's man himself, but he had morals and he actually valued the characteristics of what a relationship entailed.

As they got off of the bus, King and Harry were the last two teammates walking to the buffet. They noticed a group of individuals standing in front of a camera for what appeared to be an interview of some sort. The individuals were dressed in business attire with their backs facing the direction in which King and Harry were walking.

"See now that right there is a nice ass. And she on her sophisticated shit," Harry said in a voice that was so loud that the women overheard him.

King was so embarrassed that he quickly turned his head and sped up as she turned around to see where the voice had come from. Harry looked directly at her and smiled with his not-so-perfect grill. His front teeth had a gap and when he opened his mouth wide enough you could see the two silver caps on both sides in the back of his mouth. The lady looked at him but then over to King who she noticed was walking at a different pace from Harry. She saw Matthews on the back of his shirt.

Harry slightly jogged up to catch back up the King. They waited in the entrance of the door with the rest of the team to be seated. The buffet was huge, but it was packed today as families often filled up the place following church. After being seated, the team lobbied the place like small kids in the candy store. The boys could eat a lot. They were hungry as they deserved to be after the way they played on the field earlier. King had just finished his second plate. His favorite food was pot roast and he almost always got mashed potatoes and macaroni to go with it. He was walking near the dessert line when he saw the group of nicely dressed people from the parking lot. They seem to be getting coffee and chatting briefly.

King spotted the woman with a nice body again from a back view. He stared at her ass as she bent over slightly to grab napkins. He stared so hard that he didn't even notice the ice cream overflowing from his bowl that he was filling until one of the workers walked by him to notify.

"Oh shit. I'm sorry. I'll clean it up," he promised.

"Oh, it's okay. I got it," the young worker said.

She was a brunette with green eyes that smiled during the whole interaction. The young girl picked up the ice cream from the metal countertop and placed it into the bucket of sanitary water that she used to wipe tables and machines. She continued to flirt with King, but he didn't know how to react. He had never conversed with the white girl, so he didn't know what to say. Eventually the girl walked away disappointed as you could imagine.

"Fucking idiot," he called himself under his breath.

He looked back at the beverage station. The woman was still facing away from him talking so he walked over to the eating utensils that were directly next to where she stood. He didn't look at her, but he saw through his peripheral that she was looking at him. He pretended to be grabbing a plate and something to eat with. The woman eased her way from the group and walked over to King.

"Hey you," she said as if they were close friends. To King's surprise, the face did look familiar when he looked up.

Damn the girl from the wedding, he thought himself. Still lost for words, the woman spoke again.

"You don't remember me, do you? LJ, from the wedding you went to with your Aunt Jane last year."

"Oh, I definitely remember you. Who are those people you with over there?" he asked.

"Oh, those are my future investors. I'm trying to expand my business," he responded.

"What business?" King asked.

"I make natural washes and creams for your skin and conditioners for hair to help it grow and keep it moisturized. It's called the Beyond Beauty Collection," she described.

"Oh wow. I might have to try some of that," he said.

"I hear you. So, what brings you back to Maryland? Are you following me still?" she joked.

"No, I just left this football camp," replied King.

"So how old are you now like 15?" asked LJ.

"I'll be 16 soon," King responded.

"Oh my god. So young," LJ muttered.

"We're about to head out," one of the men from the group said to LJ.

"Here I come," she responded quickly. Then she reached in her purse and pulled out her set of keys. She disconnected the key from the ring and handed it to King along with her address that she had just written on a napkin.

"Come over later when you get a chance so we can finish this conversation cuz I gotta go," she said before exiting the buffet.

He looked at the key in the napkin. He was set to leave directly following his lunch outing, but he didn't want to pass up on this opportunity. He thought of this woman every day for about a week after their first encounter without even knowing her name. He knew there was no way that he couldn't show up to the address. King had to do something fast. He quickly grabbed the ice cream and went to the booth where his coach was sitting. Coach was on the phone, so he sat there and waited for the call to end. It seemed like the longest phone call ever. Or maybe he was just too anxious.

"Mr. Matthews, what's up soldier. What was that recruiter back there talking about?" Coach asked.

"Just that they were interested in me and if I knew where I wanted to play," he replied.

"What you tell em?" he asked

"That I was keeping my options open," King responded.

"Good," said Coach.

"So yeah, Coach. I'm gonna stay back. I'll be back Tuesday for practice," King presented to his coach.

"What are you talking about?" he asked.

"You know I have family out here, Coach. I just saw my aunt and she gave me her house key. She's gonna take me back in the morning," King improvised.

"I didn't know you had family out here. I forgot you were from Baltimore. Ok, where is she?" he asked.

"She just went to a meeting with her coworkers. That's why she gave me the key. I know where she stays. I came to visit last summer," King continued.

"Ok, you need a ride there?" asked Coach.

"Yeah," King replied.

King had no idea where she lived but he had to pretend, so that his coach wouldn't be suspicious. He had the team's bus driver take him to a random street. King picked a random house and pretended to walk to its back door just until the bus pulled off. He waited for a minute then walked down the street not even knowing where to go. As he continued to walk, he eventually pulled out his cell phone and googled the recs nearby. He caught a break because there was a gym within walking distance.

It took him seventeen minutes to get there which stalled out the time to 6 p.m. King wondered if LJ was home yet. He wasn't sure so he decided he would play basketball for a little while as he waited. King was so competitive that one game turned into two because he lost. Two games turned into three to break the tie. Afterwards, he checked his phone for the time. It was 7:03 p.m. so we figured that LJ would be home or at least on her way. He told the guys he was hooping with that he'd check them out another time because he had somewhere important to be. They asked him where he lived. King didn't want to tell them that he was from out of town because he didn't know how they would react. Like trying to rob him or beat him up for example. He hadn't lived here since he was 8 years old and he needed to answer quickly before they knew he was lying.

"Over by MLK," he responded.

He knew that Martin Luther King was so popular that he had a street named after him everywhere.

"What time does the rec close today?" King asked.

"8:00," one of the boys responded.

King went to the pool area where the showers were found so that he could get cleaned up. The showers were disgusting. Each shower was separated by a single wall. The walls were dirty, and they seemed to have mold growing from them. The room had an awful order. He looked around to make sure that it was a shower room and not the bathroom. He was actually afraid to get in and he refused to allow his bare feet to touch the ground. It was a good thing that he always brought his flip-flops whenever he played sports to put on because he knew his feet would probably hurt afterward.

He put them on before getting in the shower and he stood in one spot to ensure that none of his body would touch the walls. After that he called a cab to come take him to the address on the napkin. The cab driver was a black guy in his mid-thirties. He offered King some weed, and he declined at first but then he must have thought about how nervous he was because he grabbed the blunt and hit it not two but three times. He was already high before he even passed the blunt back and it felt good. No lights were visibly on when the cab pulled in front of the house.

"Damn, she's still not home," he mumbled.

"Huh?" the cab driver yelled over the Little Wayne song that was playing on the radio.

King just handed over a fifty-dollar bill and stepped out of the burgundy 2004 Ford Escort that had an American Eagle trim on the sides. Ironically, King became more confident as he walked up the stairs of the front porch. He grabbed the single key from his gym bag and used it to get in the door. The house was pitch black. The only thing he could see was a small red LED light from the 55-inch television in the living room. Not trying to walk or step on anything, King walked ahead slowly with the only sound coming from his footsteps touching the fairly new hardwood floors. He kept walking forward until he was in the doorway of a room. He used his hand to feel on the wall for a light switch. As the sounds of the lights flicked, variety boxes and cans of food became visible.

Oh, just a pantry, he thought.

He turned around to walk back in the direction of the door. On his left side was a set of stairs. He figured the bedroom would be upstairs and that's where he would wait until she came home. King crept up the steps with his hand gliding on the walls beside him. The upstairs was pitch black also, so he went up to the room closest to him. He twisted the doorknob as the door squealed while opening. He heard music playing softly but he just figured that she maybe left the radio on. King was caught off guard by the sound of the light switching on and the color that appeared.

The bedroom lit up red. King's eyes did as well with LJ standing right in front of him with all red lingerie set barely covering her glistening chocolate skin complexion. All King could was stare but not for too long. With no words said, not even a simple

"Hey," LJ rushed King with an array of kisses.

King had never tongue kissed a girl, but he learned quickly in the moment. His manhood stiffened up against her petite stomach and he squatted down a little to lift her up by the back of her thighs. He continued to kiss her while holding her up by her round tight ass. LJ stopped kissing for a moment to whisper something in his ear. She leaned her head over and said, "now this is a nice ass. Isn't it?" This made King palm and rub LJ's ass with his big hands.

"Perfect ass," he responded back before carrying her to the bed.

He placed her on the bed smoothly as if he had experienced an older woman like her before but really his arms were beginning to burn from holding her. LJ laid on her back at first staring at King as if he was her newlywed husband on their honeymoon. She used her index finger to circle her nipples with one hand while slowly taking her free hand down her stomach until she found what she was looking for. Then, she pulled her panties to the side and began to play with herself as King watched.

"Get undressed," she said seductively as King started by first unzipping his Bape hoodie.

King revealed his freshly developed chest and abs he had worked hard for over the past year. He had also just began to grow hair on the lower part of his stomach where his belly button was. LJ thought that was so sexy as she placed her finger on the tip of her clit using circular motions that made her nipples harden. King then unbuckled his pants, causing his jeans to drop to his ankles. He kicked those off. LJ laid on her stomach and crawled closer to him until her face was directly in front of his boxer briefs. She could see his dick print and she was impressed. She yanked his briefs down and his dick almost bounced up her face from the impact. When she saw it whole, she couldn't believe her eyes. Through all her years of fucking, she had never seen a dick that size and for it to belong to an almost 16-year-old boy baffled her. But she didn't want to seem too surprised, so she just put it in her mouth.

King watched her suck it and then looked up at her body, mainly her ass and dropped his head back. The head was feeling good, but he was honestly in disbelief from what was taking place. LJ was sucking and gliding her hands on his dick at the same time. Until she couldn't go any further, but she forced herself to go further than the last time causing her to gag leaving a thick glob of saliva on his dick. She then increased her speed until he stopped her, and she raised up on her knees and looked him directly in the eyes while biting her bottom lip. King couldn't resist any longer. He pressed his body up against hers, backing her backwards before pushing her on her back and then her legs back as he began tongue kissing her pretty pink pussy. He ate it until she couldn't take it anymore while she begged him to stop, letting him know that she had to have him inside of her.

"Please baby, please," she cried while still enjoying his delicate lips pleasing her. He then instructed her to climb further up the bed and flipped her over on her stomach again. LJ laid there anxious to see how it would feel when King entered her vagina for the first time. He entered her slowly as she bit down on her lip to contain her moan. He plunged in deeper and she couldn't help but to tell him how it felt.

"Oh shi, shit. Baby just like that. Oh my god," she sang uncontrollably.

She kept getting wetter and wetter. He felt the sensation getting close to the tip of his dick, so he pulled out and tapped it on her butt. He laid down and she climbed on top. She came down on his pole slowly at first just to tease the head of it until her pussy started to pulsate. Then she started going down further and faster, squeezing her walls every time she landed causing him to lose control. All she heard him saying was "damn girl, what the fuck you doing to me?" Hearing those words must have brought out something in her. She started going up and down more rapidly.

"I'm boutta cum," he said.

LJ turned around backward with his dick still inside and bounced up and down less rapidly. She felt King grab her hips and lean forward as he was cumming hard in her pussy. She still didn't stop yet because she was only a few stokes away from cumming herself. It was like King knew her body well because he reached around her hips to rub her pussy in a fast circular motion while she continued to ride him. At last, she exhaled a deep breath and creamed all over his dick. She was so out of breath that she fell forward but still managed to turn around and saw King clenching his hands tightly from the sensitivity he was feeling from his dick. She crawled up to him and kissed his lips before laying down while using his chest as a pillow. King couldn't even fathom what had just happened, but he knew it did because he could still feel it in his dick while lying there with the excellent smell of conditioner coming from LJ's hair. He still didn't know what it was that she saw in a 15-year-old boy and he didn't care anymore at that point. In LJ's mind, she had been waiting for this to happen a while ago.

King didn't awake until the next morning. He noticed LJ wasn't beside him in the bed anymore. He looked around for his underwear to put on so he could go to the bathroom that he didn't even know where it was but before he could step one foot out of the bed, LJ came in smelling good. And it wasn't her. Well maybe she did smell good after showering but what King smelled was breakfast; pancakes, eggs, bacon, and sausage with a glass of freshly squeezed orange juice. She made it herself. King acknowledged her cooking skills when she walked over with the food on a platter.

"Good morning, love. I hope you like pancakes," she said softly.

King nodded his head.

"Ok good. Fuck, I forgot the syrup," she whispered before turning to go grab it. She was fully naked and again King was mesmerized by her nice ass while remembering the night before and what she whispered in his ear while he held her up. It made his already hard dick become more stiff. When she came back, King finished his food and thanked her. She asked him when he had to be back home and volunteered to take him. King accepted and got up and showered before they headed out. They spoke the entire ride to NYC just getting to know one another more.

LJ quickly picked up on King's charming ways and great sense of humor. He was still a young boy, but she liked him, especially after seeing what he could do in the bedroom. When they pulled up around the corner of Jane's house, she reminded him that this had to be kept a secret. King agreed. He had a girlfriend already anyway so that was mandatory.

While he was opening the passenger door to get out, LJ stopped him and planted a kiss on his lips that turned into a tongue wrestle.

"Ok bye, baby," she said as he waved back at her. He walked home feeling super confident. And in that moment, he knew that he was that nigga.

Chapter 15

The Final Verdict

December 12th, 2010 was the twins' 17th birthday.

Tiffany and Jane made big plans for them to enjoy their

birthday in Jamaica, but King had to pass on the invitation.

It was D-Money's final day of trial when the jury would be

reading the verdict. As much as he wanted to spend a week

in Jamaica, he knew he had to be there. D-Money bonded out in the summer of 2009, but had it revoked when he violated the guidelines set forth under his bond conditions. Rucker's Island jail had taken a look at him as he stood in the courtroom looking like a caveman. You could tell her hadn't shaved in who knows how long. He stood there showing no emotion; no fear, no nervousness, no confidence, nothing.

His lawyer knew they had the case won already and so did the people in the courtroom. The facts were the facts. D-Money had a solid alibi during the time of the murder and the car had no license plates on it during the video shown. Also, one of the arguments from his defense was that D-Money had no motive to commit this crime.

"Why would a thirty-seven-year-old man want to murder a sixteen-year-old boy?" Joseph asked the jury.

King and the majority of others in the courtroom nodded their heads in agreeance to the question proposed, proving that D-Money didn't have a motive. The courtroom

got completely quiet as the bailiff read the verdict from the

jury to the judge. Even the lawyer looked calm and relaxed.

The state's prosecutor appeared nervous. He was a new hire

who had been a lawyer in the county for seven years. This

was the first case he was in where the defendant decided to

go to trial.

When the judge opened the envelope, the prosecutor

crossed his arms, and you could see his face turning red.

"The state of New York vs. Darius Morgan, the jury finds

the defendant... guilty of count 1 aggravated murder with a

five-year firearm specification," the judge read. The

courtroom got loud really fast. The judge had to hold the

rest of her statement so that the sheriffs could escort people

out of there. King felt terrible as he put his head down.

"I sentence you to 23 years to life at the

Warrensfield Correction Facility," the judge continued.

The courtroom erupted in emotion again. Everyone besides the victim's family was in disbelief. D-Money just shook his head. Joseph tried to talk to him, but the words just went through one ear and came out the other. He could still hear the judge's voice saying guilty and 23 years to life. He turned to look at King who was in tears.

"Imma get you out," King mouthed to him.

King waited around for Joseph to walk into the lobby. When he saw him, he approached him with questions.

"Man, you didn't even argue the main fucking point!" King shouted.

"And what was that, Mr. Lawyer?"

"His alibi you fucking genius. He was in the hospital during the time of the murder!" he yelled some more.

"Look kid, I did what I could do," Joseph said now speaking calmly.

"Man fuck you!" he said calmly using the same tone of voice Joseph had.

King was furious as he walked away. He saw Mrs. Morgan and their children. He stopped to chat.

"Adoree,' I don't even know what to do now. I'm broke, my husband is still away," Mrs. Morgan said.

"Don't worry about the money. We're going to make this right," he assured her. He got closer and began to talk really quietly. "When you go home, go into the basement and push the washer over to the side. There's going to be a small compartment door with a keypad. The code is y'all wedding year. Open it up and it'll be money in there for you. I'm gonna call you something later this week," King explained.

"Ok Adoree,'" she responded

King felt that he had to look out for D-Money's family while he was away. He knew that he would do the same for him. King's senior year wasn't quite what he expected it to be. His vacation was vacated, his OG was sent away to prisons, and he didn't get any offers from the schools where he wanted to play college ball. But on the bright side, he was making more money than ever. He was able to buy himself and Queen vehicles a few months leading to their birthdays. Queen picked out a silver 2007 Pontiac Grand Prix. She loved it. King bought himself an all-black Lincoln truck. Driving D-Money's Tahoe inspired him to get a truck. He got lots of compliments for it.

His relationship with Amara was going ok, but her and her family moved to Washington, DC. So, her and King rarely saw each other. Also, Amara wasn't the brightest. She didn't even know what she wanted to do in life and King disliked that. It was the one trait she had that reminded him of Destiny. Destiny, who still kept in contact with Queen, still hadn't passed one of her graduation tests. She worked at a fast-food restaurant and the word on the street was that she was messing around with a pimp. King hadn't talked to her in over a year. He was way over her.

When he wasn't in the streets making money or at practice,

he was with LJ. King had fallen in love with LJ and so did

she. She would come down to visit every other week, but

they kept their relationship a secret. That was mainly

because King didn't want Jane to find out about them. But

more importantly, he didn't want his girlfriend to find out.

When King went home after the trial, he sent five

hundred dollars to D-Money's commissary and sent one

hundred dollars for phone time. D-Money called once he

got back to his cell.

"What up, big bra? How you holding up?" asked

King.

"Man lil bra, this shit crazy. You know I'm solid

though," D-Money said with dignity. "Fasho dat. I

just put some bread on yo books and phone son," he

responded.

"I appreciate that," he replied.

"No doubt. You gon be good, bra. Imma get you outta there. And imma look out for yo family till you get back," King assured his OG.

"I know, bra. My nigga. This lil shit ain't bout nothing. Imma call you back tonight cuz they bouta count," D-Money said.

"Bet," King finished.

***

School resumed a few weeks later. Queen had been offered a scholarship by eight colleges to run track as well as academic scholarships. If she got at least a 3.7 g.p.a this last semester of high school. She could still graduate with a stellar 4.0 g.p.a. At this point, she was the most popular girl in the whole entire high school. She hadn't decided where she wanted to go to school yet. Tiffany wanted her to stay close, but Queen told her that she wanted to go wherever she felt was the best fit for her. She was secretly waiting for King to commit to a school before she did because she wanted to stay close to him or even at the same school if possible.

Throughout their childhood, she was used to King having all the spotlight and the attention but now that she had it as well, she didn't want it. As good of a runner that she was, she didn't want to run track her whole life. Queen knew the life of a professional athlete and she knew that it wasn't for her. She was more of a family-oriented woman. She saw a future with TJ who had several offers as well. Queen was so proud of him. He expressed to her that he wanted to graduate from college with a degree in law and that was like music to her ears because deep down she didn't want the baggage that came with marrying a professional athlete. But still she wanted the best for him so if that meant getting drafted to the NBA then so be it.

Last year, TJ transferred to the high school where King went because their athletic programming was more polished, and the staff had more connections with college coaches. He averaged 19 points, 6 rebounds, and 6 assists. He was also able to get to know King better.

They became good friends. King had an amazing senior season in football. He became the school's all-time leading tackler and in interceptions. His team won the state championship. His best offers were from Ball State University, Indiana, and the University of Maryland. His dream schools were Michigan because of his father, Ohio State, Alabama, LSU, and USC. TJ would always tell him that those offers would come and if they didn't then he'll just have to roll with one of the offers on the table which weren't bad schools.

Two months after the twins' birthday, Tiffany received a devastating call. King had been arrested for possession of an illegal substance. He got caught with a gram of heroin. Tiffany couldn't believe it. She went to go visit him that next morning in juvenile. There was a glass that separated them at the visit. Tears raced down her face while she sat there shaking her head at him. He knew he had fucked up as he just put his head down.

"You ain't got nothing to say, huh?" Tiffany asked.

"I'm sor…" cried King.

"I don't even want to hear it. I told you that it was only two places you'll end up from doing what you do. Right here where you are now, or in a grave like your dad. Why can't you just play sports and go to college then get drafted? Why do you want to just fuck your life up?" she questioned.

"I don't, mom," he mumbled.

"Look where you are. Look around you. Is this what you want for your life?" she asked.

King sniffled from crying before saying no.

"Well, you gotta make some changes. Starting with you moving back in ASAP," she suggested.

King nodded his head as the tears continued to roll down his face. He knew that everything his mom was saying was right. It was a weekend so King couldn't bond out until the following Monday. He had never been to jail before, so the environment was way different. He had already seen more fights and riot in his first day there than he had seen his whole life. The kids in juvenile were wilder than the adults in the county jail. King went to shower at around 8 p.m. There wasn't anyone else in there at the time.

"Perfect," he said to himself. But just before he could finish getting undressed, three white teenage boys came out of nowhere. The boys looked at each other and smiled. King quickly put his pants back on.

"What's funny?" King asked. The taller boy with tattoos on his face was the first to speak.

"Who laughed, son? We just tryna figure out why the stupid lil black kid is getting in the shower after 6 o'clock," the boy responded.

"Stupid? Little black boy? Man y'all got it twisted. I do what the fuck I want," King yelled.

The boys rushed him. They were all pretty small compared to King. King was about 5'11," one-hundred and eighty pounds and neither one of them were taller than 5'8" nor did they weigh over one-hundred and fifty pounds. So, them rushing King didn't go quite as planned as he punched the one who did all the talking right in the nose. Blood poured from the boy's face as the other two grabbed King. Eventually, they wrestled him to the ground where he was still able to grab a hold of both of them. The other boy finally recovered and kicked King in the stomach twice and once in the head. King saw stars. He could longer defend himself.

Out of nowhere, another black kid ran in and punched two of the boys and threw them off of King. The boys got up and headed back to their cells.

"You cool, son!" he asked King.

King sat up and squinted his eyes from the head pain he was experiencing. He just nodded his head. The boy said something else to King while his head was pointed at the ground and King recognized the voice. The boy standing at 6'4," two-hundred and twenty-five pounds reached his hand out to King to help him up. King stood up and stared.

"Ronald, what's good, man. You came at a perfect time. Thanks ,man," he said.

"No problem, slim. Man, you fucked dude up. His nose is broke fasho. They was fucking you up when I came in though. Man forget all that. What the hell you doing in here?" Ronald asked.

"I could ask you the same thing son. But first let's get out of this shower," King responded and they both laughed.

Ronald walked with King to his cell. He stayed there and chatted until it was count time. Ronald told him some of the guidelines of the place and the first one was to not shower after p.m. The second was to stay away from the white kids.

"Black and white don't mix," Ronald said.

The next morning, King woke up with a headache. After eating breakfast, he called LJ. She answered the phone as quickly as she could.

"Hey baby," King said.

"Oh my god. What happened, bae?" she asked with extreme concern.

"Some stupid shit, come down to visit me tomorrow at noon. Bring your I.D," he told her.

"Ok, how are you doing?" asked LJ.

"I'm ok. It's cool I guess. I….Ima call you back babe," he hurried and said before hanging up.

"Wait, where you go…," LJ attempted to ask before hearing the dial tone.

King ran over to the nearby table where he saw the two white boys jumping a black boy. He tackled one of them and started choking him. Then he felt someone trying to pull him off. The incident quickly escalated into a riot. King didn't even realize what he had gotten himself into. As he was getting back on his feet, he saw the chaos. He quickly backed himself up to a small corner of the room. Right in front of him were two black boys stomping out a white boy. Over to his right he saw a chair fly by and hit a small teenager who couldn't be no older than 14 right in the head.

"Oh shit," he whispered.

The atmosphere was so loud that he couldn't hear himself. At this moment, King was terrified. He used the wall he was near to get across to the other side of the room without being spotted. An alarm sounded and King saw the white lights flashing. His head was still hurting from last night, so he squinted in pain. As he got closer to the other side, several men dressed in all black body armor rushed through the doors. They were yelling loud.

"Everybody get down, now!"

The boys continue to fight causing the SRT man to begin pepper spraying. The spray quickly clouded the air. King was one of the first to be affected by it. His eyes started burning and so did his nose. He repeatedly sneezed and coughed. King lifted the top of his shirt over his mouth to navigate throughout the battlefield-like room. As he was leaving out the room, he felt a slash across the back of his arm. Then on the same side of his body he felt an even worse pain. One of the boys had stabbed King twice and would have continued if the SRT didn't stop him. Blood sprinkled from King's rib cage like tiny raindrops. He took off his shirt to press against the wound while he finally made it out the room. The jail staff quickly approached King to get him medical attention; he was taken to the closest hospital.

***

Queen and two other girls from her track team were spending their last night in Alabama. They were visiting the University of Alabama. It was a college trip and each of them were planning on going to college next year, so they decided to party. One of the school's fraternities was hosting a huge purple and gold party. Queen and the rest of the girls noticed that this particular frat had a lot of cute, muscular boys so they had to be there. One of the boys kept checking out Cassidy while they were there touring the campus. The girls told her that she had to talk to him.

"He's an upperclassman and he's fine as fuck," Queen convinced her.

It was just a coincidence that all the girls had brought their purple spirit pack shirts from the previous track season. Queen put hers on with leggings but the other two wore something more revealing. They put on half shirts, showing off their newly belly piercings.

"Ok so no drinking from strangers, no walking off with strangers, and let's all stick together," Queen expressed to the other girls.

They each agreed before heading to the frat house off-campus. This would be the biggest party any of the girls had been to and they noticed that before stepping a foot inside. The street where the frat house was located was so packed that they couldn't find anywhere to park. They pulled around the street twice before peeping a car that was pulling out of a spot and they quickly filled it. Cassidy and the other girl Tiny had already started to drink in the car. Queen looked at them and smiled as they stumbled into the party. There was a guy at the door offering drinks of a mystery juice. Queen declined but the other girls shared a cup. Queen looked and shook her head.

"Rule number one!" she said to them in a stern voice.

"Lighten up, baby girl, have some fun," Tiny responded as her and Cassidy sipped the cup filled with blue fluids.

Lil Wayne's song *Lollipop* started playing from the large speakers. Everyone started dancing. Queen danced for a little, then she found an empty spot on the stairs to sit. She pulled out her phone to see if her boyfriend had called or texted her back, but he didn't. She sighed and shook her head.

"Damn girl why you all anti over here?" a boy said from the bottom of the steps. Queen smiled.

"I'm not, I was just checking my phone," Queen responded.

"Ok ok, what's ya name pretty," he asked.

"It's Queen, and yours?" she replied.

"A queen you are for sure. And just call me CJ," he responded.

"Yeah I should probably get going. I have to call my boyfriend," she said as she recognized his name sound too close to her boyfriend's.

"Whoa Whoa, slow down baby. It's pretty loud down here. It's way more quiet upstairs if you wanted to call him," CJ suggested.

"That's a good idea," she said.

Queen followed CJ upstairs. When they got in the room, he closed the door and asked her if it was quiet enough. She nodded and made the call. She called three times, but TJ never answered so she texted him.

"Is everything all right?" CJ asked and Queen responded.

"Yeah."

"He's probably just busy," CJ said.

He poured a drink and asked her if she wanted some. Queen looked at the bottle of 1800 and told him that she didn't like that. CJ pulled out a bottle of Hennessy.

"How about this?" he asked.

Queen nodded her head. She was so upset that TJ wasn't answering the phone that she threw the drink back faster than she wanted to. CJ offered her another and she took it, throwing this one back faster than the other. Not even ten minutes later and it had already hit her… fast. Then her stomach began to burn. Queen tried to remember what she had eaten that day, but her brain wouldn't allow her to because her head was spinning uncontrollably. She felt herself about to throw up soon.

When she lifted her head up, the room appeared smaller from her viewpoint. Some of the things in the room appeared blurry and others she saw two of. Then she looked over and saw CJ standing in the corner with a blank face. She couldn't remember why she was up there, let alone while she was alone in a room with a complete stranger. Then rule number two kicked in her head, which resulted in her thinking of all three rules.

Damn I broke all 3 rules. It's definitely time to go,
she thought to herself. Queen quickly stood up to her feet.
She didn't even realize how drunk she had gotten from the
two shots.

"I have to get back to my friends," she said as she
wobbled toward the door that seemed like a double door.
As she was opening it, CJ closed it back.

"Where ya going pretty. The night just started," he
said in a soft voice.

CJ was wearing a purple tank top with the year he
became a member of the fraternity on it. He had chest hair
with several gold chains. He was average height and weight
with a huge bald head. CJ's voice wasn't intimidating, nor
did she get that aura from their short conversation. But he
was still a stranger. Queen looked at him confused. She
reached for the doorknob once more, but CJ put his body in
a way.

"Just relax," he said softly.

"No, I'm ready to leave. Move!" she yelled.

She was quickly starting to sober up. CJ placed his hands on Queen's shoulder blades to move her backwards but she tussled for the door. She tried her hardest, but her strength just wasn't enough as he wrapped his arms around her whole body and slammed her on the bed. Queen never noticed that CJ had locked the door when they first came in. While she laid involuntarily on her back, CJ held her down and listened to her yell and scream.

"Stop, help, help," but no one was upstairs to hear her and the music was blasting downstairs.

She continued to yell and tried to get up, but CJ was too determined. Queen looked him in the eyes and it was like she saw a demon. He was staring at her like he was ready to cut her up and eat the pieces. He ripped her leggings off with his left hand while holding both of her hands together with his right. Then he unzipped his jean shorts. Queen couldn't believe what was happening. Her head was still spinning, and her vision was slightly impaired, but she was fully aware of what was taking place. Seconds later CJ jammed his dick in her young vagina. She wasn't wet even a little, but he forced it in her while she screamed. Her screaming was a turn on for him as he went deeper and deeper.

Queen was so tired and in so much pain that she couldn't even try to fight him off anymore. She felt defeated. Mad at TJ for not answering but even more mad at herself for violating her own rules. Eventually her pussy started to lubricate itself and it became more bearable. CJ flipped her over, using the bottom of her purple shirt as he forced entry into her walls again while pushing her head into the cushion of the bed. He continued until he came in her before getting up and zipping his shorts back up. He looked down and noticed blood on his shirt and shorts. Queen continued to lay on her stomach with her head faced down while she pulled up her leggings she had left. She was in a heap of pain, physically and mentally. Not much later, and she heard the door close. She rolled over and looked around the room to notice that he was gone so she quickly got up and called Cassidy.

"Queen, where are you? The party is almost over."

"Meet me at the car," Queen said.

"Are you Ok. Why do you sound like that?"

Click

She got up from the bed and walked toward the door stiffly. Her vagina felt like someone was squeezing it tightly. It was like she had no more strength. When she got to the front door of the house, she noticed that people were leaving. She felt so insecure that she didn't want anyone to see her. She heard people laughing and cracking jokes about her ripped pants and she walked to her car where she saw Cassidy and Tiny waiting.

"Queen, what happened to you pants?" Tiny asked in a joking manner.

Queen didn't answer. She handed Cassidy the keys and told her she didn't feel like driving. When they got to the hotel, Queen told them what happened, and they couldn't believe it. Cassidy tried calling the police, but Queen stopped her and told her not to tell anyone.

"Especially not my mom and definitely not my brother, you know how he is," Queen added. After D-Money's conviction, she had her suspicions about Kings involvement with Shelton's murder.

***

Tons of people came up to the hospital for King's support. Though he was grateful, he didn't get a chance to see the two people he wanted the most. Amara didn't have a ride home from D.C and he hadn't heard from LJ since that morning. He waited for his mom and Jane to leave before calling her.

"Hello," she answered.

"Hey, how are you?" King asked.

"I heard what happened, I'm in the parking lot. Is it safe to come in?" she asked.

"Yeah, come up, I'm in room 213," he replied.

"I'm on my way handsome," she responded.

King rushed the last two friends in the room out. He told them he was tired and wanted to rest. LJ arrived at the door some minutes later, wearing a shirt that King had bought her last year when they took a trip to Chicago. He was so happy to see her. His dick stiffened beneath the cover when she came into the room with her perfect smile.

"Aww look at my poor baby," she whined. King chuckled.

"Soooo, why you ain't come in earlier?" King asked.

"What chu mean? I left work and came straight here," she responded.

"No, I mean like straight into the hospital?" he asked.

"Oh bae, I figured your family would be in here and you know our situation," she explained.

"Forget that, they're going to find out one way or another. This would've been a good time. Well no it wouldn't, but still," he said.

"Babe, were going to tell them soon. Jane's going to be pissed," she said.

He knew why she wanted to keep things a secret, but he felt that their relationship had become too serious to continue to hide it. King knew that Jane would be pissed also and would feel betrayed, but he also knew that she'll get over it. King was so happy with LJ that he was willing to keep it this way for as long she wanted. LJ was laid back. That's probably what he liked the most about her, besides her being older. She didn't go through his phone, question him about other females, not even the one that he was in a relationship with. Also, she was financially stable, so she gave King whatever he needed and paid for mostly everything.

The juvenile jail officer who was supervising King warned them that visitation would be over in ten minutes. LJ made a sad face at King. He told her not to worry because he'll be free in the morning regardless.

"I want to feel you inside of me now," she said to him. His dick stiffened again. LJ came over and kissed King on the lips. "Call me in the morning, I'll be at the spot," LJ said to King before leaving out.

The hotel they usually stayed in was located in Brooklyn. It was a nice hotel and it felt like a second home for both of them. They fucked in nearly every inch of the suites they stayed in.

***

The twins had a month left before track season began. ESPN ranked Queen as number three women's track runner in the nation. She still hadn't decided where she was going. King had brought his rank from number fifteen to number eight after his junior year last year was projected to be even better this year. Him and Queen held the title as the fastest male and female in the state of New York. King wanted to focus on football and track this year. But he wasn't sure if he was going to risk getting hurt while playing basketball. He promised his coach that he would play, but deep down he didn't want to risk it.

Last year, he sprang both of his ankles during the season. Tiffany hadn't come to any of his sporting events since his sophomore season, and Queen maybe made it to two or three of them. Jane didn't make it to all of his football or track meets, but she made it her priority to attend his basketball games. After seeing how shined in a varsity game as a freshman she loved watching him play ever since. King was still out on bond for the drug possession charge. His lawyer was working out a deal for him to get an alternative to getting convicted. The prosecutor was willing to work with him because he had never been in trouble before. With this in mind, King knew he had to walk on a straight and narrow path. He had a nice chunk of money saved up and he decided to move back in with his mom and sister. He stopped selling drugs and spent his extra time going to visit LJ.

One weekend, while he was visiting in Baltimore, Tiffany called him early in the morning. King was still asleep aside of LJ when he got the call. He answered in his morning voice, still sleepy until he heard the anxiety in his mom's voice. So, he hurried to a sitting position. His mom told him that she didn't know what he had planned today but he should make it back to NYC as fast as he could. Jane had been rushed to the hospital. Her son Adonis had made the ambulance call earlier that morning after walking in and seeing Jane unresponsive on the couch. King asked her what had happened, and she told him that Jane had been keeping her illness a secret. A few weeks prior, she was told she was in stage 4 lung cancer during a scheduled doctor's appointment.

"I don't know if she's going to make it," Tiffany said in an almost crying voice. Tears escaped King's face instantly following Tiffany last couple of statements. He immediately got dressed to head back the way before LJ held him for a brief moment.

"You coming?" he asked her. She shook her head no and told him that she would come down later that night.

"I don't want us to get there at the same time. It'll look suspicious," she responded.

King agreed and kissed her before leaving. The kiss gave her body a warm sensation. King's presence alone caused her body to react a certain way every time he got near her.

King couldn't believe that Jane was near death. Before going to the hospital, he stopped at a drug store and bought a card along with flowers. When he arrived to the ICU room, where his family was, his mom smiled at him. With everything going on, she was just happy to see her son showing care for his aunt. She reached her hand out for the card and flowers and sat them beside Jane. King looked up at all the machines that she was hooked up to. There were so many numbers and different colors lighting up and a constant beeping noise. Then a nurse came in and he asked her what was going on with Jane. She concluded to him that the ventilator was the only thing keeping her alive. But King still had faith that she would survive.

When they lived together, she sometimes shared stories about her rough childhood, so he knew she was strong. The family sat there mostly quiet throughout the night. His mind was in a gaze that he forgot that LJ was supposed to be driving out there after work. At 4:19 a.m.,

King was awakened to the sound of Queen talking on the phone.

"Oh my god, are you serious?" she asked.

This eventually woke up Tiffany, causing her to ask Queen what had happened as she hung up the phone.

"Mom I got it. LSU just offered me a full ride scholarship!" she yelled.

"That's great, baby."

King closed his eyes in an attempt to go back to sleep, but for some reason he couldn't. He looked over at the ventilator and it showed that Jane was taking two breaths a minute, which was more than 75% less than average. Then he looked to Jane who had taken in one deep breath and then exhaled. King looked back over to the machine that now showed one breath per minute and the time, 4:24 a.m. The long deep breath would be the last breath that Jane would take. The machine sounded off.

Tiffany called the nurse into the room. The nurse claimed that Jane wasn't dead yet, but the family knew she was.

"What the fuck do you mean she isn't dead? She isn't even breathing nomo!" King shouted to the nurse.

Tiffany politely asked the nurse to leave. After everyone cried, and Tiffany spoke to the mortician, they left. King was the last to leave the room. He kissed Jane on the cheek one last time and grabbed the flowers to place inside of her arm. As he did, he saw teardrops drop onto the flowers and that's when he knew it was time to go. He made up his mind at that moment that he was done playing basketball.

Chapter 16

Beauty lies in the eye

National signing day was here, and Queen sat alongside her family and friends. Three hats laid in front of her to choose from. Tennessee on the left, LSU in the middle, and UConn on the right. When it was her turn to choose a hat, she reached for the UConn hat to build the suspense of the crowd, but then grabbed the LSU hat directly in front of her and put it on her head. The crowd stood and cheered for her. New York City hadn't seen a runner of her caliber since the eighties.

After the photographer snapped pictures of Queen and her family, she received the biggest hug from King. He was so proud of her. The hug lasted about ten seconds before Queen shed a tear on King's shoulder. After everything they had been through, they were finally on their way to college. But they were about to be away from each other. King chose not to sign on signing day. He was still stuck between two schools. He wanted to finish out the track season to see if he could land a better offer. Though his ACT score was well above average, his grades had slowly declined over the last two years. His final track season ended great but there weren't any signs of an offer. Prom was right around the corner, so he didn't want to stress himself anymore. He wanted prom to be special with someone special to him. So he phoned his cougar.

"Hey handsome," LJ began.

"What's up, baby. What you doin?" King asked.

"Um, nothing. Trying to lotion my back. I wish you were here to help," she said.

"Oh yeah, I miss our shower sessions," he responded.

"Damn I just got horny from thinking about it, bae," she added.

"I'm driving down there this weekend baby," he said.

"I know, I know. I can't wait," she responded.

"Fasho. But look babe. Prom is next month. Have you decided if you were coming or not yet?" asked King.

"King, you know I can't do that," replied LJ.

"Why?" he asked.

"King, I'm 40 something years old. I can't go to your prom. Plus, you already know our situation," she explained.

"Bout time you mention your age," he said with a laugh.

"Oh shit, I wasn't supposed to say that," she responded back with a slight grin.

"Damn bae, you're almost my mom's age. Wow you look amazing," he praised.

"Thanks, babe. Well, I know there's a ton of girls that want to go to prom with you. Find one of them and I'll pay for everything. As long as it is not with that Amara girl," she proposed.

King just laughed and said ok.

LJ was right, a lot of girls had been asking King to be his prom date since last year. He thought of all the girls that asked and one in particular who came to mind. But it was someone who hadn't asked... Cassidy Morgan. Not only was she a close friend of the family, she was also one of the family's main supporters during D-Money's incarceration.

After giving it some thought, King decided to phone Cassidy. She was doing laundry when she answered. She nonchalantly accepted King's invitation to prom, but deep down she was ecstatic. She always had a crush on King. But she never thought they would have a chance because of all the females that were all over him. And the fact that Queen was a bitch about her friends liking her brother.

Similar to Cassidy, King thought Cassidy was cute, but since she never showed any interest in him, he never paid her any attention, especially after the big ordeal with Sierra.

Well, it's just prom, they both thought to themselves as the phone call ended.

***

After a romantic weekend with LJ, King and Cassidy met up at a library near Cassidy's home. The library was practically empty since it was noon and kids were in school. When they saw each other, it was like they were meeting each other all over again. He'd been so busy over the past year that they haven't really seen each other. They hugged briefly as King got a whiff of her sweet-smelling perfume.

"What's up stranger?" asked Cassidy.

"Stranger? Ha ha. How you been?" he responded.

"Ugh, stressed out with this whole college thing. And now prom. So we got two proms to go to right? Aww Queen will be there too. We can all take pictures together," she answered.

"Whoa Whoa, slow down. Queen doesn't know that we'll be dates yet," he warned her.

"Oh my god. That should have been the first thing you did. You have to do that ASAP, like right now. Call her," she replied.

"I know, I'll tell her when I get home. Well, technically you were my big homie's niece before you were her friend so she can't be upset," said King.

"You know how she is. We'll see," said Cassidy.

"Yeah. But anyway, what day is your prom?" she asked.

They discussed the prom arrangements for the next thirty minutes before King dropped her off home. He stopped at Mrs. Murgain's house before heading home to see how she was. The mood in the house was depressing.

The lights were dim when she opened the door to let him in. King could see the hurt on her face. She didn't look like herself and King knew that he had to uplift her, not just for D-Money, but for the kids. He opened the blinds and cooked a meal for everyone. Before leaving he looked D-Money's wife in the eye and said, "stay strong."

When he got home, he had an even bigger task ahead of him. He went straight to Queen's room after his arrival. She was laying in her bed on her laptop.

"Hey sis, what you doin?" King asked.

"Watching this movie. It's good," she replied.

"What movie?" he asked.

"Um, The Road North. I think that's what it's called," said Queen.

"Ok, pause it for a second," he said.

"Okay. Everything cool?" she questioned.

"Yeah look, I gotta tell you something but you can't get mad," he responded.

"What?" she asked.

"I want to go to prom with Cassidy. We're not dating or anything like that. I just want her to be my prom date," he explained.

"Ok that's cool. Be honest though, do you like her?" questioned Queen.

"Nah, she's cute. Not my type though," he assured her.

"Boy, I done see you with all types of girls. You don't have a type," she stated.

They both laughed. King couldn't believe how cool his sister was about the situation. The old Queen would have flipped.

He texted to Cassidy when he got to his bedroom. Queen had two proms to attend herself, and what a coincidence that they would be the same ones that King, and Cassidy were attending since TJ had transferred to King's school a year ago. TJ had committed to Bowling

Green State University on a basketball scholarship. He had been asking King who he was taking to prom for months as they hung out regularly. TJ would always say that King was going to take Amara, but King always refuted that idea. Queen and Cassidy's prom was first. Queen and TJ wore grey and pink, while King and Cassidy were black and teal. The weekend went alright. The four decided to enjoy the prom weekend festivities at the boys' prom so that they wouldn't have to twice. King wanted the weekend to be great. Since LJ offered to pay for his prom, he would help Queen pay for hers. The last weekend that he went out to see LJ, she had given him fifteen hundred dollars. But either way King had started back hustling in the streets. He would still sell weed here and there but he made the majority of his money from heroin. His clientele ranged from the inner NYC to surrounding cities.

***

May 13th was the day of the prom. Cassidy and Queen had gotten custom made dresses. Queen's followed the color scheme from her future school, purple and yellow. So, King wore navy blue and orange as a hint to where he decided to attend school, but no one picked up on it. No one knew, but King had finally made up his mind. TJ pulled up to the twins' house prior to prom. He had his dad rent a purple Range Rover. Cassidy and Queen were still getting dressed while King went downstairs to answer the door for TJ. They dapped up and smiled when they saw each other.

"Boy you almost look as fly as me," King joked.

TJ laughed and they walked to the backyard where family and friends were all waiting to see them off to prom. Mrs. Morgan was the first person that King spotted when he walked out back. The sight of her quickly made him think of his big homie. He gave her a hug and they chatted briefly because King felt his eyes watering under his all-black Gucci shades. He knew without a doubt in his mind that D-Money was supposed to be there. The thought quickly evaporated from the awe of the people in the backyard. Both King and TJ looked at the back doorway to a pleasant sight. Queen and Cassidy looked amazing; dress, hair, make-up, everything was on point. King always knew that Cassidy was a pretty girl, but today she was beautiful.

He walked up to her and each of them put the corsage on the other. King put hers on first. As she put his on, he couldn't take his eyes off of her.

"What?" Cassidy looked up and asked. King just shook his head as Cassidy proceeded to put the corsage on his tuxedo jacket.

"Ok let's get some pictures!" someone shouted. After they took pictures, Tiffany hugged the four of them and told them to have fun. King pulled out the key for the orange 2010 Porsche truck that LJ had rented for him. The inside of the truck was trimmed orange. The two trucks drove to the high school's parking lot first for about 20-30 minutes to take pictures with teachers and coaches and some of their classmates,' and their parents before heading off to prom.

The venue was nice. They got the most attention. Everyone complimented their attire and asked for pictures. For King and Cassidy, it felt awkward because everyone assumed that they had just began dating while telling them how cute they looked together. For King, he had a secret relationship of his own, but Cassidy was as single as a slice of cheese. But still it was awkward for her as well.

The party after prom was at the Durlin's Hotel. They stayed long enough to get a few drinks and something to eat. TJ and Queen went back to TJ's where they would stay for the rest of the night. Cassidy wanted to stay with King, but they didn't know where to go. Neither of their parents would let them stay the night, so they decided to stay at the hotel and book a room.

King knew that Cassidy had strict parents, so she didn't get out enough and that's why she wanted to stay with him. First, they went to the liquor store where he grabbed a fifth of Hennessey before they headed to the bowling alley. He had Cassidy put the liquor bottle in her purse. They sipped on the liquor in between bowling while having a good time. Eventually, they got drunk and went back to the car and smoked two blunts. Next, they went to get fast food and then back to the hotel. Cassidy was so drunk that she kept hugging King and touching his face. It was beginning to look like they were going to more than just prom dates this weekend.

A few weeks ago, King had no intentions of being intimate with her, but after that first glance of her after she walked out the back door of his home and now seeing how open she was at the moment he was ready to explore her body inside and out. After prom, Cassidy had changed into a short skirt that repeatedly rised up while she laughed and giggled with King. King couldn't help but to feel underneath the skirt. Cassidy's ass felt soft as a pillow in his hands as he caressed just one cheek at a time. Eventually, King stood up to grab his cell phone from the nightstand that had rang several times in the past thirty minutes.

As he turned back around, she tried to kiss him, but he turned quickly, leaving the room filled with awkward silence. King was definitely caught off guard as he found himself stuck in place staring Cassidy in her eyes. He had never realized how beautiful she was until earlier that day, but certainly at this very moment as she stood there looking lost with her doe shaped eyes. Her skin was flawless with a tone so perfect it seemed as if it had been sun kissed. Her full set of pouty lips adored her round angelic face which in turn set off her smedium curvy body frame, he thought to himself as he glanced downward towards the floor examining all five feet of her. He knew deep down that no good could come from what he wanted to do to her, but in that very moment he didn't have a care in the world. He wanted her now and there was nothing or no one that could apprehend his desire. King placed his hand on her shapely hips as she stood there frozen and slightly confused since he had just rejected her moments ago. She looked into his eyes for answers as they lustfully starred at one another with mutual hunger. They both leaned in for a kiss with one being quicker than the other and bang! Both horny teenagers yelled out in pain from the collision of them accidently headbutting each other.

"Damn move your clumsy ass out of the way," King jokingly said as he massaged his forehead.

Cassidy giggled and said, "dang boy watch your big ass head, you about to give me a damn black eye," as she began walking away.

While King glanced at her perfectly round ass, his manhood began to rise. As she tried to take another step, she noticed that something was holding her back. She looked at her hand to find King holding it. He stepped in closer to her leaving no room for air in between. Then he grabbed the bottom of her face and stuck his tongue right in her mouth. The atmosphere suddenly became hot causing them to rip off each other's brand-new clothes while she moved backwards and him forward until they fell on the queen-sized bed. And from there that night faded sensationally.

***

A few months later, the twins were off to college. Queen was first. Her family and boyfriend dropped her off in Baton Rouge on August 12th, 2011. Queen instantly fell in love with her new school. Her roommate was a second-year basketball player from Toledo, Ohio. Exactly one week later, Tiffany dropped King off to her alma mater; Morgan State. It was her first time being near Baltimore since they left a decade ago. She didn't tell King, but she was a nervous wreck. She got in and out of the city the minute King was unpacked.

"This is it, son. Make me proud," Tiffany said before kissing King on the forehead and taking off.

King was roommates with another first year football player from Glacier Hills. The boy's name was Kenneth. He recognized King the minute he saw him. He had moved in a few months prior.

"Adoree'! Man I remember you. First grade Mr. Robinson's class. His wife taught your twin sister's class and then she skipped like two grades or somethin," Kenneth said.

"Oh yeah, what's up bra. How you?" King replied.

"I'm good man. Ready for this season. You ready?" he asked.

"Am I? I was born ready," said King.

"Yeah well, I know I'm late bra, but I'm sorry about your dad," he said.

"Oh, it's cool man. Were any of the kids in the school talking about it when I left?" asked King.

"The kids, the teachers, the parents too. They kept saying something about your dad had robbed someone," Kenneth replied.

"Robbed someone?" he questioned.

"Yeah for some drugs I guess," Kenneth finished. King just stood there looking astonished..

Chapter 17

Pros and Cons

Track conditioning kept Queen busy. If she wasn't training or doing homework, she was struggling to maneuver because her whole body was in pain. She took ice baths and tried other remedies for her soreness, but she was still hurting. For the most part she stayed to herself. Her only desire was to run track and finish school.

After being there for a month, she met a guy whom she enjoyed being around. He was a rapper from New Orleans that was starting to get radio play. At first, she told him how she was dating someone, but the rapper was consistent. He didn't attend LSU, but he was there often enough to promote himself and to see Queen walking through the school's student center.

"Hey angel," he would always yell when he saw her power walking to her destination.

This particular time she decided to stop to see what he had to say since she would always find herself blushing when he called for her.

"Where ya heading, baby girl?" the rapper asked.

"Back to my dorm so I can get ready for practice," Queen replied.

"Hell, you so perfect you don't need no practice, angel," he said.

"Thank you. But I run track," she said.

"Ok now," he said as he looked her up and down examining her body's physique.

"Well, I have to get to practice. Nice chattin' with you," Queen said.

"Wait wait. Before you leave, what's ya name?" he asked.

"Everyone calls me Queen," she answered.

"That you are. Ok Queen, I'll see you around," he said.

The college experience was going the same for King. He had to practice harder than everyone since he came late to the workouts. He didn't know the players or anything for the team's first game, so the coach made him sit out. But the next two games he balled out with a total of 21 tackles, a forced fumble, and two interceptions. He had high school film playing cornerback and safety, so the coach trusted him to play man coverage against the opposing team's best receiver, as well as covering the center of the field. King was never a partier back home but now he enjoyed it. The football team there threw a party every weekend at the football house. And so, did every other big organization on campus. He would finish his homework either during the team's mandatory study session or sometime during the day but definitely before it got dark out. His phone calls home to his mom gradually decreased. But he made sure to call at least once a week to her and to his sister. Like most other star players on the team, King had a bunch of groupies that followed him around when he went out. He slept with only a few of them.

When the season ended, King visited LJ in Glacier Hills. They went out to bars often, mostly in places where not a lot of people know of. This was cool for King because he was able to get a good balance of the high and low intense type of crowds. He actually enjoyed being in an older scene. One day the two went to a restaurant that was also a club. They were dressed casually from head to toe on the spot that LJ had decided on. She was tired of going on the same type of dates and by King looking a little older now with his facial hair finally starting to grow, he was able to sneak in bars and clubs.

The restaurant was playing smooth jazz when the two walked in. LJ gave the host their names as she had made reservations. The short white waitress seated them at a table near the bar.

"Thank you," King said to the woman. She walked away smiling.

"Always have been a flirt," LJ muttered.

King laughed and picked up his menu and after eating they went over to the bar. It was around 10 p.m. and the restaurant closed at midnight, so it was beginning to get packed.

"Order our drinks, babe, I have to go to the lady's room," LJ said.

King sat there confused for a minute because he knew that LJ knew he wasn't old enough to buy drinks if the bartender was to ID him. He watched her as she walked to the restroom envisioning her naked and as he did, he could see someone staring at him out the corner of his eye. It was a woman who he had caught staring at him at various points throughout the night but this time he stared back at her. The woman stood up and made her way over to King considering that she had seen LJ leave his presence.

"What you drinking?" the woman asked.

"Umm, nothing yet," answered King.

"Hey Kelly,"she hollered.

Kelly walked over to them.

"Can we get two long islands and two shots of patrons?" she asked Kelly.

"My brother owns this place so I'm always here."

"Really? This is a nice place," he responded.

"Yeah it's alright. Is that your woman that you've been with all night?" she asked.

"It is," he answered.

"Don't take this the wrong way but she is so pretty," the woman added.

"Thank you," he replied.

"The club session will be starting in a few and I have a VIP section over there," she said while pointing in the direction. "Y'all should stop by if y'all want to," she included.

"Ok what's your name by the way?" he asked.

"Oh yeah my bad, Joseline and I already know who you are Adoree'," she said before getting up and walking to her section.

Not even a full minute later, LJ came out of the restroom.

"Damn bae you alright?" King asked. LJ just laughed.

"Yeah, I had to fix my make-up, babe," she responded.

They both took a shot then started their long islands. A few minutes later, they heard the club music beginning to play. King left a one-hundred-dollar bill on the counter under the empty glass cup and grabbed LJ's hand. He walked her over to the dance floor where they danced. She pressed the back of her body up to King and grinded on him. King wasn't much of a dancer, but he just followed LJ's movement by holding her hips.

After the song ended, King spotted Joseline over at her section sitting alone so he turned LJ around and they kissed.

"Babe, I have a friend over there with a VIP section and some drinks. Let's go over there for a hot second!" King yelled over the loud music.

LJ nodded and King grabbed her by her hand to head that way. When they got a couple feet away from the section, LJ noticed that King's friend was a pretty young female and King felt her stop walking so he turned to face her.

"What's wrong, babe?" he asked.

"Who the hell is this girl? You said a friend," LJ inquired.

"She's a friend from school, babe. Just come on. Let's have a good time," King explained.

LJ looked at King like he was crazy, but she went along. He introduced the two women to each other, and they sat down. King offered LJ a drink, but she declined. She was quiet for the most part. King gave her a kiss then got up to use the restroom himself. Joseline scooted over closer to LJ.

"So how do you like it here?" asked Joseline.

"It's nice," LJ replied.

"Yeah it's cool. That dress is incredible. It shows all of your curves," Joseline complimented.

"Oh thank you. Yours is cute as well."

Both women were wearing tight fitted body dresses. "Don't take this the wrong way but you and your man are fine as hell."

LJ was flattered. She thanked her and took a drink and from her peripheral she noticed that Joseline was looking in her direction still. She turned to face her and Joseline was staring at her seductively. Joseline then placed her hand on LJ's thigh saying, "girl I just love this dress. You have to tell me where you got it from."

LJ responded saying, "I got you," and before anyone knew it, Joseline had leaned in to kiss her. LJ had never been into females but shockingly she kissed back.

They kissed like they were in their own private rooms. They kissed so passionately that neither of them noticed that King had made it back to the section. King cleared his throat to get their attention and they both looked up at him smiling as he sat down and handed them both a glass filled with champagne. It was quiet until King said, "Shid, don't get quiet now. What all did I miss?" In unison they both responded with, "nothing," and each of them broke out laughing.

The DJ started playing a twerk song causing Joseline to grab LJ from the sofa and dragged her to the dance floor. After the drinks and sound of the music, LJ was ready to shake her ass. Her and Joseline were having a great time dancing while LJ kept looking over to the section to watch King, watching her with a look that only she knew. It was the "girl I want you right now" look.

When they walked back over to King, he saw LJ whisper something in Joseline's ear. Joseline stood right in front of him and began to move her hips precisely and alluringly. King looked at LJ for confirmation and she smiled and blew a kiss. King turned back to Joseline but this time he was biting his bottom lip. Then she sat on his lap while circling her hips to the beat of the song that was playing. LJ sat there staring at Joseline thinking how perfect she was. At this point she knew she had to have her, she had to have him, and she had to have him while he had them both together. So she got up from the sofa to whisper I want you in Joseline's ear. Joseline didn't respond, she just bit her lip and LJ took that as confirmation. She immediately grabbed Joseline's hand to walk away before stopping to look back at King to say, "come on baby let's go."

Shortly after they arrived at a hotel, the same hotel that he and Jane stayed when they went to her best friend's wedding. The women walked in behind King as he held the door open to the room. LJ quickly cut on the light and kicked her shoes off before flopping down on the bed due to her aching feet. Joseline was still standing by the door so King told her to get comfortable and LJ patted the bed for her to come sit down next to her. Joseline smiled and did so. King began to remove his silver watch and placed it on the nightstand. Then he took off both his polo short sleeve shirt and white beater that was underneath. LJ had brought in the bottle of patron that had been in the truck already. She grabbed three cups and poured 3 double shots in them.

The three made a toast before throwing them back. Next, LJ walked over to King and planted a kiss on his lips.

"Baby I'm about to shower. Put on some music for us please," she told him. Then she gave Joseline a peck on her neck and whispered, "start without me" in her ear. Her shower lasted for about ten minutes. As she walked out of the bathroom with her hair down in an attempt to dry some of the dampness, she called out for King saying, "Babe."

"Huh," he said, causing her to look up and what she saw next made her nipples stiffen instantly.

King was sitting at the foot of the bed with Joseline butt naked standing right in front of him. *No wonder he responded like that,* LJ thought to herself because his mouth was filled with one of Joseline's perky pierced titties.

She stood there and watched for a second before King signaled for her to come over. LJ took another shot then walked in front of King while letting her towel drop to the floor. King placed his left leg in between Joseline and his right leg in between LJ. While holding one of Joseline's titties, he leaned over and put one of LJ's nipples into his mouth. He took turns tasting both of them making sure he kissed and sucked one as good as the other. Then he stood up and told LJ to lay down as he pushed her onto her back making her giggle nervously out of curiosity of what he was going to do next.

As she scooted up the bed toward the head of the bed, King grabbed her feet and pulled her back down toward the foot of the bed. King kneeled down while opening her legs and placed his head right in between them. He knew her body so well that the first lick made a moan escape from her lips. He feasted on her vagina like it was his last meal. LJ's eyes were rolling to the back of her head from the sensation she was experiencing. Then she felt another set of lips on her nipples. She opened her eyes to Joseline devouring her titties. Her body started getting hotter and more intense, so she pulled Joseline's head up bringing them into a kiss. She felt King move so she looked up to see him hovering over them both with his third leg stocking out.

Joseline's face froze in amazement while LJ rolled onto her stomach so she could take him into her mouth. She started at the tip and took him in further with each motion. The further she took him in, the wetter her mouth got. She pulled King's dick from her mouth and held it up to Joseline's lips. Joseline was thirsty to take him in and she tried to go as far down as she could which wasn't far. LJ just smiled at her thinking how that was her dick, and it took months and long hours of practice to strengthen her jaws to slay that snake. She continued to watch as it did in fact turn her on.

She leaned in to lick his balls while Joseline continued to suck. King mumbled, "damn baby." LJ stood up because she suddenly had the urge to taste Joseline. She walked on the side of the bed where Joseline's ass was up in the air and stuck her middle finger in her mouth before beginning to finger her pussy.

She looked up at King who was already looking at her. *Damn I love this man,* she thought to herself. Then she put her face right in between Joseline's legs and stuck her tongue into her opening and licked all around her walls as she slurped her juices. Next, she began to lick her hardened clitoris using up, down, and circular motions.

Eventually, LJ laid on her back while Joseline turned around and put her pussy on her face. LJ felt her legs pry open as King began to taste her briefly before sliding inside of her smoothly since she was drenched at this point. While dipping in and out of her it sounded like macaroni in the pot. Her body was going crazy. King leaned in and started kissing Joseline's neck while caressing her titties. Both women moaned, turning King on even more causing his strokes to speed up.

"That pussy tastes good, bae?" King asked.

Unable to speak LJ mumbled. "Umhm."

The harder King became, the more LJ sucked Joseline's vagina. Joseline started moaning louder while yelling.

"I'm bouta cum."

"Not yet beautiful," LJ told her as she stopped and instructed her to put her ass in the air.

She did as she was told, and King grabbed her hips to pull her closer towards him. LJ watched as King placed her exactly where he wanted her. When he got inside of her all the way she grunted loudly with her mouth wide open. He plunged into her pussy roughly causing her moans to become louder.

"Eat that pussy," King told her.

Joseline ate LJ's pussy as if it was her profession while stopping momentarily to moan from King's thrust.

"I love you for this," King said.

LJ smiled and continued to watch him fuck her faster and faster. Her moans became even louder but she still managed to eat LJ's pussy good at the same time. LJ couldn't take it anymore.

"I'm about to cum, baby. Fuck the shit out of her," she yelled.

She reached around to rub Joseline's clit which made her throw it back faster as she heard King saying, "take this dick."

First LJ came, moaning loudly. Joseline came seconds later and King hurried to pull his dick out of her, busting all over her back. They all paused for a minute and all that could be heard was loud breathing from the work they had just put in. They were so tired that they couldn't move. When they finally climbed to the top of the bed, King looked at LJ.

"You know I love you right, baby?" King said before kissing her lips.

"I love you too, baby," she responded and they all fell asleep.

At 5 a.m. the following morning, King got up to grab a drink of water. He was dehydrated from the day before with all the alcohol and not much water. When he looked over at the bed, he saw LJ laying there with one leg under the sheet and the other not. His dick began to rise which let him know that it wasn't over just yet. King walked over and pulled the cover up just enough to kiss LJ between her legs. With each lick he could feel her getting wetter while her body tensed up. So, he looked up at her to find her looking down at him.

"Good morning," he said.

LJ muttered it back as best she could. King smiled at her and started kissing it more intensely. LJ glanced over to Joseline who was still asleep. She took her hand and slid it between her legs just to feel her still delicate vagina. King heard Joseline moan softly followed by LJ's moans, making him slightly hornier.

"Put that pussy on my face," LJ said to Joseline and she did without hesitation.

"Baby, come fuck me," LJ said to King.

King fucked her missionary briefly until she got on top and straddled him as he instructed her to. Joseline then sat on King's face. LJ started slowly making sure to cuff the dick every time she slid back up. Her and Joseline were now face to face, tongue kissing as King was too occupied with LJ on top; he didn't recognize Joseline's moans were now few in between. King grabbed the bottom of LJ's ass, and held it up slightly as he fucked her harder. LJ put her head to the side and exhaled. She was cumin again, and so did King. He came in her hard while LJ rubbed Joseline's clit to make her cum. When LJ got from on top of King, she noticed that she had creamed all over his dick. She crawled up to kiss him once more and they all passed out. What a night!

***

After football season, King and his roommates hung out in Baltimore on weekends. He started dealing again and even worse he began using them. He formed a drug ring between him and a few other players on the team. This meant that King met new people and with doing so he learned things. Guys that had been in the drug game for a long-time recognized King. Some mentioned that they knew his father and others kept their mouths shut. After one guy pulled out a picture of, he and Kobe from 1990. King had to call Queen and let her know and she asked King to send it to her.

Besides that photoshoot years ago and only a few pictures that Tiffany had of him, the twins didn't really have pictures of him. Everyone that King met always spoke highly of Kobe. If they weren't talking about the athlete that he was, they were talking about how he loved making money. It wasn't until he ran into Issac when he heard something similar to what his roommate had told him.

"Yeah, it had to be like 1996 or 97, one of those. Your dad had came up on this lick and he wanted me to come with him. We went, did what we had to do, and that was it. A couple years later, I saw him getting shot at his wedding," Issac explained.

"So, is that what my dad was into? He was a jack boy?" King asked.

"Naw, hell naw. I want to say that's the only time he ever did something like that. I was the jack boy so he probably just felt more comfortable if I was there. Ya know what I'm saying?" he asked.

"Yeah. So they still haven't solved the murder, huh?" King asked.

"Nope, not that I know of. They just had something in the paper a few years ago talking about it still being unsolved. They never got any leads or anything," said Issac.

"Alright, I appreciate you patna," said King.

"No doubt. How's your mom and sister doing by the way?" Issac asked.

"Oh, they good. Sis got a full ride to LSU on a track scholarship," he replied.

"Oh damn. Yeah, yo dad was the shit in sports man. Oh, and if you ever need a connect, I got you lil bra. You like family," Issac responded.

King nodded and walked to his car. Everything in him was telling him that Issac knew more about Kobe's death but King didn't want to jump to any conclusions. He phoned his mother once he got back to his dorm. Talking about Kobe's death was something that never took place in the Matthew's household. So, the phone call was quick. Tiffany simply didn't want to talk about it, and she didn't want King trying to investigate.

***?

In the summer of 2012, Queen had been selected to run in the U.S.A Olympics. She had the top three fastest time for the 100m dash in the whole country, so it was only right that she highlighted her speed for the whole world. The event was to take place in Beijing, China. The family got all their traveling expenses paid for by the government to allow them to support Queen. Cassidy came along too. Tiffany always tried to match them together since seeing them go to prom together. They just always told her that they were friends. But they both knew that they had more of a connection than that and were happy to see each other. Neither of them mentioned to anyone what happened prom night and they hadn't messed around since then. Cassidy ended up getting a boyfriend down at the community college that she attended in NYC.

The Olympics was a long eventful week that included tons of parades and parties. King bought a gym membership for a week. One night he was in there working out when he noticed Cassidy and Queen walking in so walked over to speak. Cassidy was wearing tights and a sports bra. Just watching her walk in sent chills down King's body. He quickly snapped out of it, well at least he tried to. But she kept smiling at him when Queen wasn't paying attention. So, he pulled out his phone and texted her.

Coming over to my room tonight? she responded and winked. When she got to his room, she just sat there quiet. King tried kissing her on the neck, but she moved away.

"What's wrong?" King asked.

"I tried calling and texting you a few times and you never responded," she responded.

"I uhhh...well I do have a girlfriend. I told you that," stated King.

"No King, you never ever told me that," she yelled.

"I thought I did," said King.

"So why did you invite me over here?" said Cassidy.

"The same reason why you accepted and came," King threw out.

Cassidy smiled and rolled her eyes. She cared that King had a girlfriend only because it meant that they couldn't be in a relationship at that moment, but it wasn't stopping her sexual desire for him. She thought about him every day after they went to prom.

The next morning, the family went for breakfast. Queen was aware that Cassidy had left the hotel last night and didn't return until morning. She wasn't stupid. She knew that King had a thing for Cassidy the minute he told her that they were going to prom and she knew that Cassidy liked him as well. She could see it in their eyes when they took pictures before heading off to prom.

"Soooo how was you guys' night?" Queen asked really loud to King and Cassidy who were sitting on opposite sides of the table.

"It was cool," King looked up and said.

Cassidy pretended to not have heard the question. Tiffany sat at the table giggling. She liked Cassidy so she didn't care about what they had going on. Then King got a call from D-Money, so he stepped away from the table to answer. D-Money had some decent news to share. His appeal was granted, and he was set to go back to court in a month, but King was already aware of this because he had communication with the lawyer; he had hired for him. Getting the appeal granted was great but he still wouldn't be free unless the state reversed his conviction.

When the phone call ended, King headed back toward the table and saw a man with a bunch of jewelry standing and talking to his sister. He had never seen this guy before, so he assumed it was one of the Olympic participants. Whatever they were talking about kept Queen smiling. When she walked back over to the table, she still had a slight grin on her face.

"Who was that?" King asked.

"Some guy I barely know from school. He's a rapper," Queen responded.

"So, some guy you barely know came all the way to China to see you?" Tiffany and Cassidy both asked in sync.

"I guess so," Queen said and chuckled.

The rapper seemed like a nice guy to Queen but after the incident in Alabama, she wasn't trusting smooth talking men anymore. Her and TJ would talk occasionally as they were beginning to outgrow each other. It probably was the distance but neither of them seemed to care about their current status. Her desire stayed the same. She wanted to graduate from college and start her career.

The next season, King had another position change. He packed on an extra fifteen pounds because he wanted to play running back. When asked why he said that he always wanted to, but just never did. He fit the criteria of a running back excellent on paper. He was big, fast, and quick. He could make all the cuts. But the biggest question during the offseason was if he could take a hit. Coaches were soon to find out at the team's first scrimmage that was coming up. King wanted everyone there. He told LJ to come without telling her that his family would be coming as well. He knew that if he did, she wouldn't want to come. It was still summertime, so the sun was shining bright.

When LJ arrived, the scrimmage had just began. Morgan State was on offense and King had received a toss to the outside. He made a cut inside and ran behind his two blockers until he scored. Tiffany, Queen, and Cassidy all stood up to cheer wearing their number eight Matthews jersey. LJ knew that they had to be King's family, so she quickly walked back to the parking lot. Tiffany noticed the sudden misdirection when LJ walked off. She recognized her face but couldn't remember where she had seen her before. After the scrimmage, Tiffany asked King why his girlfriend, that he was supposedly going to introduce, didn't show up and he said that he didn't know.

"She texted me and said she was here earlier and now she's saying she's back home. I don't know what's going on," he said.

Tiffany never mentioned to him that she saw a woman walk off who was wearing a number eight Morgan State t-shirt similar to the jerseys that the family was wearing. After the family, and Cassidy parted ways from King, he headed straight to LJ's house; he was pissed. He used his key to unlock the door and met her in the kitchen after slamming the front door. LJ was startled and confused.

"Well damn don't break the door. What's your problem?" LJ asked.

"Why the fuck would you stand me up in front of my family like that," King hollered.

"King you never told me they were coming. I'm not ready for that yet," said King.

"Well, when will you be ready?" he asked.

"Soon bae," LJ said.

"I've been hearing that forever now. So, when is soon?" he questioned.

"   Soon baby, I promise," he assured her.

"Yeah ok," he said.

"You say you're ready to marry me but you're not ready for that yet. You're fucking all those girls at the school. Oh, and don't think I didn't see that girl you went to prom with, with your family. Is that your side hoe?" she asked.

"Nah, just a friend," King responded.

"Oh, just a friend, huh? A friend that you fuck from time to time, right?" she asked.

"What are you talking about?" he asked.

"Oh stop it. I saw those text about her coming to your hotel while you were in China. Don't play with me," said LJ. "Exactly, nothing to say. Told you that you're not ready," LJ added.

LJ stormed upstairs and King followed behind, watching her perfect ass as it switched through her leggings with each step. He was determined to show her that he was in fact ready, but in all actuality he wasn't. King hadn't even reached the prime of his life yet. As he followed her into the bedroom he sat up against the dresser while LJ sat promptly on the bed. The room was filled with silence and tension. They both stared at the floor for a moment until King broke the ice.

"Well maybe I'm not ready to get married, but I am ready to have you, like really have without hiding and being secretive. I want everyone to see us together," King explained.

LJ looked up still in silence at first. She understood what King was saying. She just wasn't ready for people to know yet. LJ stood and walked right in front of King, staring him into his eyes. She smirked slightly at the fact that King was so stubborn. She shook her head and thought, *just like your dad*, but she said it out loud.

"Like my dad? What do you mean?" King asked.

"You look like your dad, from the picture you showed me," LJ responded with a quick cover up. Her thoughts had slipped out of her mouth.

"Well, maybe you know my dad. Y'all probably are around the same age. His name was Kobe Matthews and he played for the Ravens for a few years. He's from Baltimore too," said King.

"Name sounds familiar, but I didn't recognize him from the picture," she replied before wrapping her arms around King's lower back. King put his arm around LJ's neck and kissed her on the forehead.

Chapter 18

Back to the basics

"Faster, faster. Come on man. Don't let them get you."

Bullets blazed in his directions. Before he took off running, he noticed the gunman holding a gun that he had seen before. He hit a corner and ran past the parked cars on the street. He no longer heard any gunshots.

"Ok, breathe, breathe."

Down the street was a gate that looked open. He ran inside to catch his breath. The man was relieved. His breaths were rapid as he entered the gates. He looked around and he got goosebumps. He had been to this place before, but he couldn't remember when or where. Once he got to the center of the platform, he heard a voice. A calm but deep voice called his name. The person sounded powerless, as if he was calling for help.

The man walked toward the voice. His heart sped up tremendously as he didn't know what was happening. It appeared as if everything around him was dark but all he could see was a light glaring on the walkway in front of him. As he walked, the voice became more and more loud and clear and what he saw next blew his mind. It was Kobe lying on the ground in a pool of blood. He was reaching his arm up in hopes of help. The man heard someone call his name from the opposite direction. The voice sounded so close in proximity, it startled him causing him to jerk before turning to see who it was. It was the gunmen pointing the familiar looking gun right at his head. And as he pulled the trigger.

Boom

King woke up from the nightmare, sweating like he had just finished a twelve round boxing match. His dream was mind blowing, confusing, and horrific all at the same time. King, who was now 20 years old, had never seen his father in his dreams before. But it was components of the dream that made his mind ponder.

Today was a special day. D-money's conviction had been overturned and he was being released from Rickers Island. King made plans to go pick D up from county jail. He was hosting a huge party for him that night at his home. Everyone was going to be there, even Queen, who was set to graduate a year early in the summer. King hadn't told anyone yet, but he decided to forgo his senior season and enter the NFL draft. The last person he wanted to tell was his mom. All he could hear was her telling him how his father had made a bad decision with doing the same thing. But King believed that he was making the right decision. His love for the game was demanding and no one, even his mother, could stop him. Plus, he felt an obligation to his father's legacy.

He and his father always talked about football and he remembered them, although the conversations were from his early childhood years. He remembered them almost verbatim. He didn't feel that his latest dream was a coincidence!

When King arrived at the front of Rikers Island, Mrs. Morgan and their children were already waiting.

"Hey Adoree,' " the family said almost in unison. Mrs. Morgan had a huge smile on her face. King had been there for them since day one and he never let up. They hugged long before stepping away and she put her hands on his head while continuing to smile.

"Well, here we are," King professed.

"Here we are," Mrs. Morgan responded.

King high fived the kids. It was a chilly January morning, but it wasn't snowing. However, it was cold enough to see the mist coming from one's breath when they spoke and a ton of it came out of D's oldest child when she screamed his name and ran in the direction of the facility.

When they saw D step foot outside for the first time in almost 5 years as a free man, it was like some sort of dark cloud vanished away. D hugged his kids, his wife, then it was the moment of truth with King. He stood there nodding his head at him for several seconds before hugging him as well. A tear fell from his eyes onto King's shoulder. Throughout the five years, King had probably only seen D three times aside from court appearances. But every time he did see him, he assured him that he would shake back soon. The long hugs showed a sigh of relief for everyone.

King visited the Morgan's household before returning back to his mother's home. Tiffany was excited to see her babies. She only saw them together on holidays and usually their birthday but neither of them visited for their latest one. Queen was on a second plane when King called her, so it was still going to be a few hours before she arrived.

"Just one more year boy. You ready?" Tiffany started.

"Yup, one more. What's been going on momma?" she said.

"Oh nothing. Work work work you know me. Did I tell you that I was the director of nursing now over at the VA center off of Switzer Rd?" asked Tiffany.

"Oh naw. That's wonderful ma. Why didn't you tell me?" asked King.

"It kind of just flew over my head. But man it's good to see you. You got everything ready for this party tonight?" she asked.

"Yeah. Just a few more things to grab. Man, you should have saw D-Money when he got released. He grew his hair out in his beard. He's chubby now too," said King.

"Really? I know he's happy to be home. His family too. Y'all fools better not tear down my house. Oh, I just finished paying off that too by the way. I've been thinking of moving and renting this place out," Tiffany explained.

"Where would you move, ma?" he asked.

"Haven't thought about that part yet. Somewhere not too far though," responded Tiffany.

King thought about where he would get drafted in comparison to where his mom would move to. He wanted her to be close to him because they had a strong bond, one that couldn't be broken. After their short discussion, King went up to his old bedroom and went to sleep. Just like before, he woke up and he was startled. But this time from the sounds of his loud alarm clock on his cell phone screaming. It was 6:30 p.m. An hour and a half before the party was supposed to begin. King's intended nap turned into a five-hour sleep. So, he quickly began setting up for the party with the help of his mom and sister.

"Oh King, let me see your tattoo," Queen said over the music being played.

King took off his shirt. His entire back was covered in black ink. The number eight was the centerpiece of the tattoo and on his upper back was his last name. In between the two was background shading related to football and like a jersey. He had his father's signature at the bottom. With his shirt off, he also revealed his chest piece. His tattoos spread all the way out to his muscles. On the left was a portrait of his father that read "in loving memory of..." on the right was a portrait of his aunt Jane.

"Damn!" both Tiffany and Queen muttered.

"Those look exactly like them," Tiffany added.

"You like them?" King asked.

"They look great," she assured him.

King lifted his arm to show her the tattoo of her name he had gotten with a big heart surrounding it.

"You know I couldn't forget you," King said with a smile. Tiffany smiled and came closer to examine it. As they continued to chat, they heard a knock on the door. Queen answered. It was her friends from high school.

"Heyyy Ms. Matthews!" Cassidy yelled when she saw Tiffany. They hugged briefly.

"What's up?" King greeted Cassidy.

She gave a shy smile and hugged him as well. It had been a while since they had seen each other but their feelings for each other remained the same. Even the mild hug gave him an erection and gave her flashbacks of nearly every sex encounter that they've experienced.

"Oh, King, this is Tiny. Remember her?" Queen asked.

King shook his head and shook Tiny's hand. He honestly didn't remember meeting her before. Tiny was really short in height with short hair. She usually left memorable impressions with people whom she interacted with because of her smile. But her and Queen didn't hang out much because she was a known hoe in the schoolhouse and in the neighborhood.

As it got late, the house became more party ready. Folks were beginning to flow in like crazy. People that neither member of the family had seen in years. Though the celebration was for D-Money's homecoming, the people flowing in gave the impression that the party was for the twins. At around a quarter after 8, D-Money arrived. He wore a pair of black Bauman jeans with a black and gray Louis Vuitton belt under his gray Louis Vuitton v-neck shirt. The bottom of his jeans were tucked away in a pair of all-black Louis Vuitton boots that matched his Michael Kors jacket and skull cap. To top it off, D-Money sported a chain and watch that complemented his entire outfit that King bought for him. D-Money caught everyone's attention when he walked in. The shots of Hennessy were also a factor in his buoyancy. King was the first to greet him.

"Man. Welcome home my motherfuckin boy!" he yelled over the speakers.

Random folks at the party welcomed him home as well. Queen and Tiffany did so also. Tiffany actually couldn't take her eyes off of D. After welcoming him home, she continued to host the party while Queen indulged in a few drinks and reflected on her life. Seeing all her old friends made her happy that she had chosen to go to school and finish. Here she was an almost college graduate with a job already in her field, driving a 2014 Lexus truck. And here were her friends working minimum-wage jobs with no education further than a high school diploma besides the ones who started college and dropped out. In a way, she was proud of herself, but she knew she had much more to accomplish.

Meanwhile, King and D-Money were drinking and smoking. Enjoying each other's company as King's first time being an adult.

"Dis party goin crazy lil bruh," D-Money shouted.

"Man what. It's definitely lit," King agreed.

"My dawg TY pulled up on me too. He trying to put me back on. Back in da game but I don't know man," D-Money said.

"Shit. It's up to you OG. You got to decide if that's what you want to do again. But I feel like if you do decide, it's only right if you let yo lil prodigy put you on. I'm tearin' the streets up right now," King proposed.

"I'm already hip. Shit niggas in the joint was braggin' about you. Actin' like they knew you and shit," said D-Money.

"Oh yeah? Well, what you think? You fuckin' with me?" King asked.

"You already know son," assured D-Money.

King grinned.

Bonding with someone, who he looked up to, meant everything to him. Like a father and son relationship, King wanted to further impress D-money. After the handshake to confirm it, he invited D to take a drive with him in the morning. The two finished conversing until he saw Queen waving her hand in an attempt to get his attention. King signaled for her to come over to him as she walked up with a familiar looking smile that he knew to be suspicious.

"Guess who's here?" she asked humorously.

"Who?" he questioned with confusion.

"Destiny. She's over by the side door," Queen responded. "Go over there," she added.

King grabbed his cup and headed in her direction. The party was dark, but there was a light in the hallway near the side door. This area was packed, causing King to have to maneuver through the bodies with difficulty. That was until he felt a hand grab his arm and he turned back.

"You walked right past me boy," Destiny said.

"It's packed in here my bad," King said.

"What's in the cup?" Destiny asked.

"Kool-Aid" he responded.

They both broke out laughing.

"Whatever," she said.

She grabbed the cup from his hand and sipped it.

"So, what's up? How have you been?" King asked.

"Whew, a lot! I have a son now. He turns two in April. I'm going to school at Northstar Community College. Uhhh, oh and I've been with my boyfriend for almost 3 years," she shared.

"Whoa. Congratulations. Where you live now?" he asked.

"I ended up getting an apartment over on Everette St. It's all right, nothing fancy. How about you Mr. Football Player? I've seen you all over ESPN," she said.

"Yeah, I'm trying man. Just football and school just like old times. No kids. I am dating someone though," he replied.

"Don't try to downplay your life… King. I be hearing about you. Everybody from the hood be talking about you. Shit the whole city for real," said Destiny.

"You know that type of stuff never excited me. Come on though, let's go get you something to drink," King said.

They weaved their way to the kitchen where they poured drinks and chatted with others they knew. Essentially, everyone enjoyed themselves. No drama and nothing negative brought up from the past besides the hilarious story that King, Queen, Destiny, and Ant told Tiffany about when they snuck and threw a party here at the house before high school.

"Feels like it was just yesterday," Ant said, and everyone agreed.

King went to pick up D-Money early the next morning. They were both hungover and still tired. D-

Money practically slept the entire ride until he was awakened from taps on his shoulder. When he opened his eyes, he was in the driveway of a green and white house. The grass was freshly cut to compliment the flower garden that was fenced off.

"Wake up, old man," King jokingly said to D as they walked to the back porch. D-Money noticed that King was carrying two Louis Vuitton duffle bags.

This nigga love, Louis, he thought to himself.

A younger female opened the back door for them. She was pretty with shoulder length hair and a nose piercing. D-Money observed the woman as her and King hugged examining her thick shape.

"This my peoples D or D-Money. D this is Liandra," King introduced them before going downstairs to the basement.

Liandra smiled and nodded at D. Then she pulled him to the side for interrogation since King never brought anyone here before and especially not to the basement.

"Yeah this family baby," he assured her.

Liandra then went into another room where she came back holding two bricks of white. D-Money's eyes got big. He wasn't expecting King to front him that much. Hell, he hadn't been in the game for years, so he didn't even have clients. King signaled for Liandra to hand D-Money the bricks. He tossed one of the duffle bags to him and another to Liandra where she took in another room. This time she returned with the duffle bag filled with vacuum sealed bags of weed. She handed that bag over to D as well and they all headed back upstairs.

"I'll text you Li," King said to her before he and D headed to the car.

"Damn who was shawty?" he asked.

"That's just the homie. I stash everything here with her and her girlfriend," King replied.

"Girlfriend? Damn does she look as good as her?" he asked.

"Hell yeah. They both nice. I met them 2 years ago. The other one first at a restaurant," he added.

"You doin' yo thang fasho boy," said D-Money.

They discussed other things in King's life that he had going on for the rest of the ride to D's house. King also handed him a cell phone that had a bunch of contacts that would be D-Money's clientele. D-Money thanked King over and over during the car ride but King told him that it was the least he could do.

Over the next few days, he wouldn't waste no time. He started trapping immediately, spending long hours out of his home. This caused some conflict between him and his wife, but it didn't slow him down. D had lost everything he had over the past 5 years and he was determined to get it back. So, spending time with family came secondary to "working" he would often refer to it as to them.

King returned back to school following the road trip with the D-money. He needed to finish the semester and stay healthy post draft day. A lot of teams were interested in his skill set. The teams that show the most interest were the Pittsburgh Steelers and the Cleveland Browns. Both teams would be ideal for him because it was still in the area and that would mean that he could potentially move his mother in the same city as him. His talents at running back captured a lot of attention from NFL scouts which was a plus because running backs typically have higher draft stocks than safeties. This meant that he could potentially be a top 10 draft pick which meant a higher signing bonus if he made the team.

In February, he found an agent to represent him. His agent found him an athletic trainer to work with leading up to the draft. The scouting combine was a huge focus on teams drafting requirements. Though he was one of the better running backs coming out, he had to stand out in the combine. So, his days consisted of working out, taking professionalism classes, school, and 'working.' He had given some of his homies who he trusted some of the demands of getting rid of the product.

Liandra and Joseline grew the weed in their basement. They also drove out to California to pick up the shipments of other drugs while TJ and Anthony made the sales. The operation grossed nearly twenty thousand per week. He was easily sitting on one-hundred fifty thousand that he kept tucked away at a secure location. His home life was steady. He and LJ now lived together and committed to each other. Neither had met the other's family and King had become content with that. Well at least for now because he had plans on everyone meeting soon; he wanted to propose to her. He was totally in love with her; he couldn't imagine spending life with anyone else. When thought about her age and where she was in life, no kids, no husband, he concluded that his future wife just wasn't really a family-oriented person and he was ok with that. They had spoken about having children and she was willing to have some so King knew he had to move quickly.

Now that the D-Money was working under King, they were around each other a lot. But not in the public eye. They would meet up at either the two women's houses or at another woman's house where King kept things stashed. King was precise about how he moved, having being caught as a juvenile and seeing other people around him getting jammed up.

For the time being he was connecting with the guy who owned several corporations in the DMV area who he would use as a security blanket for income if he was ever under investigation. The guy would often keep King in his computer system as an employee worker. He even printed out paystubs and income tax forms for validation. This was only until he got drafted and hopefully endorsed by a big brand-name. His plan would then be to handover ownership of his operation to D-money. It was like perfect timing that D was released from prison just in time to get a feel of Kings sting while he prepared for the biggest moment of his life; the NFL draft.

When the day finally came, he sat in Nashville, Tennessee with Tiffany, his newly college graduate twin sister, D-money, and other friends of the family. Tiffany even brought the newest member of her household, Adonis, who she just recently took out of foster care and picked up guardianship roles for.

The family went with King, each sitting there impatiently waiting for that lucky team to call King's name. The Cleveland Browns had the 3rd pick in the draft. When they went up to select their pick, Tiffany and Queen closed their eyes nervously, anticipating hearing his name.

"With the 3rd pick in the 2014 NFL Draft, the Browns select; Timothy Ball Jr," the commissioner shouted.

Tim and King were cool with each other, being that they played each other three consecutive years. He was a quarterback which gave him a higher draft stock than any other position. "With the 7th pick in the 2014 NFL draft the Pittsburgh Steelers select; K'Won Jordan," said the commissioner. King knew K'Won too. He was an offensive tackle who played at the University of Maryland.

At this point, King's hopes of getting picked in top 10 were gone. The Browns and Steelers were in contact with him more than any other team. But King continued to sit there optimistic about his opportunity to even be in the position that he was in. "With the 10th pick in the 2014 NFL Draft, the Baltimore Ravens select....Adoree' Matthews. Running back out of Morgan State University," the commissioner said. That sent King's family in an outpour of raw emotions.

Tiffany watched tears roll down her only son's eyes. She had a rainfall of tears as well as others from his entourage too. The cameras that were being nationally televised got closer to King and his family so he wiped the tears away so he could walk on stage to receive his jersey. The Ravens had shown some interest in him, but never did he think that they would draft him. They currently had a good running back who ran for over 1000 yards the previous season.

He wasn't sure of what the Raven's plan with him was yet but to be drafted number 10 to the same team that drafted his dad a little over 20 years ago meant a lot to him. The family took pictures and King was interviewed by a reporter before he called LJ.

Chapter 19

It's only right

Standing in an all-black and purple sweatsuit with a Nike winter coat that was the same colors as the sweatsuit on the sideline of the freezing cold game. It was week five and the Ravens were playing a division game against the Cleveland Browns on their home field. It was a game he wanted to play in badly ever since they passed up on him in the draft. King, who was already sponsored by Nike and under a five-year $25 million contract with 15 million guarantee, was leading the entire NFL in rushing yards. But he was on the sideline for this game and would be for the rest of the regular season due to a tear in his rotator cuff he obtained while working out. No one saw this coming.

He was having such a great season. In fact, a great year. So, he knew exactly what to do with his free time during his rehab period and that would be to make things legit between him and his future wife. His first step was for them to meet each other's family and he knew that this would be hard. He decided that on his first night free of responsibilities he would take her out somewhere nice. It was late in the game and his team was up two touchdowns when King felt his phone vibrating. It just happened to be a text from LJ who he had just been daydreaming about for the past several minutes.

I see you on the sideline looking handsome, she wrote.

King smirked at his phone and then over to LJ who was watching the game from the Cleveland stadium. King had recently been discussing his plans for he and LJ with his sister and that helped give him an extra insight on things. Seeing things from a woman's perspective gave him the opportunity to submerge in their taste even though Queen was less than half of LJ's age. Them discussing the plans also gave them a reason to communicate since they were always busy and away from each other. Queen hadn't seen King since the draft.

After graduation she and Arnez, the rapper from Louisiana, got a place out in New Orleans together. Arnez, who is also known by his stage name as Yung Snupe, had become a mainstream rapper signed under a top record label. He signed a deal worth $7 million for three years. Queen supported his rap career heavily. She continued her career in law as she worked as a paralegal and planned on going to law school soon. She and TJ didn't work out after high school. They were just in two different places in their lives and they knew it.

Following the game, King and LJ drove home together in her new Maybach. LJ hadn't missed one game yet and she didn't have any plans on doing so. She was his backbone and spare tire. As she drove, King glanced over at her admiring her delicate features. He still was in disbelief of how well she looked for her age.

"What?" she smiled and asked, noticing his intense stare.

"Just trying to figure out what it is you're doing to me. Why is it that I have all the faith in the world that you're the one for me and vice versa?" King said back. LJ was at a loss for words. Not knowing what to do or say at that very moment but couldn't help to blush for the rest of the drive to the hotel suite.

After getting help from the hotel staff with bringing in their bags they showered, and LJ streamed a movie from her MacBook onto the television. It was a newer movie that she had already seen but King hadn't. He must've enjoyed the movie because he was locked into it. He didn't even notice that LJ had been hawking him for the past few minutes she simply just needed to be touched. Touched by him specifically. So, she placed her hand on his resting dick and started massage through his shorts all while continuing to eyeball him. King moved in closer toward LJ to kiss her lips, but she had other plans.

"I see somebody's awake," LJ said, referring to his dick that was brick hard.

LJ used one hand to pull the top of his shorts down while grabbing his manhood with the other. She was so turned on at this point that she had to taste him. She began by circling her tongue around the head of his dick before taking him in as much as she could. King grabbed the back of her head forcefully to direct her exactly the way he wanted her to suck him. She sucked faster and better.

"Babe, stop before you make me cum. Come sit on this mothafucka," he whispered, and she did just that.

She lifted her thigh length sleeping shirt and sat her warm pussy on his dick. She slid up and down slowly as her body shivered with every descending motion. King thrusted his hips forward so deep that he transported her body up some so he could be positioned leaning backwards against the vanilla seat cushion and her holding herself up using her hands on the wooden coffee table. The speed of her strokes increased but it wasn't enough for him. He wanted those strokes to feel as efficient as if he was just fucking her in a normal position. King grabbed the bottom of her ankles tightly and began fucking her from the bottom up as she raised and sat on that motherfucka, as he had told her to previously. The more intense, the more her juices dripped down to his balls. She felt herself about to explode as King watched her ass move in sync with his thrust.

"Baby I'm about to cum," she cried. And so was he so he fucked her harder. LJ came so hard that a loud moan escaped her lips on the silent part of the movie causing the sound effects to sound even louder. She continued until she felt a jerking sensation of her body.

Seconds later, LJ snuggled up to King on the couch and wrapped the blanket around both of them. They hadn't been spending as much time with each other due to King's adjustment to his professional athlete life. So, this night alone was just what they needed, especially for King and his motive. And he knew this, so he made his move.

"Babe, I'm ready for you to meet my family," he spoke calmly. "And I want to meet yours," he added.

LJ sat silent. Initially she didn't even lift her head until the awkward silence ate her conscious. And the fact that King randomly started rubbing her back. As much as she didn't want to be a participant in this particular conversation, she knew she had to say something.

"Ok let's do it," she responded, not wanting to disappoint him any longer. King was shocked. He didn't say anything but the thoughts that were roaming their minds during a period in which they never made eye contact, made their hearts skip a beat.

Seems as if King's love life intact. Queen's not so much. Her and Young Snupe were beginning to argue nonstop. Most of her problems with him was that he wanted to party and be out all night which was typical young rapper shit. But Queen never really enjoyed that lifestyle even while in college and the little that she did enjoy, she had outgrown. Snupe's problem with her is that he partied heavily when they first started dating so she was already aware of that. He just couldn't understand why it was a problem for her now. Since Queen worked eight hours a day, she wanted to come home to her man and spend time. However, when they did spend time together, she enjoyed it. Snupe was far from boring.

He used various party drugs when he was on the road and prior to performing. He had a show tonight at LSU's football stadium. For the first time in a while, Snupe asked Queen to come to the show with him. Queen accepted the offer and went to get dressed as she put on a dress with a fur coat covering it. Snupe, Queen, and his team all hopped in the sprinter bus and headed to Baton

Rouge. Queen wanted to enjoy herself as the others were doing so, so she partook in the liquor and the weed.

When Snupe set the stage, Queen stayed backstage to watch. She had been to some of his performances before and she always admired when he went into his stardom mode. Snupe was musically talented. He could rock the whole crowd by his written lyrics or just by freestyling. He started the show with one of his songs that was buzzing on the Internet. Halfway through the show Snupe took off his white beater and threw it into the crowd. His body was filled with tattoos dating back from when he was just 13 years old. The sweat crept down his body as he vibed to his own words. Queen loved watching this side of Snupe.

As she watched him, she envisioned their future together. He didn't have the ideal career that she always dreamed of, but he had money. And with the money Queen knew that she could help make smart investments with it.

After Snupe's performance, he went backstage. He wiped the entire top part of his body with a towel and drank some water. Queen looked around waiting for the rest of the team to show up. When they didn't, she asked where they were and Snupe told him that they would be back later. Then he stood over her why she sat slightly up against the countertop. He picked her up by her thighs and sat her on top of it.

"Well how was it?" he asked.

"You did great, boo. Now let's go. I'm tired and you should be too," she answered. Snoop agreed.

He grabbed her hand and the bodyguard escorted them to the back exit where the driver was waiting. Queen's thoughts begin to run even wilder considering that the drugs had fully sat in. Regardless of what she thought about his career, he was looking like a snack to her. He sat there worn out from the three-hour performance he had just given, on his twitter account. Queen scanned Arnez's whole body in the back of the dark limousine. After locking his phone, he placed his arm around her and closed his eyes. It could have been the drugs, but Queen was extra horny. She slid Snupe's hand to her lap so that he could touch her vagina just to realize that he was dead asleep. Queen was distraught. She smacked her lips and rolled her eyes in the direction of the backseat window as they rolled past cars and highway signs.

After some time passed, she heard Snupe snoring, so she removed his arm from around her shoulders and scooted closer towards the window. She was bored and just wanted to talk to someone. Queen went down her contact list and pressed the name that read "Twin" with a bunch of emojis around it. It was late but she figured she'd try and give him a call. The phone rang maybe eight times and Queen was pulling the phone away from her ear to hang up when he suddenly answered. Queen could hear the bafflement in his voice when he answered.

"Are you ok?" she anxiously asked him.

King took some deep breaths before answering as he tried to calm his breathing. Then he explained to her the dreams that he had been having since the morning that D-Money was released. This was news that he hadn't shared with anyone until now. Queen thought that the dreams, or nightmares rather were strange as well, being that he mentioned seeing the gun and that setting before. This most recent nightmare was of him chasing the man who shot their father, but he only saw his backside.

"Did you tell mom?" Queen asked.

"Nah, I don't want to worry her. I don't even want to bring dad up. You know how she is," King responded.

The conversation lasted until the driver stopped the car in front of their home. Her last question to King was how he had decided on proposing to her and how she wanted to be there when it happened. King promised her that he would invite her before the call ended. This gave

King an idea of how he could slowly introduce LJ to his family by starting with Queen.

He texted Queen afterward and asked if her and her boyfriend would visit for a weekend sometime soon. She responded to accept the invitation. She, like Tiffany, was eager to meet this woman that King had been messing with for years now. He never told them that she didn't want to meet. Instead, he would make up excuses. Just as LJ would when King tried bringing up her family. To King's knowledge, this was where LJ was at, this weekend which he figured she'd mention something to them about meeting up. He let his thoughts float around before falling back to sleep.

The upcoming Sunday, when LJ was back, they went to an adventure park. They had more fun here than they did in a while. It was fun for them to interact outside of being home like they had been ever since King's preparation for the draft. After a game of miniature golf and go-cart racing, they stopped to grab a quick bite. They sat down under a shed near the go-cart track to eat their food.

"I'm having fun, baby," LJ said.

"We definitely needed this for sure. I love you," King added before LJ said it back.

They finished eating and talking for a bit then King told her that his mom and D-Money were planning to move out near Baltimore. LJ pretended that she had heard good news. It wasn't really the kind of news she cared to hear. On top of that, Queen and her boyfriend were visiting next weekend and then Tiffany and Adonis right after. LJ felt that King just threw a lot of information her way at once, but she kept her composure and smiled. In her mind, she knew that she had to invite her parents soon as well. After a bathroom break, the two headed to the batting cage where LJ was able to show off some of her batting skills. She played in a small softball league every year with some of her girlfriends. They both laughed as she out-batted King.

Queen and Snupe flew into Maryland the following Saturday morning. King picked them up from the airport. Both Snupe and King were fans of each other, so they got each other's autographs and took a picture before even leaving the airport. Queen thought this exchange was so funny because in her eyes, she didn't see celebrities, just her brother and her boyfriend who were regular people with good intentions.

"So, where's the future Mrs.?" Queen asked once they got to the airport's parking lot.

"At home still asleep," King responded.

It's 7:30 in the morning, Queen thought to herself.

When they got in the house, they smelled the delicious aroma of breakfast. The dining room table was set up with black and purple kitchenware. No one had eaten so after everyone met, LJ invited them to the table. She had made over a dozen pancakes, French toast, bacon, sausage, and eggs. King usually ate a lot by himself, so she made enough for seconds. Queen didn't want to be obvious, but she couldn't help but to quickly glance at LJ every so often.

No way she's 40 anything, she thought to herself.

LJ has recently cut her hair into a shorter hairstyle and you could tell that she still worked out. Queen admired everything about her and the fact that King wanted to propose to her made her admiration even stronger. LJ was oblivious to Queen basically staring at her, but King wasn't. He sent her a text at the table.

Why you lookin' like you see a ghost? he wrote.

OMG she's beautiful. Queen texted back.

Most of the conversation at the table was of King's injury and how his rehab was going. That was until Queen asked LJ what she did. She told her how she worked in downtown Baltimore at the board of education. Then she and King showed them around the house.

Queen and Snupe would be staying in a room downstairs that had an empty bedroom set. It was an old chest in the closet with a huge master lock on it. King had previously seen the same chest in their bedroom before, but he didn't remember the lock being on it. When LJ showed the guests to their room, King noticed that she stacked a few boxes that were in the room into the closet on top of the chest to create more space.

That night they all went to the bar for drinks. It ended up being King and Snupe on a date with Queen and LJ instead of the norm. Queen was so infatuated with LJ that she wanted to know everything about her. So, as they kept drinking the deeper their conversations. Turned out that Snupe had been a fan of King since he was in high school. King had several highlights of him playing all three sports that surfaced the web. King was also familiar with Snupe as an underground rapper when not too many people were. The two drunk a ton, almost forgetting that their

women were just a few feet away.

Queen requested that the bar play one of Snupe's hit

songs and her and LJ went over there. Without even

checking to see what Snupe was drinking, Queen grabbed

his glass and took a huge gulp. Snupe started laughing and

so did the other two when they saw the look on her face

after the gulp. This was the first time in a while that Snupe

went out without a bodyguard with him. It felt good being

regular for a night. King drove them back home. Both

couples practically ran to their bedrooms and had drunk sex

to end the night.

King had to be up super early the next morning so

that he could be with his team for another division game

against the Pittsburgh Steelers but this time they were at

home. LJ, Snupe, and Queen were all hungover from the

night before, but they still made their way to the game that

started at 1:25 p.m. King stood on the sidelines frustrated

about not being able to play. This was all he ever wanted to do since a child. The team was winning and losing games without him. King felt left out. On top of that, his mom had only made it out to his debut game and that was it. All she ever did was work since Kobe died. King knew that he needed her to move close to him, so she didn't have to work and attend more games. And in that moment, he made up his mind that he was going to fly her out here next. Crazy thing is Tiffany and Queen texted back and forth that whole weekend she was down there so that made her eager to visit for herself. She actually called King and told her that she would be flying out in two weeks.

When she got to LJ and King's house, she instantly remembered her from the game.

"I've seen you somewhere before," she proclaimed.

LJ looked back with confusion shaking her head.

"Maybe at a game or something. Nice to meet you, I'm Tiffany."

The two hugged and sat down in the living room. Of course, the topic of age arised as a concern from Tiffany, but LJ assured her that she was madly in love with her son and age was nothing but a number. She did however admit that her avoiding this meeting was due to the issues surrounding their age difference. Now, King just had to meet her family, and everything would fall align perfectly. When King mentioned that to her before bed, she told him that she would call them tomorrow morning to see if they were available. Surprisingly, at short notice they were. King told her to invite them to breakfast at Lee's diner which was the newest section of the restaurant, Lee's Eatery.

As they walked inside, Tiffany caught a flashback. She remembered coming here when she was nineteen with the future love of her life on their first date. The agony came over her all again, but she maintained her composure.

After everyone met, she mentioned to King how she remembered coming here before he and Queen were born.

"Wait a minute. Aren't you Adoree' Matthews?" LJ's father asked. King smiled and said yes. Her father was astonished. He didn't keep up with sports much but everyone in the city knew about King's rising stardom even being that he was injured.

"He kinda looks like someone I've seen before," LJ's mom added.

After breakfast, everyone went to LJ and King's home. Tiffany saw her old home on the way back and thought to herself maybe that's' where she had saw LJ before when she spotted her at the game depending on how long she lived here. King waited for LJ to leave the room with his mom so he could talk to her parents privately to ask the big question. Her parents were stunned. They weren't aware of their daughter's love life and they hadn't since she was dating back in college. But just from meeting

King for these few hours, they knew that he was well put together, so they were on board.

***

Weeks later was New Year's Eve. The Ravens hadn't made the playoffs so King had a long time before he would step foot onto a field to play. His injury ended his rookie season early, but he had his sights set on an even better second year. One thing he didn't want to do was go out like his dad, who had all the talent in the world but couldn't display it on the biggest field due to his injuries.

For the past eight months, he heard different things about his dad's legacy and his death. He often wondered if his dreams ever offered any clues to what had happened. The curiosity ate at his conscious just as it did his whole life without his father around. He saw the effect that one person could have on multiple people. He felt that Tiffany's whole life was changed following Kobe's death, that's why what he would do next made a lot of sense to him.

The plane to Louisiana arrived at a quarter to 7:00 a.m. Neither had gotten much sleep over the past week and with the big holiday being tomorrow sleep wasn't in their future plans either. Both fell asleep as they were driven to the mansion. Out in front was a yellow Lamborghini with a license plate that read Snupe. The driver walked around to open the door before grabbing the luggage from the trunk. The burning marijuana smell crept from the door cracks. He must have heard them pull up because he was already there to open the door before they could knock. His neck was still gleaming red from the tattoo he had gotten recently of his grandmother who had just recently passed away. You could smell the alcohol on his breath when he spoke. Queen came from the back of the house when she heard Snupe talking. She grabbed LJ's luggage from her hand and told them to follow her. It was a five-bedroom mansion that stood on the outskirts of New Orleans. LJ wasted no time. After speaking to Queen and Snupe for a bit she laid down. King laid with her until she was asleep then he went back downstairs. Snupe tossed King a sack of week and some backwoods.

"Roll up," he smiled and said. He grabbed the sack and looked over to Snupe.

"Queen said she enjoyed her b-day. Thanks for showing her a good time," King said.

"No doubt," Snupe responded.

King rolled up and the two of them blew the whole backwood. Before he knew it, he was into a deep sleep dreaming about playing basketball in high school. He wasn't having the best game, but Jane was there to uplift him during and after the game. He was happy to see her. It felt like she had come back to life or as if went back in time in some kind of way. They were on their way out of the gym laughing and talking just like old times when suddenly, everyone even Jane disappeared. King was puzzled. He looked around for the sight of anything or anyone, but it was just empty.

A light popped on in the center of the court, so King walked toward it. The light flickered on and off like it was about to blow. When he was right under it, he heard the voice again.

"Help," the man cried.

He tried to turn in the direction of where the voice had come from. Then the man appeared right there next to him with a bag over his face tied to a chair. He lifted the bag up and saw his dad's face. King hurried to untie him. He didn't seem to have any injuries, cuts, or bruises, so King asked him what happened. Kobe never answered and instead just looked at him with a blank stare. Then he heard footsteps. A woman with a long trench coat walked alongside a man with the same gun from his previous dreams. This time King wanted to make sure he saw a face. He started walking toward the two. The man lifted the gun and fired it right at King. But it was like the bullet had gone right through him. When King turned to see where the bullet had gone, he was awakened by the sound of the entertainment speakers.

"Oh my bad, I was just testing those babies out. You coo my nigga?" Snupe asked.

He saw the startled look on his face when he woke up. "Yeah bra. I'm straight," he responded before looking to see if the women were around.

Tonight, everyone was to go down to Bourbon St. and watch Snupe perform. The entire ride there King couldn't stop thinking about the dream. The biggest question he was stuck with from this dream was who the mysterious girl in the trench coat was.

"What's wrong, babe?" LJ asked during the car ride.

King just shook his head. Bourbon St. was packed with people, mostly adults. There were parades and small acts going on the entire day. Snupe was set to perform a little after the ball dropped. It was probably 11:50 when he grabbed the mic. He got a huge round of applause.

"Before I start, I want to call a good brotha of mine up. Make some noise for the Baltimore Ravens star running back; Adoree' Matthews y'all," said Snupe. The crowd simmered down a little. He was popular in the sports world, so some people there knew who he was, but a lot didn't.

"It's been an amazing year, am I right or wrong?" King said into the mic as the crowd clapped. "They say everyone has someone for them. Someone whom they are compatible with. Someone who thinks they're the best looking person in the world. Well besides themselves," he said before chuckling . "Someone whom you want to spend the rest of your days with. So when you find that person why wait around without doing what's right?" King stated while looking directly into LJ's eyes as she stood in front.

Queen had her arm around her, recording the special moment.

"LJ, I don't want to waste another day with you as my wife. I want to wake up to that smelly morning breath of yours every day from now on. I want to tell you how beautiful you are every day from here on out. And most importantly, I want that M.S. in front of your name to become M. R. S," King looked at his custom-made Rolex to see that it was 50 seconds until the new year.

"Well, I guess I should probably pop the big question now right?" he kneeled down and pulled out the diamond ring. His dad had given to his mother when they renewed their vows.

"Will you marry me?" he asked her as she stood motionless with a pool of tears in her eyes and the crowd counted down the remaining seconds of 2014.

"5...4... 3... 2...1! Happy New Year!" the crowd roared and the music blasted.

Chapter 20

The infamous tool

The game had become easy to him. He had it mastered. D-Money was easily pulling in twenty to thirty thousand a week himself. His marriage had collapsed and so did his relationship with his children. Hell, he barely saw either of them. Now after saving for a whole year he decided to move to Maryland. He was leaving nothing behind but his family. Getting his life sentence overturned instilled green tendencies in him instead of humbleness.

During his incarceration, he met men who were really getting to some money on the streets. He learned a lot from them. The most important teaching was how to stay low key. Staying out of the eyes of law enforcement. King was also very prestigious about keeping a low profile, so D-Money took some things from him as well. D-Money bought a small $120,000 right outside of Baltimore but was still the next city over from King's new mansion. He and Tiffany were both moving so they drove to Maryland together. You can imagine how that car trip was with Tiffany being widowed for nearly 15 years and D-Money who was now separated following being incarcerated for almost 5 years. Tiffany was so excited to be moving. She decided to sell her house as she did her beauty salon years prior. She was now on her way back to the place where she started her family. But now she was ready to enjoy life. She would be staying in the guest house of her son's mansion, but she didn't plan on being home much.

Tiffany's goals were to travel the world with money she had been saving since the last time she lived in Maryland and to also just get out of the house more. She was tired of living the boring and lonely life of a once married woman. Basically, she moved out of town without any of the normal responsibilities of an adult. All she had was her phone bill, car, and car insurance to worry about.

Speaking of cars, King had a pleasant surprise for Tiffany before she could even move in her section of the home. The pink custom made Ashton Martin lit up her garage space with "TiffDa1" on the license plate.

"Boy this must have cost a fortune," she stated in an anxious tone.

King just laughed. Something Tiffany noticed immediately was that LJ wasn't around much after she greeted her which meant that she wasn't around King much either. That seemed odd to her because when her and King spoke on the phone LJ would always be around. That was one thing that she liked about her. There wasn't any girl King dated that his mom didn't like but LJ was the best fit for him in her eyes. Though she was much older than him, she had her own job, her own money, but most importantly she was stable and settled in her own life with or without King.

After Tiffany was moved in completely, King went to D-Money's new home to assist him with unpacking. There were two totes that D sat aside to bring in last. Once they got to them each brought one of them to the bedroom.

"Man, what the hell you got in this tote? A dead body?" King jokingly asked.

"Nah but they got some dead bodies on em," D responded.

King put two and two together. He always knew the D to keep multiple guns but when he peeked inside the two totes, he saw a mad arsenal of handguns, shotguns, and assault rifles. They spoke often so he knew how well D-Money was maintaining the drug operation. Now he had the most important people in his life living near him beside his twin sister. Tiffany knew that King would be gone for some hours, so she figured she'd chat with LJ for a bit until he got back. Tiffany made small talk. She told her how beautiful the engagement ring looked on her and how she was happy for the both of them. The conversation eventually led to wine tasting. The glasses became continuous and before either of them knew, they were drunk telling each other stories and watching videos on the internet.

Tiffany had to go use the bathroom, so she asked where the closest one was since they were right outside the bedroom, LJ sent her to her their personal bathroom. It had been a while since Tiffany drank that much as she stumbled slightly to the bathroom at first and then she bumped into a chest that was on the ground.

When she saw the bathroom and sat down to pee, she noticed a piece of LJ's mail on the sink. Something on the envelope caught her attention so she reached eagerly to grab it where she then heard King yell her name for the bedroom. Tiffany hurriedly tossed the mail back toward the sink and got up to wash her hands. She headed out the bedroom where she saw King.

"Boy do something with that chest. I hit my toe on it. You know I got bad feet," she said causing them both to laugh.

Once Tiffany left out of the bedroom, King grabbed the chest by the handles and carried it into their huge walk-in closet. He sat it on one of the shelves that was around LJ's eye level and when he did, he wondered what was in it after hearing the lock hit against it.

King peaked toward the bedroom door to make sure the women were still outside of it then he took a closer look at the chest. He had seen his classmates pick locks all the time in high school so he knew that he could. He put his index finger through the lock's hole from behind but before he could finish through with the pick, he heard LJ calling for him, so he quickly pushed the chest back and headed her way. She came inside the room and shut the door behind herself. King tried not to seem suspicious. He wasn't sure if she would notice the chest being missing from its original spot, so he instantly started a conversation.

"Y'all having a good time?" he asked quickly.

"Yessss…. your mom is so fun. She's funny too," she replied with a huge smile.

"She's alright. You had her try that new wine from Jack's?" he asked.

"Yep, she loved it. We drank almost two bottles," responded LJ.

LJ started walking toward King as she continued to tell him about her time with Tiffany. The wine was hitting her hard and she was feeling herself. She wrapped her arms around his lower back and stared up at his baby face. Without any hesitation, LJ unzipped his hoodie to reveal exactly what she was looking for; King's muscular body frame that stood zip tight beneath his all black v-neck. She pulled his shirt up and began kissing his stomach, then chest as he finished taking off shirt. He could smell the sweet wine on her breath when she rose on the tips of her toes to reach his neck and lips. His hands smoothly gripped her hips as their lips met.

"Where's my mom?" he whispered in her ear.

"She's already asleep babe," LJ responded back in her soft voice before continuing with the kissing.

The hair on her arms and legs stood up when he remembered a similar scene where they stood and kissed in the bedroom. But now he was older, more experienced, rich, and they were engaged so it made her attraction to him that much more as she kneeled down to pleasure her King. Over the next few months, LJ and Tiffany continued to build while King was away at practice. He was able to make a full recovery and was finally able to work toward his offseason goal of putting on an extra 10 pounds of muscle. At two-hundred and five pounds, he was one of the smaller running backs weight wise but he was 6 foot tall so that made him one of the taller backs in the league. He hired a strength training coach to aid him in accomplishing his goal.

Tiffany met a guy who was a personal trainer, and she began spending time with him. King wasn't okay with it, but LJ convinced them that the guy was good for her and that she needed a man. King wasn't trying to hear that either, but he let her do her. He started going out more by himself. Well not alone, but not with LJ all the time like he had been. He had D-Money, who lived 20 minutes away, and he had close friends on his team. King obviously had more fun with the guys, but he hated always having security and bodyguards around him when he stepped out. It made him feel that he had become too mainstream when in actuality he was just a regular kid who wanted to follow in the same footsteps as his dad.

One day, he chose to go out with just D-Money and himself. D-Money drove King's infinity truck as they club hopped all over Baltimore. King wore regular street clothes and shades to keep a low profile so everyone wouldn't notice who he was. They hit up a few strip clubs as well where King had his first moment of really splurging money. The two of them through over $100,000. They had it like that and they both knew that it could be made back with a blink of an eye. But what they didn't know was that their moment of fun was all being closely watched by a group of guys in there who couldn't even afford a lap dance. Their observations were driven by jealousy, envy, and hatred. The traits that prevented African American men from being united. It wasn't until King and D-Money were leaving when one of them noticed mean mugs coming from the entire group.

"You saw dem niggas lookin' all aggressive in there?" King asked.

"Man, fuck dem niggas. We just tore that bitch up. They prolly was just some hating ass broke niggas," responded D-Money.

King laughed as they jumped into Infiniti truck. The music blasted while they were stopped at a red light. They were both drunk and ready to call it a night. King pulled out his phone to call LJ and told her he was on his way home. He pressed the button to call her and a picture of the two of them covered the screen bringing his mouth into a smile.

"I'm like 5 minutes away," he spoke into the phone.

"Okay babe," she responded before hanging up.

While putting his phone away and turning the music on the car speaker back up, he could see a car through his peripheral. Then the car's window began rolling down. The first thing visible to King was the barrel of a shotgun.

"Pull off!" King demanded.

D-Money slammed on the gas and he blew through the red light. He didn't even know what was happening, but he sensed the urgency from King's shout. He sped up the main street and made a left at the next intersection and that's when he finally perceived the car who was after them.

"Grab the tool from the glove compartment," King did so and pulled out a .38 revolver. He looked at it for a second. Hesitant of making a bad decision that could fuck up his life, he didn't make a move.

"Shoot, nigga," D-Money yelled. King rolled down his window and fired three shots at the car but didn't hit anything. "You only got six shots son. Make em count," D-Money warned King.

The car had already shot the back of the Infiniti truck twice. King didn't want to get hit. He pressed the button to roll down the sunroof and he rose through it with the .38 in his right hand. He pointed it just a tad bit below the driver's chin and fire. After firing King hurried back down to the passenger seat as he watched the car swerve off the road. The bullet hit the driver directly between his eyes resulting in an instant death. The music continued to blast while D-Money cruised back to the mansion.

"Who the hell taught you to shoot like that?" D-Money asked anxiously. King shrugged his shoulders. His adrenaline was still racing. He had his driver take the D-Money back home.

It seemed as if the following morning arrived quickly. LJ woke King up to breakfast, but he didn't have an appetite. He was more nervous than he had ever been.

"What if someone saw what happened? What if they wrote down my license plate?" were the kind of questions that clouded his mind.

When he told her he wasn't hungry she was concerned so he just told her that he had a hangover. He couldn't tell her what happened the night before. Hell, he didn't even want to believe it himself. He had done things in his younger days that were just as bad or worse but now he had made it and there wasn't any room for error.

It was 9 a.m. Saturday morning, April 6th. He had to be at practice in less than an hour, so he hurried to get dressed. The paranoia ate at him as he brushed his teeth. He stopped at D-Money's house on his way to the practice facility to tell him to go back to the mansion and get the Infiniti truck destroyed. Luckily, it was a smooth practice day where the guys just conditioned. He was drained when he got back home. The first thing he did after kissing his fiancé was got into the shower. Then he finally had an appetite once he smelled LJ's cooking. They ate together then went to lay down. It was still early. Only 6:30 p.m. So, they weren't about to go to bed though King was still tired from the night before, on top of practice. King laid down with his head on LJ's leg as she sat up and rubbed her hands through his short curly afro. She knew she had to spend as much time with him before the season started. LJ had spent the day cleaning up which reminded her of King's clothes on the bedroom floor.

"Oh, babe I put that gun from your jeans last night inside the nightstand," LJ mentioned. The gun she was talking about had actually been in the back of King's mind that entire day. He didn't even know that he brought the gun home. Since it was a small revolver it fit right in his pants pocket.

"All right thanks babe," King responded.

"Why did you have that anyway? You're not living in the hood anymore. You're an NFL player now. And a damn good one," she made him aware of.

"I still have to protect myself. No one's going to spare me because of who I am," he replied.

Ironically, an article of the driver of the truck that was chasing King popped up on his twitter account.

"You see that babe? No one spared him. Probably didn't even think twice about it," he said.

"I guess you're right. At least be legit. Get your gun permit and register your gun," she responded.

"I will," said King.

LJ was right and King knew it. He woke up later that night and took a closer look at the gun as he went to the bathroom. The same model gun from his dreams.

"No way," he said to himself. But why this gun is what he couldn't get over. It looked exactly the same. Silver and black with the scratches on the right side of it.

"Man are you serious? You trippin' son," he said jokingly to himself before hearing LJ's voice.

"Who are you talkin' to?" she muttered. King laughed and went back to the bedroom.

"I was talking to myself," he said with a slight grin on his face.

"You are right?" she asked. He responded by nodding his head and kissing her on the lips before they fell back asleep.

No practice today, he thought to himself when he first woke up Sunday morning.

He went next door to the guest house to see what Tiffany was doing. She was up reading scriptures from the bible while sipping her hot coffee. A typical Sunday morning for her in which she tried to invite King to study but as usual he declined. LJ had yoga and dance class till around 1 p.m. so he was alone till then. He decided to get in a quick 30-minute workout before showering and heading to D-Money's. It was somewhat chilly outside as he shivered knocking on the door. He only knew D was there because both his cars were outside. D came to the door with his eyes squinted.

"Damn nigga why you ain't call first?" he asked. King started laughing.

"Nigga it's almost 11. We to the city," King declared.

D-Money went to the back to get dressed so King you sat on the couch and waited. They hadn't spoken since yesterday morning when he visited before practice so King wanted to see what he had to say. They spoke about it briefly on the way to Baltimore but that was it. It wasn't until they started drinking when D-Money complemented King on his shooting from other night.

"That's why I fuck with revolvers; no shells," D-Money added.

"What you mean?" he asked.

"Revolvers don't leave shell casings. You ever looked at how it's made? No clip or slide. Like them old western movies where they gotta put the bullets inside the spinner," he explained."

"Damn, I never peeped."

"Yup, shid I got away with all types of shit with that joint. Matter of fact, where my shit at anyway son?" he asked.

King took a drink from the bottle of D'usse.

"I got you son," he responded.

Later that night, he called Isaac so they could meet up sometime that upcoming week. He had some questions for him, and he was the only person he knew that could answer them. So sometime later that week, he took another drive to the city but this time alone. He met with Isaac at a gas station near an alleyway and hopped in the car so that they could talk in private.

"Young Kobe, what's up man? You doing it big now. I've been seeing you on the screen," Issac said.

"What's up Unc. I remember this gas station. My dad used to take us here and step outside to smoke sometimes. He thought he was doing it on the slide but me and lil sis knew all along," said King

"Aye you know what's crazy? That alley right there is where me and your paps robbed dude at. Kobe was nervous as fuck afterwards. I don't think we spoke for a week or two after that cuz he was so shook," Issac said with a laugh.

"Man that shit still crazy how he ain't here nomo," he added.

"Did they ever say what type of gun killed him?" King asked.

"38 Special. I'll never forget. No shells left on the scene. Which was crazy cuz that gun isn't even the type of gun that people shoot from long distances. That's about all we know for real. Nobody saw anything like if the person was on foot or in a car," he explained.

"Do you remember what the nigga looked like dat y'all robbed?" asked King.

"Honestly lil bra, I never saw his face," Issac responded.

"Did my dad ever see dude again?" he asked.

"Naw not that he ever mentioned. See he knew dude, I didn't," Issac responded.

The stuffed backwood was on its way out so they wrapped up their talk and King drove back home. He knew better than to jump conclusions but still he had a lot to think about. In addition, D-Money lived in New York during Kobe's death. His hypothesis was like everyone else's. The man who they robbed came for pay back. But how could he ever find him? The question lingered his mind the entire ride home.

Pulling up to his mansion, and then seeing his beautiful fiancé who appeared more glowing than usual today, helped distract his detective intellect. She sat on the top balcony with their Bluetooth speaker playing old school R&B songs. King came up from behind and began massaging her traps and shoulders. LJ placed her hands on top of his hands and rubbed.

"King," she called him.

"LJ," he responded back. LJ didn't say anything causing King to stand in front of her.

"What's up baby?" he asked now sounding concerned especially after seeing a tear roll down her face. She looked up at him.

"I'm... I'm pregnant." It got quiet on both ends for a moment before broke the silence.

"Oh wow?"

"Oh wow, huh?" she repeated with an attitude.

"Yeah wow. When I saw you this morning before you left it was just something blowing about you. Then when I walked in just now you looked so beautiful. Now that you don't always, but today is just something about you. You had to just find out today," King explained.

"An hour ago actually," she added.

"Wow, babe, are you serious? This is the happiest day of my life," he assured her.

LJ breathed a sigh of relief. At first, she thought he was mad about her being pregnant. But she felt the excitement from his response, and she knew they were

going to be good.

Chapter 21

What's next?

Some sat but most people stood quietly in
anticipation for King to run down the grass field and spike
the balloon shaped football. He did so with force just as he
did sometimes when he scored touchdowns. The blue
confetti sprayed from the balloon signaling that there was
potentially an Adoree' Jr to come. Their families and
friends clapped while King and LJ hugged each other with
enjoyment.

Tiffany couldn't believe that she was a soon-to-be
grandmother and Queen, a soon-to-be aunt. With the season
about to start in a few weeks the two wanted to have
everything ready for the baby ASAP to alleviate stress. The
wedding had been previously set for the middle of next
year, so they didn't have to take on the complications of
that until after the baby was born. But King had a hidden

agenda. He felt that his life was ascending so well and that was due to his father. He didn't discredit his mom taking care of him and Queen all alone, but he knew that his father dying when he was just a young child was what inspired him to accomplish the things he had. So, for the past four months King spent days on end and long hours investigating his father's death just to come up with nothing more than he already had. All he knew was the gun used and that he had robbed someone prior to his killing.

After the baby shower, Queen helped LJ decorate the baby's room. Since LJ wasn't able to drink, King didn't drink around her. When he wasn't with her, he was at the D-money's house. He and D drove over there following the baby shower and they began drinking immediately.

"Damn son, can you believe you about to be a father?" D-Money asked.

King smiled and shook his head. He wasn't lying, he really couldn't believe it. They discussed parenting a little then D brought up how he missed his kids back in NYC. King told him that he should have them come out to visit sometime soon. D-Money agreed knowing that it would take a lot of explaining to do to his wife before that would happen. He told King how his mom raised him all alone on top of his two other siblings. King added how he wished that could have been there his whole childhood and definitely now to see how good he and queen turned out. He also expressed his gratitude for d for being a father figure to him and how that helps him along the way as well as they continue to drink, they discussed more and more topics. One in particular was D's violent childhood.

He served juvenile to life for killing a police K-9 while in high school. Once free he committed robberies on banks, car jackings, and home invasions. He even mentioned carrying out murders for hire. This news was shocking to King. He wondered if it was just the liquor talking.

"You did a lot of hits?" he asked.

"Probably over 10 for sure," D-Money responded.

"How much was they paying you?" King asked.

"5 stacks usually. I made the most on the last one though. $15,000," D-Money recalled.

"Why so much for this person," D-Money explained.

"It was some popular dude from out here actually. They really wanted him dead, I guess," he explained.

Those last two statements instantly made him think of his dad. What were the odds of him carrying out a hit in Baltimore when he lived in NYC. On top of that? He bragged about getting away with a live dirt by using that same revolver. King took it all in and sat his cup on the ground. He looked over at D-Money who was more drunk than he was and just pondered.

"Nah, this nigga has been too good to me," he mumbled to himself. His segment on ESPN had just come on so they tuned into that. The analyst asked, "better than his rookie year or worse?"

D-Money yelled, "are they serious? Better for sure," before looking over to King for validation but he never acknowledged.

"You feel me, son?" he asked King. King just nodded his head without even turning to look.

"What wrong, bro? I know that drink ain't put you down like that," D said.

King shook his head and said nothing. But deep down D knew what was wrong. He felt bad for him as he sat there thinking back on his past and the man he was now.

"Hey little bro, I got to tell you something," he said softly. King didn't respond but he did look up at him.

"Man, I don't even know how to tell you this. I didn't even know until a few years after I met you when you told me how your dad died. You know I don't watch sports, so I didn't know who he was. I got a random call to kill a man on a certain day. He was getting married and the person knew his location, the time, and all. They offered $15,000 to take him out. Man I had to take it. I was about to propose soon then have a baby. I rode past the street twice to make sure I had the right guy, then I took my shot. Bam. One shot and that was it. I drove back to NYC that same day," D-Money explained.

King stared at the ground with both eyes full of tears speeding down his face. All the signs added up, but he still couldn't believe that this man that he looked up to for the majority of his life, in his father's absence, would be the man that took his life. It was more than anger that he felt. A built up hurt that now came to a head. But now with his father's murderer sitting right next to him, it became rage.

King pulled the .38 from his waist but D must have known what he was about to try. He smacked the gun from King's hand, and it flew across the room. King quickly grabbed D's shirt and pushed him off the couch onto the floor. With the anger he had built up, he handled D-Money as if he was a child. He punched him over and over until his eyes shut. Then he looked over at the gun and went to grab it. Before he could take his second step, he felt D grab his leg with both arms and bent it as he stood up. Now King was hopping on one leg to balance himself while still trying to retrieve the gun. It seemed that D had gotten a boost of strength but really, he was just trying to stay alive.

He yanked King back towards him and then jumped on him and began choking him from behind. D squeezed with everything he had and with the perfect angle he had on the choke hold, he felt King going out. Well at least he thought so, before King flipped him over and elbowed him over the head. He stood over D-Money and when he saw he wasn't moving he tried to grab the gun again. He pointed the gun down at him and watched D as he stared down the barrel of the infamous revolver.

"I knew you since I was eight years old. I loved you like a father. Made sure you had money when you were locked up. You and your family. Made sure you got freed. Put you on when you got out. And never one time, could you have mentioned what you had done to my father," King said as the tears continued to pour. Blood rolled down D's forehead and nose.

"I'm sorry man! You should at least know the person who hired me," D pleaded. But King had too many emotions spinning throughout him.

"I've heard enough son." He squeezed the handle of the revolver tighter and pulled the trigger.

"Their name is LE..." was all King heard before the .38 caliber bullet took D- Money out execution style.

This death was too closely related to him so he knew it would raise suspicion if he just left. His adrenaline was racing but he was still able to move accordingly. He hurried to remove the camera system in the home then he called the police from D's house phone. He wiped his fingerprints from the revolver and hid it in the fireplace. Moments before the police arrived, he was able to take a pair of D-Money's shoes from his closet and tracked shoe prints using his hands, with blood to make a trail that led all the way to the porch.

Once the police was there, he gave a statement claiming that someone had come in and tried to rob both of them. In those few seconds, he had thought of a good story that they actually believed. He called his fiancé and mom to come pick him up. When they got home, he went straight down to his mancave and locked it. He grabbed his weed and immediately sparked it up. His phone ranged from a bunch of people, but he just let it. What started as a great day had turned into a murder. As he smoked, he began to feel a bit of relief. His father's killer was known and dead. King replayed the last moments in his mind right before D-Money died. The confession, the scuffle, and the final shot.

It all brought back tears. He hadn't cried this much since his father had died.

"Damn," he yelled. It all hit him at once as he began to roll up another blunt. Then he remembered something else. *You should at least know the person who hired me. Their name is LE...* replayed over and over. That made him frustrated again. The man that Kobe and Isaac robbed, name must have started with Le, was his thinking. "Larry, Lester, Lex..." He brainstormed. There were so many names it could have been and now he wondered if he should have waited one more second before pulling the trigger. He thought the killing would be closure but in the end, it only brought him more questions and frustration. Now he was on his second blunt and as high as a kite, so he put it out.

His phone rang again but this time it was Queen. She was literally the only person that he wanted to talk to at the moment. He didn't tell her what actually happened, but he gave her the main gist of the made-up story because he didn't want to say too much about it over the phone. Queen had only flown down for a gender reveal party, but she was willing to come back down asap. She knew what D-Money meant to King and D even had a positive impact on her life at one point. She felt sympathetic for him, being that he was there when he died and had to witness it.

"See you soon brother. I'll call you tomorrow," she said to end the call.

King heard a knock from the top of the steps, so he went to open it. It was LJ with a plate of fresh cooked food. A well-cooked steak, fresh broccoli with butter and a sprinkle of cheese, and seasoned mashed potatoes; King's favorite.

"You have to eat something babe," she recommended.

King grabbed the food and held the door for her as an invitation for her to join him. LJ walked down the stairs slowly examining the man cave. She hadn't been down there since he was putting it together and not because didn't allow her. It was just an environment for him to get away without actually being away. On the walls were paintings of him playing ball, his favorite retired athletes, and some were of vicious animals. The carpet was soft like cushion and the sectional was black and purple. The TV was so big that one could have mistaken the man cave for a movie theater.

King demolished his plate of food. He still hadn't said a word since the ride home.

"Babe, you want to talk about?" she asked. He continued to stare at his plate with a mouth full of food and shook his head. She knew that he needed her during this time. She sat closer to him and began rubbing his back.

"I'm sorry for your loss. I know how close you guys were. He was like family. Actually, he was family. But baby I'm here for you. I need you; your family needs you, we have five more minutes until this baby is born. D-Money will definitely be there for us in spirit. We're all in this together," LJ expressed. The thought of him being there disgusted him but he looked up and nodded his head.

"I know. Thank you," King responded. He put his arms around her, and they relaxed for the rest of the night.

A few days later, King was at practice running plays. The season was starting in two weeks, so they were just tightening up on their playbook. His coaches were telling everyone how the offense would run through King and that he was the face of their franchise. As he jogged back to the huddle his coach and the man in the suit was standing there waiting for him.

"Matthews, this is Detective Hutchens. He said he got some questions for you about a homicide that took place a few days ago. Go handle that and we'll see you tomorrow," his head coach said.

King shook the detective's hand and headed towards the station with him. King stayed calm and composed the entire car ride but eternally he was scared straight. He knew what he had done, and he was just praying that he had all his tracks covered. He has his story memorized so well that in a way he believed it himself. When he got into the station, he followed the detective who had a piece of paper with a pen, into an empty room.

"I need you to tell me again what happened during the night of August 28th," demanded Detective Hutchens.

"Darius and I left my house to go to his, after my gender reveal. Then…" told King.

"Whose idea was it to leave and why?" asked the detective.

"It was my idea. We wanted to drink and since my fiancé couldn't, I chose not to drink around her. I've been going to his house to drink for the past six months," he continued.

"So yall went to his house, then what happened?" he asked.

"Then we started drinking and watching TV. He drank a little more than I did, like usual. I'm not really a drinker. Maybe like an hour later there was a knock on the door. Darius walked over to open it. He never said he was expecting anyone but he rushed to the door like he was. I continued to watch TV. It was a segment of me on ESPN. They asked if I was going to be better this year than I was last year," he said with a smile. "I looked over to tell Darius what they were talking about and I didn't see him or hear anything. So, I got up and started walking towards the door when a man rushed through with a gun pointed towards me while holding Darius by his shirt from behind. I froze right there, and he yelled for me to lay down, so I did so. The man pushed Darius on the ground near me and demanded we emptied our pockets and told him where things were. He put the gun toward my head and went through my pockets, but I had nothing in them. Then Darius next, and he pulled out a small stack of money and put it in his bag that he pulled from his waist. As he was turning around to go to the safe Darius grabbed his leg."

Then King stopped to put his head down and began shaking it from side to side.

"How did he know where the safe was?" asked Detective Hutchens.

"Darius told him as he went through his pockets. I think he just didn't want him to kill him," King answered.

"So why would he grab his leg instead of letting him go to the safe?" he asked.

"You're asking the wrong guy. I can't tell you his thoughts. Only what I saw detective," he said.

"Well your story isn't adding up. We have a homicide with a so-called eyewitness, with no fucking leads or anything. No gun or no DNA from the so-called perpetrator," he said.

"Look man, I told you what happened. If there's no further questions can I leave?" he asked.

"I want you to take my card. If you remember anything or want to tell me anything ELSE, give me a call. And you're free to go Mr. Matthews," he concluded.

"Will do sir," replied King.

King waited in the entry room for LJ to come get him. He sat there wondering if the detective would buy his story or not, or if he was just fishing for information. One thing he knew for sure was that law enforcement could pull all types of antics on people to get a conviction. He saw that with D-Money. How ironic!

"It's been a few days now. You want to talk about what happened?" LJ asked.

King gave her the detailed made up story. She was just happy that King was able to avoid getting killed. It would have crushed her if he died on the day that they found out the gender of their unborn child. For the next weeks law enforcement harassed King even after the season started. They would pop up directly following his games, sometimes before the games they parked outside his home. They just didn't have enough to charge King with anything. But a judge did give them an order to search his home. Still, they had no luck. King was walking on eggshells.

In addition to the baby on the way and the wedding, King wasn't performing to his fullest potential on the field. To others and to his team he was doing well, but to him he knew that he could do much better. In game three of the regular season, he broke a run for eighty-two yards and rushed for over 200 yards and three touchdowns. It was the first game that he was able to put all his problems to the side and focus just on the game he loved so much.

Following the game, a female reporter jogged over to him as he was walking to the locker room. She wanted to talk to him about his performance. The reporter was a younger woman from Trinidad. She was slim with green eyes and a soft caramel skin tone.

"Matthews what a performance today. Would you say that this game was your coming out party?" the reporter asked.

"Nah. I think the people who know me and have watched me play since high school know how good I am. This game was just one of many," King boasted.

"How were you able to run the ball so well today?" she asked.

"Uh, just good play calling and my teammates did hell of a job blocking and creating holes for me to hit. Just good team ball today," King explained.

"Mr. Matthews, do you have any comments about the homicide that took place while you were there?" asked the reporter.

King looked at the beautiful reporter and shook his head. She had no business asking that, especially being that this interview was being televised live. He was usually good about keeping his composure, but he snapped this time.

"Check this out Miss whoever you are, don't ask me no dumb ass question like that. I'm pretty sure they don't teach you that in journalism school or wherever you went. Matter of fact, I hope you lose your job after this," he said as he pushed the mic down and walked off.

The interview would air on ESPN for the next few weeks with analysts giving their opinions on his reaction and her question. It was the incident that made King go find the lawyer from D-Money's appeal and call him up. He knew how the public would emphasize his questionable involvement with the story he provided. The lawyers were able to talk to the detective and police officers to find out what all they knew and was trying to dig up.

"They found the gun, but it was all burnt up. No DNA of anyone outside of you and the victim. And only your DNA is on his body. I'm not sure why they haven't pursued any charges yet. They definitely have enough for an indictment," the lawyer explained to King.

King was surprised himself. The detective called him down to the station soon after this conversation so of course he showed up with his lawyer present. He brought him into the same room where they had spoken weeks prior. When they got inside the detective left out and an older white man walked in. King and his lawyer looked at each other in confusion. They had no clue of what was going on or who this man in the suit was. He sat down and stared at King. The stared lasted for seconds until he finally spoke.

"Big fan of yours. Nice to meet you, I'm the district's attorney for Madison county," the man said.

The three shook hands and King introduced his lawyer to the DA though they were pretty familiar with each other already. The conversation consisted of everything King's lawyer was telling him about what they had on him and more. King sat there listening, getting more afraid with everything being said. He felt his stomach drop. He already began to come up with his defense in his mind. Even the best lawyer couldn't convince a jury that this wasn't him according to the evidence they had on him.

"I've been a DA in this county for thirty-one years. You will easily get a life sentence and it'll be twenty-five years before the parole board even considers letting you," the DA said in a stern voice. King shook his head and looked over to his lawyer for reassurance but even he no longer seemed confident.

"Kobe Matthews, that's your dad isn't it?" he asked King.

His head snapped over quickly to the DA and he nodded. "That's one we wish we could have solved. Sorry about your pops man. I at least owe you and your family for that. Let's forget this ever happened and get the fuck out of here. I don't ever want to see your name pop up in any bullshit or I'll make sure you never see the light of day myself. You're welcome," he voiced.

King nodded again and he and his lawyer rushed out of the room. King felt a sense of relief. He knew he dodged a bullet. Better yet a grenade. The lady working at the front desk of the station informed King to pick up his property that law enforcement obtained when they conducted the search warrant of home and vehicles. They had taken a few laptops, an iPad, two iPods, a phone, weed paraphernalia, and a chest. His lawyer helped bring it all to his car and after he signed for it the two spoke for a few minutes about their blessing and King drove home a relieved man. He was excited to tell LJ how they wouldn't be getting harassed anymore and how he could finally sleep at night.

Before he could even get in the house to share the news, he saw the chest on his passenger's seat. He noticed the huge lock that was previously on there was unlocked. Out of curiosity he opened it and what he saw, he couldn't believe. Pictures of he, Queen, Kobe, and Tiffany that all appeared as off-guard photos from a private investigator or something. The pictures were from fifteen years ago.

But why..how? he asked himself.

He looked up and saw her car parked in front of his. Her license plate read Leslie J. Then everything made sense. The "Le" from D-Money's final seconds were for Leslie. How they met, how much older she was, how she didn't want their families to meet and go public, how his mom remembered seeing her before and so did he after seeing an older picture of her. The exact day popped in his head when Kobe officiated, he and his cousin's foot race when they were kids. He remembered looking from the front door and seeing Kobe talking to her. It added up now. But why would she hire someone to kill him? He thought about it for a moment and then he remembered something else. A comment that LJ's mom made when they met during breakfast.

"He kinda looks like someone I've seen before," he recalled her saying.

"They must have messed around or something," King said under his breath. Now here was the murderer of his father dead, and the person who hired him, who he's about to marry and give birth to his son. So, what's next?

Chapter 22

The Finale; love hurts!

In a rush to brunch, she knocked over her cup of coffee on the counter.

"FUCK!" she yelled before running to her car. She met up with three of her friends at Lee's Eatery for a planned meeting that she desperately needed.

"Damn that belly is getting bigger by the moment," her friend said when she saw her walking in. Leslie laughed and sat down.

"So, what's up girl?" another friend asked.

Leslie exhaled noticeably through her mouth. With both life changing events in the near future, she wasn't comfortable with how King had been acting for the past month, especially being that his behavior was a new occurrence. She shared this with her friends over brunch and like the good friends that they were, they listened. One friend added her input.

"Girl, he just has cold feet. He's about to get married to someone who's older than him. He's young. Plus, his first child is on the way. He's nervous and scared. It's normal. You know how men are," she said as if she was in a happy marriage with longevity. Leslie took in what she was saying. She was hoping that her friend was right, and it helped that she believed what she was saying to be true.

"Just sit down and talk to him. And fuck him good," another friend added.

"Oh, I always do that!" Leslie responded with confidence as they all laughed.

After brunch, she went to the store to buy things to decorate the living room. Rose petals, candles, champagne, lingerie, etc. When King got home from practice, she filled up a glass for him and asked him to sit and talk. He looked around and said he was tired from practice.

"Let's talk in the room," he said, sounding exhausted. Though he shitted on her plans, he agreed. She followed King in the bedroom in the brand-new lingerie set that he didn't even acknowledge. And King loved when she wore new lingerie. This was the first time she had bought some since being pregnant. So, she thought maybe her oversized belly, thighs, and facial features weren't attractive to him. Even still, the sudden change was bothering her.

She stood there and watched him as he gathered his clothes for a shower. The room was silent with the only sound being the water bubbles from the eighty-five-gallon fish tank.

"What are we talking about?" he finally said, sounding irritated. Leslie's face instantly squinted up in reaction to his attitude.

"I know you noticed things have been different between us lately. I just want to know how you're feeling about everything," she responded.

King continued to grab his clothes without even looking in her direction one time. He did so intentionally. After returning the chest back to the closet with the lock returned in its locked position, he waited days to see if she would say anything about it. Even just about it being returned because she had to know that it had been moved more than once, since it was a heavier chest.

"Shit, I'm cool. You cool?" King said carelessly.

"No I'm not cool. What's the matter with you?" she asked.

"I'm cool. What are you talking about?" he returned.

"Adoree', we've barely spoken for the past few days, weeks even. You haven't even touched me in almost two weeks, and we use to have sex almost every day. Is it because I'm fat now? Are you not attracted to me because of that?" she asked.

"Listen, I think you're over thinking things. I love you, I can't wait for you to have our child, and I can't wait to marry you," he assured her.

That was music to her ears. She needed that reassurance so after they hugged, she gave King his time in the shower and afterwards she took her friend's advice and put it on him. King continued to shine on the field. He led the league in rushing yards through the first half of the season.

Despite figuring out that Leslie was the person in charge of his father's death, his life was going cool. Since D-Money had died, he gave the drug game up. It was part of his development. His team of people tried to get him to bounce back but he had his mind made up. He was having his first child and he wanted to change his ways. But he wanted to go all the way with it. Not how D-Money did when he first handed King the pack as a child. So, he stopped talking to everyone who he had drug dealings with and became actively involved in his community.

He began working toward starting a non-profit organization called Greater Youth, for children and teens. The foundation would offer free meals, free extracurricular activities, and free clothing. King's goal was for this organization to become huge in the Baltimore area and for it to get a lot of recognition from other popular figures. King had tons of ideas for the inner-city Baltimore. And this was just one of many. Though he stopped selling drugs he had been saving for the past four years. He had made well over a million dollars. Combined with his contract money and money from his endorsements, King opened a restaurant, a food truck, and started a clothing line. He knew a few females from college that were graphic design graduates that helped with the ideas for his brand logos. These projects were ones he was able to focus solely on once the season ended in December from a playoff loss to the New England Patriots. He and

Leslie had the majority of the wedding task taken care of already, so their main focus was the baby being born next month. Leslie decided that she wanted a natural birth, so her birth was painful. King stood in the hospital room holding Leslie's hand as she pushed as pushed for over and an hour. The baby boy came out weighing eight pounds, two ounces.

King clipped the umbilical cord and stared at his baby boy with the biggest smile on his face. The instant love he felt for his first child was unexplainable. He was in his own little world holding him forgetting that Leslie had just carried him for a little over nine months and sat in pain for hours giving birth.

"Born January 18th, 2016. So, did you finalize the name yet babe?" Leslie asked.

King handed their son over to her and responded.

"Yup… Kobe Prince Matthews," he said with pride.

He looked to see if Leslie's facial expression would show any emotion from hearing his father's name, but she had become so content with what she had done that it didn't faze her. Though she did what she did, her love for King was undeniable and so was his love for her. Due to the baby, King skipped out on the pro bowl game. His stock as a player was increasing and he was already recognized as a top player in the NFL. They were only a few pieces away from being a championship team.

After the baby was born, King helped Leslie to lose all her baby weight and got her nice shape back. When they weren't exercising, they were with the baby. When the baby was with Tiffany or Queen, they spent time together planning for the wedding that was approaching quickly. They were inseparable. At least that's what their families and friends said when they saw them interacting. They knew that their marriage was going to be everlasting. The wedding invitations had been sent our months ago and over ¾ of them had responded and RSVP'd their spots. King had decided to try something different. He and Leslie agreed to have their wedding on a cruise, so there was a one hundred eighty people capacity limit.

One evening, while King and Leslie were bathing little Kobe, he got a call from Destiny. He hadn't heard from her since D-Money's party and even before that it had been years. She wanted to attend the wedding. King was surprised by her question but he asked for her address so he could send the invitation to her. Leslie had gone to change the laundry load over from the washer to the dryer. Little Kobe was dried and waiting for his clothes to get put on while King held him. He had just bought him a Louis Vuitton outfit to wear and he was going to his closet to grab it. He spotted the small shirt and pants on the shelf next to the chest. When he grabbed it, he noticed that the outfit was slightly under the chest which meant that the chest had to have been moved recently. He kept that in mind as he finished getting little Kobe dressed to take next door to Tiffany.

It was days later before he got the chance to play with the chest. It would have been nearly impossible for him to guess the code for it, so he ripped it off without breaking it. The pictures he had previously looked at were still sitting on top. The pictures had blown his mind so hard when he saw them the last time that he never even figured out what brought his attention to the chest which was how heavy it was. As he moved the pictures over to the right, there was a tiara in a box with two medals. The medals read prom King and Queen on them. Then there was a picture of Leslie and Kobe at prom. They were wearing red, white, and black. They looked happy together which was why King couldn't figure out why she had hired someone to kill him.

As he kept rumbling, he saw a photo album. It was filled with pictures of a man from when he was a boy until now King was assuming. There were certificates in there from school, but there wasn't a name, birth date, or anything around to identify who the pictures were of. After looking at all the pictures, he fixed everything back to how it was, locked the chest back, and sat it on the shelf.

The wedding started at 3:00 p.m. but everyone had to be there by 2 p.m. because that's when the cruise was taking off. King's friend Anthony had taken D-Money's spot as the best man. Ronald had shown up. King's college roommate was there. A few guys from his college and high school football team showed up. But the face he was most surprised to see was Destiny. Never in a million years did he expect to see her attending his wedding. His first love there supporting him for who was hopefully his last and final love. They both cheesed hard when they saw each other and gave a long hug.

"Thanks for coming," King said softly.

"You know I couldn't miss this," Destiny responded back in the same tone.

King was out mingling with the crowd. He hadn't seen Leslie since that morning. So, when she walked up to the altar with her dad, his mouth almost dropped to the ground. For a 49-year-old woman she looked excellent. She looked no older than 35 and that wasn't an exaggeration. Leslie wore a fitted dress that showed some cleavage but not too much. The diamond bracelet on her wrist cost over ten thousand dollars and so did her diamond earrings. King wore a diamond watch as well with an all-diamond choker necklace that displayed above his open cut dress shirt that lied beneath his tuxedo jacket. Separately they looked extravagant, together they were amazing. When she stood across from him staring into his eyes, he couldn't do anything but smile and neither could she. Leslie said her vows first. King's was last.

"Through thick and thin, ups and downs, good and bad, I promise to love you through it all. If we tilt, I promise not to let us fall. I promise to be faithful, trusting, and most of all, honest," King continued with his vows.

He placed emphasis on the words honesty and trusting. After they kissed and exchanged wedding rings, they started the reception right there on the ship. They danced together with their families, and with their friends. Leslie hadn't drunk much since before her pregnancy, so she got drunk fast. Queen made sure to pour a cup for Leslie every time she went and grabbed one for herself. Everyone was having a good time. King kept thinking about little Kobe who was at home with their nanny. He figured he'd give her a call, but the music was so loud there. He began heading toward the cabin.

"Babe, where you going?" he heard Leslie yelling.

He waited for her to get closer before telling her that he was about to check on little Kobe. Leslie was wasted at this point. She was cheesing hard.

"I wanna talk to him too," she added and they went up to the cabin.

Little Kobe was asleep when King called, so the phone call was short. He had completed what he went upstairs to do so he went toward the door to leave but Leslie stopped him. She knew that no one was around so she figured they could get a quickie in. She turned him around and started kissing him while unbuttoning his shirt. The alcohol made her more aggressive than usual. She forced King up against the wall and rushed to unbuckle his belt.

As she unbuckled his pants, Queen and Tiffany busted through the door. Leslie turned to them with the lipstick smeared on her lips. Queen threw a stack of pictures on the bed.

"You got a lot of explaining to do," Tiffany said.

Leslie looked confused. She looked at King then walked over to the bed. It was the first set of pictures from the chest. Leslie bit her lips and looked at each of them individually. The room was filled with silence. King walked over and grabbed the pictures from her hands.

"So what's up? Why do you have pictures of us and my dad? I asked if you knew him a while ago and you said no," King barked.

Leslie opened her mouth to speak but couldn't make out the words to say. When she did speak, she talked very softly.

"Do we have to do this here?" she asked.

Queen smacked her lips.

"Look, I already know everything. But I'll let you explain," King added.

Leslie took two steps backwards and sat on the bed. She breathed in and exhaled.

"Well, you looked in the chest, so you know everything. Your dad and I dated in high school and college. We loved each other. A lot! His parents loved me and mine loved him. Out of nowhere he started acting differently. Like he stopped calling, stopped coming around. Just different. Well, by then I was one month pregnant, and he didn't know. I never told him. He broke up with me soon after and that's when he and your mother started dating." She looked over at Tiffany.

"I was torn. Didn't know what to do. I ended up having the baby and giving him up for adoption. Years later, I saw your dad's sister Christine. Her and Kobe didn't get along. I told her what had happened, and she slid me some information to someone who would take him out. I was appalled. I refused but she convinced me that it was the right thing to do. So, I contacted him and Christine provided me with the information of the wedding, so I passed it on. It was the hardest thing I ever had to do. I regretted everything about it for months. That's when I hired someone to follow you all so I can know what's going on. King, when I saw you at the wedding that Jane brought you to, you reminded me so much of Kobe. It was like I fell in love all over again," Leslie explained.

The Matthews family listened with anger.

"So the photo album of the boy, is that him?" King asked.

"It is. What's crazy is his name is Adoree' also. Adoree' Johnson. Born May 6th, 1986. He lives in Boston. He's a brain surgeon. His information is in the chest all the way at the bottom under everything," Leslie finished.

The family looked at each other which worried Leslie. She stood up and walked toward King and tried to hug him. But he wasn't buying it. As much as he loved her, the cross that she brought onto his family was devastating. It changed the whole dynamic of his family. He looked at her and shook his head. Leslie stood there with tears in her eyes running down her face. Her long-time secret had been discovered by the people she had hid it from. She never thought this day would come. But just as the marriage began it was all over just as fast.

The Matthew's family walked out of the room together. The reception was over anyway, so the cruise was on its way back to land. The family was on their way to the front of the ship when they heard a loud gunshot sound off. They looked up at the room where the shot came from. Queen tried to walk in that direction, but King stopped her. He already knew what it was. The agony from a dad and his son breaking her heart was too much for her to bear. Everyone on the ship panicked. They didn't know who was shot or where the shot had come from.

Eight months later, King celebrated his son's first birthday. Little Kobe had grown so much so fast. He ran around the party's venue with a baseball in one hand and a small football in the other. He resembled King so much, but you could also see shades of Leslie in him. The family made sure to get professional photos taken to hang in their homes.

Queen was there with her fiancé Arnez and Tiffany was there with her "male friend" is what she called him. Though it had been a crazy year with discoveries and the result of that, everyone was living happy lives. Meanwhile, he and Destiny got closer as they had began spending time with each other.

For King, the cross he had carried with him for the majority of his life was now over. Finally, he felt complete and to top it off, he was preparing to play in his first Superbowl next year against the city where he had grew up in New York City. And after that, he would make it his mission to find his long-lost brother.

Made in the USA
Monee, IL
04 February 2021